ALSO BY DAN BARDEN

John Wayne: A Novel

THE NEXT RIGHT THING

THE NEXT RIGHT THING

A NOVEL · DAN BARDEN

THE DIAL PRESS · NEW YORK

Published in the United States by The Dial Press, an imprint of The Random House Publishing Group, a division of Random House, Inc., New York.

DIAL PRESS is a registered trademark of Random House, Inc., and the colophon is a trademark of Random House, Inc.

Library of Congress Cataloging-in-Publication Data
Barden, Dan.
The next right thing: a novel / Dan Barden.
p. cm.
ISBN 978-0-385-34340-4
eBook ISBN 978-0-679-64435-4
I. Title.
PS3552.A6144N49 2012
813'.54—dc22   2011012646

Printed in the United States of America on acid-free paper

www.dialpress.com

2 4 6 8 9 7 5 3 1

First Edition

Book design by Liz Cosgrove

This is a house I built for Elizabeth and Duke.

"Let's not louse this thing up."

—Dr. Bob S. to Bill W., November 12, 1950

THE NEXT RIGHT THING

OFFICIALLY, I STARTED DESTROYING MY LIFE that Wednesday morning. But it had been on my mind for a while.

As I drove up Pacific Coast Highway past the Laguna Art Museum, I suddenly longed for still-sort-of-disreputable Santa Ana, where there would have been a neighborhood nearby that would better reflect my mood. There's nothing worse than a beautiful town when you've got an ugly head. From every corner of always-blooming Laguna Beach, bougainvillea announced that unhappiness was not an option here.

It had been almost three weeks since Terry died, and I hadn't done a damn thing but drink espresso and avoid the people who loved me.

It reminded me of when I first got sober. I didn't want to drink, but I held the idea of drinking close, like a suicide bomb inside my heart. Just bend my elbow and a world of possibilities would open up. Bad possibilities, but possibilities nevertheless. I'd never see my daughter again, but I'd make sure that a few people paid for their sins.

I could hear Terry's voice: *Clamoring for justice again? Is that it, Randy?*

I was waiting for the light beside the Cottage to change, staring into a pack of well-dressed skateboarders pointed toward Heisler Park, when my cell phone rang. It was Wade's number, so I didn't answer. Sometimes you're too lonely to talk to your friends.

Instead, I drove my F-350 up to Jean Claude's café in North Laguna. Like every other morning these three weeks, I would park my ass in a molded plastic chair beside a molded plastic table and try to clear my mind with double espressos.

That morning the sidewalk and the shrubs were still dewy. Across the parking lot, surfers were jaywalking across Coast Highway, shrugging into wet suits, blowing their noses into the street. Above the beach access, a gray shelf of fog announced the Pacific Ocean.

At a table nearby, a couple of rich people waved at me tentatively. I vaguely remembered being introduced to them by someone who thought I might design their home. She was too old to be his daughter and too pretty to be his first wife. I'd probably been dodging their calls, but they wouldn't approach me here. I had perfected my sullenness. It was another way that my old life clung to me: sometimes I scared people.

For three weeks, I'd been pretending I was just a home designer and not that earlier, angrier version of myself. It wasn't working. Every day it got harder to pretend I was anyone but myself.

Jean Claude set down another double espresso on the flimsy table. He was hardworking Eurotrash—a contradiction I liked. Also, the only guy in Southern California who didn't look like he'd grown his goatee yesterday.

"*Ça va?*" he asked.

"*Ça* fucking *va.* How about you? Who are you humping these days?"

"An important man, works for Obama. He's too good for me, though. I want somebody bad, like you."

One good thing had come out of the past three weeks: I'd finally found a way to describe the sound of my diseased conscience. It was a Styrofoam ice chest wedged behind the seat of an old pickup. The rougher the road, the louder it squeaked, until the noise became unbearable.

My cell phone rang again as Jean Claude was clearing away my second double espresso. This time I answered: "What the fuck do you want, Wade?"

"It's not Wade. It's Tom. Wade got into a fight. He wanted me to call you."

"Tell him that I'm not coming." I hung up.

They couldn't be anywhere but the Coastal Club, one of the places I was avoiding, a place that I'd been avoiding even before Terry died. I poured my espresso into a sip cup and sped out of the parking lot. Something that had stuck with me from that lost decade of being a cop: running out of coffee shops and driving away too fast.

. . .

A simple white building in a glade of oak and eucalyptus just off Laguna Canyon Road, the Coastal Club was nicer than most

A.A. clubs because a rich gallery owner had endowed it thirty years ago. Then it took them almost half that thirty years to decide on a design. It was just down the road from the old Bhagwan Ranjeesh place—now a nursery school—and you could have mistaken it for a deal like that. The architectural equivalent of a freshly laundered linen nightgown. They'd done a good job.

I hated going there, but it was the place where my life began. Once I would have slept there if they had let me. I first met Terry in the gravel parking lot where I was now skidding my truck into a swirl of dust.

Wade stood at the front door beside Tom and several other fools from the seven A.M. meeting. It seemed like everyone but Wade wanted to tell me what had happened. But they were a little scared to tell me, too. Since Terry's death, I'd become an authorized repository for community grief. One reason I hadn't attended a single meeting since the funeral was that I was sick of people looking at me as though I might break down or explode. Wade's pal Tom, an overweight photojournalist who'd taken the highway patrol on a chase through two counties last summer, gave me a jaunty and ridiculous salute. He and a guy I didn't know at all, with dark glasses and a bomber jacket, stood behind Wade like Secret Service agents: arms at their sides but ready.

When I rolled up beside the curb, Wade said, "*Dude.*"

"In the truck," I answered.

"It wasn't his fault," Tom said. "Troy Padilla came out of nowhere."

"Out of *nowhere,*" the other guy underlined.

"In the truck, please," I said to Wade.

"His dad's a mafioso or something," Tom explained. "He knows how to do that shit."

"In the fucking truck."

When we got back to my house above Bluebird Canyon, MP—only her father calls her Mary Pat—was back from yoga training and drilling up something in the blender that I might drink if I were dying of cancer. She gave Wade a hug. They'd gone to Catholic high school together in Ranch Santa Margarita. Wade had grown up surfing and perfecting his substance abuse and brushing his blond hair out of his eyes. MP had grown up riding horses, wishing she weren't flat-chested, and steering clear of boys like Wade.

"He won't talk to me," Wade said. "All the way over here, he wouldn't speak."

"You guys are going to have to work this out," MP said. "While I'm somewhere else."

"He thinks I'm lying to him. This dude came out of nowhere to punch me, and he thinks *I'm* lying."

I sat down on the Indian daybed that MP had found for me at a swap meet. Not as comfortable as my Eames chair, but it provided me a great view of my home. I'd taken a midcentury hillside ranch-style and redone the interior as contemporary cottage. Eclectic furniture like this daybed contrasted with the white ceilings, white walls, and white plank flooring. I had used traditional materials and hadn't goobered them up with too many fixtures. Reclaimed oak beams in the ceiling were the darkest element by far. Otherwise, it was a playground for the light from the hills.

I'll always be happy to see Wade—forever, for the rest of my life—but he's the guy who finds your kitchen first. The guy who wonders if you've made coffee. The guy who pleads his case to your girlfriend. The guy who was now scanning my living room.

We'd been friends long enough that I could read his mind: *Is that a new Blu-ray player? The kind that records? How much does something like that cost?* You'd think he was still a crack-addicted surf rat instead of a guy with a modest trust fund and an afternoon job as a scuba instructor.

I'll never not love him, though. Him and Terry.

"Coffee?" Wade asked.

MP shook her head and punched up the blender again. She was the only brunette with bangs I would ever love.

"Not until you drop the bullshit," I said.

"Bullshit?"

MP had her back to me, but I could feel her smiling.

"The bullshit about how this guy attacked you for no reason."

"His father's in the Mafia," Wade said. "He's from New Jersey. He needs a reason?"

Even Wade knew better than to sit down in my Eames chair, so he passed it to stand in front of the window watching the goats across the canyon. Wildfire control: they ate everything on the hill until there was nothing left to burn.

"I think he's the guy who was with Terry," Wade said.

"That's not why he hit you. Once you've got Tom and that other bozo defending you, I know it's a bigger story than that."

Wade smiled. My friends can get mighty full of shit, but sometimes they'll drop it if you ask them. While Wade considered how to tell me the truth, I watched Yegua, my Guatemalan laborer/assistant/better half, cross the backyard with a posthole digger.

"Well . . ." Wade finally said. "I've been telling everyone he was the guy with Terry."

"Do you know that for sure?"

"No," Wade said. "But it makes sense."

"How does it make sense, Wade? And if it made so much god-damn sense, why didn't you tell me?"

Wade turned from the goats. "You were too busy hiding out at Jean Claude's. I thought I'd wait until you showed up at a meeting."

"Fuck you, Wade."

Wade stared across the room at the nook where my electronics were stacked. I could feel that MP wasn't smiling anymore.

"Okay," I said after a while. "I'll fix some coffee."

Wade looked at me. "Rick Buford at the South Coast hospital meeting said that this dude Troy and Terry had been driving around all day, checking out Terry's old drug neighborhoods. A nostalgia trip. Sometime after the funeral, Troy told Rick how guilty he felt."

"Feeling guilty doesn't mean he was with him when he died."

Wade sat down on the couch. He leaned forward, his elbows on his knees. "Rick said Troy told him that Terry fell like a tree, that he'd never seen anyone fall like that. He saw it happen, Randy. Then he must have just bailed. Didn't even call the fucking paramedics."

MP set down her protein drink and leaned against the counter. For the first time in forever, I wished that she weren't in my house.

My sponsor Terry was a big man, about six foot three, with silver hair and a pale youthful face. I've had moments when I thought he stood straighter than any man I'd ever known. He'd been off booze and drugs for fifteen years on the night that he died. *On the night he died from a heroin overdose in a shitty motel room in Santa Ana.*

My friend Terry would have fallen like a tree.

This was what I'd been waiting for. My gift from God. And not the loving God people talked about at meetings but a God, like me, who got pissed off when good men died. I'd been sitting on my ass for three weeks because I needed all my righteous strength and every bad impulse I'd been saving from eight years of sobriety to go kick the shit out of this little prick from New Jersey.

MP walked down the hallway into the bedroom and closed the door behind her.

I said, "Let's go find this asshole."

. . .

The first time I really talked with Terry was over breakfast at Corky's. He was already hanging with Wade then, although Wade still had one more drunk left. They had invited me to breakfast after the seven A.M. meeting at the Coastal Club.

Sometimes people in A.A. will say, "Let us love you until you can love yourself." I don't think it would have worked on me. At the time I wouldn't have trusted anyone—besides my SAPD partner, Manny, and my sister—who pretended to love me.

With Terry and Wade, though, it was a totally different deal.

Corky's was a great place to have breakfast, and I fell right into the food. Terry and Wade talked about people in A.A. whom I didn't yet know. Mostly I ignored them. I wouldn't admit that I needed this thing. When they asked me questions, I answered. Terry seemed like the kind of smugly successful attorney I had always hated. And Wade seemed like a tadpole who needed to be slapped every time he said the word "dude." Still pretending to be one tough hombre, I let them know early and often that I was a cop.

About halfway through my bacon, cheddar, and avocado omelet, I could feel Terry staring at me. When I met his eyes, he said, "You know, Randy, we don't hang out with you because we *like* you. We *don't* like you. Isn't that right, Wade?"

Wade nodded slowly.

"We hang out with you," Terry continued, "because it's head cases like you who keep us sober."

It was an important moment in my life. I stood up from the table, threw down twenty dollars, and walked out of the restaurant. I think I told them to fuck themselves. Wade said I did, and Terry said I just walked out.

By that night, I knew who my sponsor was going to be.

. . .

Halfway to our destination, I realized that I hadn't even said goodbye to MP.

"It's not on Temple Hills," Wade said. "And it's not on Arroyo Hills."

"I don't care, Wade, where it's *not*."

Wade looked at me like I was rushing some terribly important process—the composition of a symphony, maybe. His sunglasses were hanging from his neck by one of those Croakie doodads. I pulled them off and threw the doodad out the window.

"You don't get to wear that anymore." I tossed back his glasses. "It looks too stupid."

The asshole Troy Padilla lived in a "recovery home"—words that should be said in quotation marks. People in Alcoholics

Anonymous were always thinking up new scams, and lately the new scam was this: rent a big house and fill it with newcomers who couldn't pull together a security deposit if they owned a gold mine. Put two of them in each room, invent a bunch of bullshit rules about curfew and house meetings, and you can rake in at least twenty grand a month over the actual rent. At best, it was "stone soup": the newcomer went to A.A. meetings and didn't mind getting screwed by some old-timers. At worst, the people who "managed" the houses began to think they actually knew something about recovering from alcoholism.

In Laguna, the scam had been refined a bit, which is often what happens to scams when they reach Laguna. An A.A. member named Colin Alvarez, who'd made a lot of money as a mortgage broker, started a corporation called Recovery Homes Incorporated to administer the houses. Sober just about as long as me, Colin was the kind of guy who, unlike me, didn't make jokes about A.A. He'd come back from a meth addiction in his early twenties and, also unlike me, didn't miss many meetings.

What did I know? Maybe the "recovery homes" were the best thing that ever happened to some of these people. Terry used to say that A.A. itself was the biggest scam of them all, but it had failed as a scam, and it had become something better.

"Wait," Wade said. "It *is* Temple Hills."

Eventually, Wade steered us to a little ranch house hanging its ass over the side of a hill. This dwelling had absolutely nothing going for it but the fact that it had landed in Laguna Beach. The porcini-mushroom-and-sun-dried-tomato color scheme beneath the shake shingles was the only upscale element in the design. In Tustin or El Toro, it would have cost half of what it did here. I parked my truck pointing down the grade beside the house.

I thumped hard on the front door, which was suburban and hollow-core and made a nice scary sound. A near-teenager with a bare midriff and a pierced navel answered. In my limited experience, these recovery homes existed somewhere on a continuum between a prison and a pajama party. I saw that contradiction in the girl before me. She might have been near the bad end of Laguna Beach High, but something in her eyes was harder than that by a lot. It reminded me that in spite of the affluence surrounding them, some of these kids could be living on the street before the year was out.

"Look who's here," she said. "It's the let's-drink-too-much-coffee-but-not-smoke-enough-cigarettes-and-still-think-we're-better-than-everyone-else brigade."

I was wondering what meeting she knew us from when Wade shouted after a dark-haired kid in his early twenties peeking at us from the end of a long central hallway. The kid ran, and I ran after him. Wade and Pierced Navel followed. At the end of the hallway, in what looked like the kitchen, I saw three more twentysomethings—two boys and another girl—watching us but apparently staying put.

The kid slammed through a door into the garage, but the automatic garage-door opener was taking its sweet time letting him out. I pushed the button to send the door down again and tossed him up against an old Datsun pickup. Troy Padilla featured grungy black hair, baggy pants, and a faux hip-hop uniform that would have been current anywhere but Laguna. He was about five-ten and all worked out, but none of it was real muscle. "Fluffy" was what Terry would have called him. I was probably old enough to be his father, but also very much *not* his father: my still-hanging-in-there blond hair and slow-to-tan skin came from an entirely different gene pool. I was five inches taller and thirty unfluffy pounds heavier. My nose had been broken enough times to prove that I hadn't always been smart about who I fought.

The garage door finished closing. I could feel Wade somewhere behind me.

"Were you with him?" I asked.

"You're talking about Terry now?" the kid said.

"Who the fuck else would I be talking about?"

"I wasn't with him. Not at the end. I was with him early, when he was looking. We went to the racetrack and a few shopping centers in Santa Ana. But he never found anything. Then he got pissed off and left me at a bar."

I slowed down my breathing. I checked the garage for blunt instruments that numbnuts might grab for. There wasn't anything in here but that old Datsun pickup.

"Which bar?" I heard Wade ask behind me. He had his arms across the doorway to keep Pierced Navel out of the garage.

"The TGIF off Orangethorpe."

"That's not a fucking bar," Wade said. "That's—"

I looked back with steel in my eyes, but Wade wouldn't stop talking. "No, I'm not going to shut up, Randy. I'm sick of this guy. Tell him how tough your father is, Troy. I never heard of a mafioso with the name Padilla. You're *so* full of shit."

I stared at Wade again. This time he got the message.

"Okay," Wade said. "I'm done."

I backed away from Troy a little, but I kept my hands up in case he tried to bolt. "How did you know my friend Terry, and how come I don't know you?"

From behind us, Pierced Navel suddenly pushed Wade in the

chest, but he stood his ground. Then she got really close to him and sniffed him repeatedly, which was, well, very weird.

Troy looked me straight in the eyes. "I loved Terry, the same as you guys."

"I've never seen you before in my fucking life, Troy. So tell me why I should believe you."

"Everyone knows you, Randy. Just like everyone knew Terry. You guys were like A.A. royal—"

I pushed him back against the Datsun, not enough to hurt him but enough to let him feel how much I wanted to hurt him. "And if you loved him so fucking much," I said, "why didn't you call somebody? Why didn't you call one of us?"

"I had ninety days of sobriety. He was like a god to me. I thought I was just going to snort a little smack. That's different, right? I thought that was different. I was *insane*. If you guys don't understand that, who the hell understands that?"

"What Troy's not saying," Pierced Navel shouted from behind me, "is that you don't know him because you haven't fucking been around. It's hard to be Mr. A.A. when you don't go to any fucking A.A. meetings."

"Crazy girl"—I pointed at her—"you shut the fuck up." I turned back to Troy. "Did he talk to anyone else while you were with him?"

"He called Claire."

"Claire Monaco? Why did he call Claire Monaco?"

"It was after midnight," Troy Padilla sneered. "Why do *you* think he called Claire Monaco?" He made a move to get away.

This time I threw him against the truck hard. "What was this shit about him falling like a tree? Isn't that what you said? That Terry fell like a tree?"

"That's the way I imagined it," Troy said. "He was a big guy. You gonna beat me up because I have an imagination?"

Troy's face started to cloud. He reminded me of the tough guy in high school, which was to say not tough at all. I noticed, however, that I believed him.

"I figured Terry knew what he was doing." Troy started to cry. "Didn't Terry always look like he knew what he was doing?"

Troy's jaw began to shake, and Pierced Navel went apeshit. She kneed Wade in the groin and pushed past him into the garage. She slapped my face—hard—but her assault didn't seem to have any purpose other than to focus my attention. Which it did.

"Do I *know* you?" I said.

"You should. Because assholes like you have been stepping on my feet and ramming pencils up my nose since before I knew what feet and pencils were. You've got a big fucking truck where your soul should be, and you want to drive it over someone, but you can't because it's encased in flesh and you would die if you tried. Fuck you, fuck you both."

She swung back to slap me again, but Wade had by then recovered from her knee, and he got himself around her pretty good. She couldn't do much but thrash and spit.

Wanting to punch someone so badly that I thought my heart would seize if I didn't, I got right into Troy's face. "I think you were there," I said. "I think you were there and you were too chickenshit to call the paramedics."

"I think you feel guilty," Troy whined. "And you're taking it out on me."

I don't know if I would have hit him or not, because two things happened at once: a dark stain grew from Troy's crotch, and shame spread through his face. The smell of urine filled the garage. As I backed away, the rage settled down inside me. I pushed Wade through the door with a hand that was no longer a fist. Pierced Navel followed us to the front door, screaming. "I don't care how many A.A. enemas they stick up your ass, you're still just a cracker with a badge!" She looked familiar, like I'd seen her regularly in some other life. And by the time Wade closed the front door on her and she didn't open it back up, she seemed almost as young as my daughter.

. . .

As my truck slammed down Temple Hills, I wanted to puke from the adrenalin. I felt like the first time I beat up someone in a bar with my nightstick. My training officer had stopped at the door and tipped his hat, and I got that this was my little hazing. As the guy came after me—a big crew cut with swollen eyes— I would have sworn that I didn't need the nightstick, but apparently, the nightstick needed him. It wanted his knees and then his kidney.

My cell phone startled me. The world of wanting to smack some guy from New Jersey shouldn't have cell phones. It was Jeep Mooney, my business partner.

"Wade and I are on our way to your place," I said.

"You've been avoiding me for weeks," she said.

"Two minutes." I flipped the phone closed.

Although she now lived with my sister, Betsy—in the biblical sense—I'd met Jeep in A.A. She'd been agitating for my return to work since the day after the funeral.

When we showed up, she was standing on her driveway. "It's Punch and Judy."

Wade looked at me. "You're Punch," I said. "I'm Judy." Someone from the seven A.M. meeting must have called Jeep about Wade's earlier encounter, but there was no way she could know about Troy Padilla and me. Yet.

Jeep was wearing a slate-blue suit over a white blouse. About an inch taller than me, she was stick-thin and regal as a queen. A once-upon-a-time debutante, she'd been spared the upper reaches of Orange County society by her Roman nose and cartoonishly bulging eyes, which weren't most people's idea of beautiful. She wouldn't say exactly how she got the name Jeep, but I bet it was a taunt she transcended.

As Wade headed for Betsy's office—lots of new toys there— I walked with Jeep through the backyard.

"Have you darkened the door of an A.A. meeting since Terry's funeral?" Jeep said.

"Did that guy drop off those pavers?" I squinted as though I were calculating material costs.

Jeep stopped walking. "Have *you* punched anyone yet?"

I told myself again there was no way she could know about Troy Padilla. "Who told you about Wade?" I asked.

"I'm everyone's den mother this week," she said. "Yours, too. You look like shit."

"The thing is," I said, "I *feel* worse."

We stood near the edge of my sister's carp pond. We had both argued strenuously against it. But without Betsy's carp pond, we wouldn't have bisected the yard with a tight little man-made stream, exactly four inches across, which fed the carp pond. That got us into *Dwell* magazine.

"Am I here to look at something? Or is this where you take people when you want to ram some recovery up their ass?"

"The answer to both questions is yes," Jeep said. "You should get back to work. You're going to need money for this custody thing."

"Betsy said that Jean has to give me what I want."

"She also said that any time you walk into a courtroom—"

"Besides"—I held up my hand—"I've got fifty thousand out there somewhere."

About six months before, Terry had asked me for fifty thousand dollars, to be paid back within a year. I had it, so I gave it to him. Still, it was a lot. Terry was sometimes reckless with money, but he would have gotten it back to me eventually.

"Oh, Christ," Jeep said. "The money you loaned Terry is gone. Come back to work, and we could make that on just one job."

"Maybe I want to fly solo and I don't have the balls to tell you."

"Balls aren't your problem," Jeep said. "Your brain's too big for the inside of your skull. *That's* your problem. You need to build something, relieve the pressure."

I laughed. "When did you start quoting Terry?"

"He had *your* number," Jeep said. "I'll give him that."

"But?"

"No but."

I looked at the back of the house. The balustrade was thick with jasmine. In another lifetime, Betsy's home was a faux Tudor–ranch style, as ugly as pink concrete. Now it had a second floor and a fucking carp pond.

"Okay, then," I said. "What does she want now?"

"An extended balcony."

"An extended balcony?"

"You want me to define the term for you? Yes, an extended balcony."

"Tell me what comes after the 'but' that you claim wasn't there. Then I'll dish about the extended balcony."

Jeep set her hands on her hips. "You know he wasn't always such a good role model. He cut corners."

"He cheated on his taxes. The IRS slapped him around," I said. "Big deal. You know many lawyers who aren't a little crooked? For that matter, you know anyone in A.A. who's not a criminal at heart?"

"Me," Jeep said. "I'm not a criminal at heart."

"Which costs us money every time we do a deal. Listen— why does Betsy's brain always reach for the first cliché it can find? A patio would work. A lap pool that goes all the way into the trees would work. But an extended balcony? I'm still not sure we did the right thing adding a second floor. Let's not push it. This won't be a balcony; this will be an invitation to musical theater."

"Oh . . ." Jeep shook her head fiercely. "You can be such a *schmuck*."

She stomped across our high-tech stream toward the house. I followed her into the kitchen where Betsy and Wade were sipping from bright ceramic mugs. They stopped talking when I came in. Jeep pulled a pack of cigarettes out of the freezer. "He thinks it's a stupid idea," she said.

Wade lifted his mug. "Jamaican Blue Mountain coffee, dude."

"For him"—Betsy pointed at me—"we've got Folgers."

My sister is the most beautiful lesbian in the history of Laguna Beach. Ask anyone. Long brown hair, olive skin, green eyes that make you forget you've seen green eyes before. As she pushed back her reading glasses, her contempt for me seemed sharper than usual. I poured myself a cup of Jamaican Blue Mountain just to spite her.

She didn't meet my eyes, which was a bad sign. Then again, it didn't take much to piss off Betsy lately. I noticed her iPhone was out on the table. News of my behavior was often where the journey to being pissed off began.

Betsy used to prosecute hate crimes for the U.S. attorney. Somewhere along her trajectory, she took the advice of her Stanford pals and invested in social networking sites. She was soon able to quit her "codependent relationship with the government" to become a woman of passionate interests: like improving her already much improved house, like the huge model railroad in her attic that only Jeep and Wade had seen, like her folksinging. Her new Shawn Colvin Signature Martin guitar was sitting in the chair that no one had offered to me.

Jeep turned toward us as she lit her cigarette. "Guess who hasn't been to a meeting since the beginning of fucking time."

"Didn't I tell you that in confidence?" I asked Jeep.

"You didn't tell me *shit*." She blew smoke past me. "I knew it before you opened your mouth."

Wade lifted his nose from the coffee. "We can go right now, dude. There's a meeting at the club in, what, forty-five minutes?"

"Or don't go," Betsy said. "And we can take bets on how long he stays out of jail."

Apparently, Betsy knew about me and Troy Padilla. Once again I found myself giving Wade a look that would have killed a more thoughtful man.

"She got a call," Wade said, "while you were outside. This place is like the A.A. nerve center."

"Doesn't anyone in A.A. have a job?" I said. "Who the hell called her?"

"I'm disappointed in both of you." Betsy got up from the table. "You preyed on this kid. How's that different from a drunk working over his wife? Or a guard beating a prisoner?"

Wade pointed to the scrape above his eye.

"Don't give me that crap." Betsy poured more coffee. "I heard you were running around making him into the guy who killed Saint Terry. He *had* to hit you."

Wade dove again into his bright mug. Betsy wasn't really talking to him anyway.

"I've spent half my life on the list of people who are denied basic human rights," Betsy continued. "When we got married, they held up signs saying we were animals. I can't be around this shit anymore."

The freezer chugged from coughing up the cigarettes. Wade and Jeep both looked down. Then I got it.

"You think I jacked him up because he's Mexican?" I said. "I'm not even sure he *is* Mexican."

Betsy stared. Jeep stared. Wade kept his eyes on the floor. By asking the question, I had somehow proved her point.

"Okay," I said. "We'll kick that pigeon another time. But please, don't tell me again how Terry's death makes sense. That he was a junkie and that's how junkies die. One day he was a poster boy for Southern California A.A., and the next day he was dead from a heroin overdose in a Santa Ana motel? I know something happened, and I'm going to find out what."

Betsy shrugged, not unkindly.

"*Christ,* Betsy," I said. "Who goes out for one night and hits the jackpot? After fifteen years? Hell, before he got sober, he'd survived ten years of overdoses worse than that one."

I wasn't shouting anything that I hadn't shouted weeks ago, after the memorial. I wasn't shouting anything that I hadn't shouted at myself every day since then. What was he doing in Santa Ana? Who was he with? Why did he need to borrow fifty thousand dollars from me six months before he died?

Wade continued to avoid my eyes. Betsy watched her guitar. Jeep was the only one who would look at me.

"I thought all of us had a solution," I said to her. *"One day at a time."*

"Maybe he didn't want it anymore?" Jeep said.

A question people had asked, I was sure, but not yet to my face.

"You don't drive to Santa Ana to kill yourself. That's pretty easy to do right here. I'll never believe that."

Jeep held my eyes. She thought I should let it go. She thought I wasn't a cop anymore, that I hadn't been a good cop even then. But I was dying from the pretense that I was anyone but my old angry self. Three weeks was, it turned out, my limit for lying to myself without a Jack Daniel's to chase the lie. I had to find out what happened in that motel room. If only to prove to Betsy that I didn't assault Mexicans anymore—or whatever the hell Troy Padilla was—for no good reason.

2

ONCE, ON THE BACK of his business card, Terry wrote exactly this: "Randy Chalmers has permission to be a 'fake' until the footwork leads to reality." At the bottom, he signed it "Terry E. 1/26/04."

We were eating lunch at Poor Richard's on Pacific Coast Highway. He worked across the street. Mostly personal injury back then, but he was getting into real estate, too. I still had my disability, and I was two months sober. Terry used to call me for lunch. I didn't do much in those days but sit and wait for the time between meetings to be over.

"Chalmers. It's Elias. Meet me at Poor Richard's in five minutes." Then he would hang up. At the time I thought he operated this way only with me, but it was the same with everyone he sponsored. Letting you know that he understood you didn't have a goddamn thing going in your life. Letting you know that he wanted to spend time with you anyway. A kiss that felt like a punch.

We'd talk about how I couldn't see a future for myself, how anything I imagined felt fake. At that time, I was only an *almost-ex-cop*. The proceedings that ran me off the force were ongoing. Terry asked me what I wanted to do, what I would do if anything were possible, if God loved me the way The Big Book said He loved me. I told him, but I also warned him that I would fuck him up if he told anyone else.

He leaned right into that one. He showed me his big bland face and said, "Take your best shot, asshole. I'm a *shyster*, remember?" He backed off a little and said, "Eight years ago I sat where you're sitting, and there's nothing you can teach me about being a loser. Do you know what it took to get from that seat to this one?"

"A big fucking attitude?"

Terry laughed. "I was a heart-stopped-on-the-operating-table-three-times dope fiend. Do you know what it took to get clean and sober after four years of shooting dope in the bathrooms of A.A.? What do you think it took to get me through law school after that? As far as whiners and malcontents, you're minor league. Everyone around here wanted me dead so they wouldn't have to watch me walk through one more meeting and destroy their fragile sense of hope. I asked you a question, you asshole. *What do you think it took?*"

"A miracle?" I asked quietly.

"All the love and power in the fucking universe," Terry said. "Do you get that?"

That was when he wrote out the card. I felt like it had magic powers. When the ink started to fade so badly that you could barely read it, I had it framed.

. . .

It wasn't smart to be meeting Claire Monaco. It wasn't smart to be *thinking* about Claire Monaco. A former—but probably still—porn actress/stripper/prostitute who'd been trying to get sober for a few years, Claire was trouble.

We met later that morning at Jean Claude's. Wade came because I felt the need for backup. I knew Claire the way I knew a lot of people in A.A., but I'd certainly never met her for coffee. There were those who'd done less and lived to regret it.

Claire was a beautiful woman, but booze and drugs had not been kind to her skin, in spite of the self-tanner. If she didn't stop soon, she was going to start looking like what she was: a thirtysomething drug addict washed up on the shores of A.A.

The tight-faced ladies around us—Jean Claude's late-morning clientele—noticed her right off. Terry used to call this time of day "shrink-wrap central" because at any given moment between nine and eleven, you would see at least six hundred thousand dollars in plastic surgery sipping coffee.

I pushed my chocolate croissant in Wade's direction; he didn't hesitate. Jean Claude brought me a second double espresso without asking. I started in on Claire: "Troy Padilla says Terry called you that night."

"Terry could have been a really great man." Claire spoke through the froth of her latté.

"*What?*" Wade said.

"Becoming a big shot in A.A. was the worst thing that could

have happened to him," Claire said. "All these A.A. circuit speakers are hypocrites. All they really care about is telling everyone else what to do. One guy I met, he gave me a lecture about the steps while I was blowing him. I told him he should share it with his wife."

"Which guy?" Wade said.

"Can we talk about the sex lives of hypocrites some other day?" I interjected.

The shrink-wrapped ladies might have recognized Claire from the papers. A few years ago, she'd been a local celebrity of the Kato Kaelin variety. She'd been rumored to be involved with a judge named Fogarty in the South County courthouse who had been accused by the local papers of trading judicial favors for sex with a variety of women of Claire's ilk. None of this stuck to him, but sometime afterward, Claire became the victim of a sting operation. She spent three months in jail for prostitution and pandering. Maybe Fogarty figured that he could make himself look good at Claire's expense, but his plan backfired: *The Orange County Register* believed that she had been punished for Judge Fogarty's sins. After a protracted battle in the op-ed pages, the dust settled and Fogarty got to keep his job. That's how the world often works—what's shitty just stays shitty.

"You know, Randy, I met your girlfriend once," Claire said. "I mean, back in the day, before any of us got sober."

"Are you sober?" Wade asked through a mouthful of chocolate. "When did *that* happen?"

"Shut up, Wade," I said. "You, too, Claire. Don't talk about MP like that."

"Like what?"

"Like the two of you were *back in the day* together."

Claire smiled. I should have kept my mouth shut. It was a mistake to let her think this was a sore point for me. MP had supported her first try at college with a stint as a tantric masseuse, which was sort of like hand job from a hippie, and it was still her biggest shame from her drinking days.

When I was drinking, giving a tantric hand job would have been one of my *better* days.

I took a breather and smiled back at Claire. I moved the chocolate away from Wade so he would know not to eat it all.

"We came on too strongly," I said. "You retaliated. If I apologize, can we talk nice again?"

"I get tired of being the most disgusting woman in A.A.," Claire said. She checked the tables around us. I waited. The other customers avoided her eyes while tracking her movements.

"You gotta look into that whole nightmare with Alexander." Again she looked around. "My son? That's when Terry started to get weird. When he tried to take Alexander away from me, *that's* where the bad shit begins."

The part of Claire's story the shrink-wrapped ladies *didn't* know: when my friend Terry offered to help Claire appeal her pandering conviction—the one that Judge Fogarty almost certainly brought down on her—he also demanded custody of Claire's five-year-old son, Alexander, in exchange. She wasn't the best mother, and Terry loved the kid, but it was extortion, pure and simple. Was that the beginning of Terry's end? At the time, I was too busy falling in love with MP to notice.

"I'm leaving, Claire." I pushed out my chair. "I've heard this song before."

"I'm trying to help you," she said. "This is the background. Terry called me that last night, but I wouldn't see him. He called me more than once."

"Was he with anyone?"

"The first time he called he was with that kid from the Thursday-night beginners' meeting—"

"Troy Padilla? Did Troy get him the drugs?"

"That kid? He's just a kitten. No, it was the other guy. You remember that lawyer John Sewell who Terry used to work with? This guy—I think he was an electrician or a handyman—he used to work for John Sewell."

"John Sewell?" I recognized the name because I read the newspapers. He was as big as a lawyer got in Orange County. I'd taken him and Terry fishing once. He was also dating my ex-wife—that part made the most sense: Claire's modus operandi was to find the link between her worst instincts and your worst instincts. "John Sewell wasn't with Terry that day. A guy like John Sewell doesn't even get off the freeway in Santa Ana unless he's getting paid a thousand dollars an hour for the privilege."

"You're not listening," Claire said. "This guy, this electrician, he used to work for Sewell on some buildings that Sewell owns. That's I guess how Terry met him? He had like a dog's name or something."

"This is what you have?" I said. "An electrician with a name like a dog?"

Claire straightened up. "Look, I don't know the guy. When Terry called the second time, he said he was with some guy who used to work for Sewell, and all I can remember is that he was named after a dog."

"Was he named after a dog," Wade asked, "like Lassie or Rover? Or was he named after a dog as in he happens to have the same name as a dog you know?"

Claire and I took a moment to marvel at Wade.

"Terry called me that night," she continued. "It sounded like a booty call, and I didn't want to have anything to do with him. But he told me he was doing a twelfth step on this guy. The guy with the name of a dog. The guy with the name of a dog was having some trouble with heroin." A twelfth step was when a sober alcoholic visited a recently drunk alcoholic at his home. A.A.s did this less often now than in the thirties, when the fellowship had begun, but Terry had done more than his share.

"How stoned were you?" I said.

"I wasn't stoned," Claire said.

I didn't say anything. I held her eyes.

"I was drunk," Claire said.

Wade laughed.

"I didn't call him," Claire said. "He called me."

I stood up. From behind the counter at the other end of the café, my friend Jean Claude caught my eye. He gave me what I've come to recognize as a Gallic shrug. I said, "You were drunk, Claire. You can't even remember this guy's name. You just want to cause some trouble. You don't know shit."

"I'm on your side," Claire said. "I want to know what turned that sweet man into an unholy prick. Before that night, I hadn't talked to Terry in over a year. Since he tried to take my son away. And if an angel hadn't stepped in to help me, Terry would have pulled it off."

Today I couldn't deal with this. "Because you were willing to trade your son for money. This is a problem that only junkies have, Claire."

She looked at me and then down at the table. If she had started to cry, I could have told myself that I was trying to wake her up, help her admit what a mess she'd made of her life. But as Wade and I left the table and Claire sat there, I knew that wasn't it. I wasn't trying to help Claire, just like Claire couldn't help me. I'd hurt her only because I wanted to hurt her.

3

AFTER I DROPPED OFF WADE for his shift at Laguna Sea Sports, I drove home. On the way there, the back of my neck told me I was being followed, but my brain wrote that off to post-traumatic cop paranoia. There was a time about eight years ago when lots of people wanted me dead. Sometimes even the eyes in the back of my head have flashbacks.

Pulling up my driveway, I had an idea that MP would know more about my adventures by now. I could feel it in the way her VW Cabrio sat on the concrete. *You're an asshole,* that little silver car seemed to whisper.

She was sitting cross-legged on the patio drinking green tea. She had changed into a tank top with a picture of the Virgin Mary on it—not a subtle girl, my MP. I closed the glass door behind me and sat down in the Adirondack chair next to her mat. She offered the tea to me. I sniffed it and offered it back.

"You mad at me?" I asked.

"That's not the word," MP said.

"Disappointed?"

"That's the word."

"I'm sure it's hard to understand." The chair was easier on my back than any other chair I owned, including the one designed by Mr. and Mrs. Eames. How could there be so many great chairs and so few men worthy to sit in them?

"I don't want to live with a cop," MP said. "I want to live with a guy who designs homes and doesn't have some fucked-up obsession with righteousness."

It had been over a year since I'd heard her swear.

"Something wrong with cops?" I asked.

"That's *not* where you want to go." MP smiled tightly. "I won't have a boyfriend who beats people up."

"Who told you?"

"That's not where you want to go, either."

"Okay," I said. "I understand."

"I don't think you do." MP untangled her ankles and turned toward me. "I'm dedicating my life to peace. That's what yoga *is*. Getting closer to the source. Relaxing into the loving spirit of the universe. It's not about beating people up."

"I didn't actually beat anyone up." It wasn't a good idea to tell her what I *had* done. "I'm going to clean that up with the guy."

"Which guy?"

"The guy I didn't beat up."

MP took hold of her big toe and pulled herself down toward the deck. She'd found yet another way to tell me I was full of shit.

"Terry was my best friend," I said. "I want to understand what happened."

"Wasn't it Terry who said that understanding was the booby prize?"

"Terry said a lot of things."

"And that's what this is about. You're afraid if you don't know why he slipped, you'll slip, too." MP rose from the deck and touched my head. "Can't you see it's all in there? Everything was okay until you stopped taking care of yourself. You think your anger means something, but maybe it's just a bunch of bad transmitters. Maybe it's just . . . *alcoholism*."

I followed her inside and started to fix some coffee. "I think it's the other way around," I said. "I think my comfortable life was covering this up. It's my responsibility to Terry. I need to know what happened."

My high-tech German coffeemaker didn't have an opinion, but I heard MP walk away. Then I heard her walk back.

"This isn't about how Terry died," she said. "This is about your feeling that you betrayed him."

. . .

About a year before, I'd run into Terry at Alpha Beta. We were in the fruit section. When did either of us begin to eat fruit? I had to admit that I hadn't seen him in a while.

We did an awkward dance, and then for reasons that seem almost suspicious to me now, we hugged.

Terry smiled. I never trusted Terry when he smiled.

"What?" I said.

"Your ass starting to feel a bit tight?"

"My ass?"

"Your sphincter. That ring where all the tension goes?"

"Because?"

"Answer the question," Terry said, "and then I'll tell you why I'm asking."

"No," I said. "I don't think my sphincter is any tighter than usual."

"Because that's what happens sometimes," Terry said, "when a guy starts slacking off on meetings. His asshole starts to get tight."

I hadn't been going to as many meetings as I used to, and when I did go, I wasn't hanging out for endless hours in coffee shops afterward. For many years, I'd had no home but A.A. That year I'd discovered that I also had a home with MP. "If you don't think I'm going to enough meetings, Terry, why don't you just say so?"

"Am I your sponsor now?"

"Yes, in fact, you *are* my sponsor."

"Well, fancy that."

"Okay," I said. "I haven't been going to enough meetings. What did I miss?"

"You mean besides a feeling of peace and connection to your fellows?"

"Yeah," I said, "besides that."

"This whole eco-friendly recovery-home thing seems to be taking off."

"The what?"

"Colin Alvarez has this idea that he can squeeze a few more

bucks out of the newcomers if he puts some solar panels on his recovery homes. The man's a marketing genius."

I laughed. I laughed hard. "Since when do you applaud Colin Alvarez?"

"Where have you been? How come you don't know what's been happening in your own community? You think you don't matter, that you can go off and fall in love with yoga girl, and it won't leave a vacuum in A.A.? But it does leave a vacuum, and this is what's filling it: low-carbon-imprint fucking recovery homes."

"Look at my face"—I pointed to myself—"this is me being contrite. I'm fucking sorry. I'll see you at the meeting tonight."

I did go that night, but I don't think I went the next night.

. . .

Despite my desire for answers, I wasn't quite ready to call everyone I knew and ask about an electrician named after a dog. And, one way or another, I knew I'd be seeing John Sewell, my ex-wife's new beau and erstwhile employer of the mystery electrician, soon enough. It was midmorning, and I decided I'd better help Yegua clean out my garage. Helping him do anything was my most valued form of procrastination.

Yegua, my illegal alien assistant, smiled and flashed his teeth. I'd bought him those teeth myself, and he liked to remind me of my investment. My other laborers had given him the name Yegua—Spanish for "mare"—because there was a time between no teeth and new teeth when he had temporaries. *Large* temporaries.

We started tying all my electrical cords into neat bundles,

which always made me wonder why I had so many electrical cords.

Yegua didn't have a green card, though he'd been working for me almost the whole time I'd been working myself. Always casually but impeccably dressed—even his jeans were ironed—he had lately grown his wiry black hair out into a mullet. Sometimes I mimed scissors and threatened to cut it off. I told him that women would like him better with shorter hair. Yegua always said he needed only one woman in Guatemala and one woman here. And both of them liked his mullet.

Yegua had put two sons through college in Guatemala, where he owned a business with a third. He was a better man than any man I knew. I guess I could have asked him whether he thought I was a racist, but I didn't have the Spanish for the question. And I guess deep down I wasn't prepared for the answer.

He finished coiling another cord, then took mine, too. I wasn't doing a very good job, and he started over. He hung them from hooks under the cabinets.

"Somebody's *buscándote*," Yegua said. "*Tiene mala pinta*. He sits in the truck, watches your house. I thought it was one of your *camarades,* but now I don't think so."

Yegua was amused by the A.A. guys, like Wade, who came by to shoot the shit. He probably thought they were "bad paint jobs," too. There wasn't an ounce of bullshit in Yegua—when the couple next door adopted a baby from China, I couldn't convince him that the child hadn't been purchased. I thought about the truck parked across the street, and the bad paint job who sat and watched my house, and I had to imagine that my feelings of being followed weren't mere paranoia. If this asshole had parked in front of my house, it was a good bet that he'd been tailing me, too. There wasn't a doubt in my mind that it somehow had something to do with my friend Terry.

I held up my cell phone. "If he comes back, will you call me?"

Yegua smiled. He walked out of the garage toward whatever he would do for me next.

. . .

"My goddamn partner was Mexican," I once told Terry. "I *can't* be a racist."

"Sure you can," he said. "We all are. We all hate Mexicans and we all hate blacks and we all hate whites and we all *especially* hate women. That's why the world is such a lovely place."

That was when I had less than a year sober. We were on our way to Bare Elegance, a strip club near LAX, although I thought we were going to a Lakers game. Terry often changed his mind about destinations.

During a brief period between big luxury cars, Terry tried a Porsche Boxster. Something disturbed me about my big-boned, pale-faced sponsor driving recklessly in such a small car.

"I didn't beat him because he was Mexican," I said. "I beat him because I was mad. He just happened to be there, resisting arrest. He just happened to be Mexican."

"Sometimes," Terry said, "it's not so helpful to look at your intentions. You gotta look at what happened. Did you, in fact, beat the shit out of a Mexican-American citizen of this country?"

"I did, but—"

"There's no 'but,'" Terry said. "A big part of this deal is getting used to the idea that there's no 'but.' That's what you did.

Therefore, that's who you are. You're a guy who beat a Mexican nearly to death. Can you hang out with that for a while? It's like a can of tomatoes on a shelf. You just want to notice that it's there. There might be some corn next to it. What you're going to do is write down that there were some tomatoes, and then you're going to write down that there was some corn. Or maybe you're going to write down that you don't have any more corn. We're not going to judge any of this shit right now. We're just going to call it by name. We'll sort the rest of it out later. You get that?"

"No," I said.

"Can you do it anyway?"

"Yes," I said.

. . .

Manny Mendoza got my call at around eleven-thirty that morning. I pretended it was a whim. "I'm about to commit a crime. You want to have lunch and try to talk me out of it?"

"Why don't you stay down south with the crazy white people?" Manny said. "Maybe they'll let you found a cult or something."

"Been there, done that. But hey, I'm learning Spanish. My crew is teaching me lots of filthy words."

"Charming."

Neither Manny nor I should have become cops. Manny because he should have become a professor or a priest. Me because I have an appetite for self-destruction and violence that no cop should ever have.

I'd been telling myself all week that I wasn't headed north—in the direction of both my past and Terry's death—but after this morning's events, the gravity of Santa Ana caught me. My sister hadn't been this pissed off with me in eight years. MP had never been this pissed off with me—which made me think about how my marriage ended, which made me think about getting kicked off the force, which made me think about Santa Ana: the scene of my crimes.

A.A. newcomers are often warned to stay away from "people, places, and things" that remind them of their drinking. In the hierarchy of good advice, that's right up there with the rhythm method and using the Hells Angels for concert security. Some days *breathing* reminded me of my drinking.

Manny and I met at Knowlwood burgers near the Santa Ana–Tustin border. I paid for the big baskets of cheeseburgers and fries because I still owed him. I would owe him forever.

"You still making lots of money?" Manny asked.

"Shitloads."

"How long has it been since we talked?"

"Three weeks," I said. "I called you about Terry."

"I mean *talked*," Manny said.

"Five months, maybe. Let's say six. That bother you?"

Manny took hold of his burger but didn't lift it to his mouth. He tried on his scary look, the kind that he had perfected playing football for Mater Dei in the early eighties. His hair had been buzzed back to nothing, and he was sporting a goatee that gave his broad face a definition that I liked. He probably weighed about 230, most of it in his chest.

"You been laid since the last time we talked?" I asked.

Manny shrugged and took a bite from his cheeseburger. He finished chewing before he said, "Why do you speak to me like that?"

"It's another disease."

"Cure it."

"I bet you won't even cash your first pension check before you sign up for the seminary."

Manny laughed. He wiped the cheeseburger grease from his goatee. "That's not what I want. Too intellectually constrained. I'd only do that if they gave me a fellowship to the Vatican. Let me play with the big boys for a while."

"You could do that."

"With a degree in criminal justice from Long Beach State? Not many cardinals with that résumé."

"Hey," I said, "maybe they'll pay me lots of money to design homes in Laguna Beach? Maybe I'll live with a woman who doesn't hate me? No, you're right. Those things will never happen."

"You have a point." Manny set down his burger and commenced on the excellent fries. "That's an entire theology right there."

Manny didn't have a high opinion of A.A.; he respected it because he loved me. Still, he had to imagine it was for weaklings. Worse than that, he had to imagine it was for people who didn't really want to know God. Manny had walked away from the barrio without so much as trying a drug. I'd never seen him with a drink in his hand, either. As for God—that big idea that A.A.s thought they knew so damn much about—Manny barely understood how He could be packaged by a monolith like the Catholic Church, so he didn't understand at all how a group of people who drank too much coffee and talked mostly about themselves could hope to understand Him at all.

He knew what Terry meant to me, though. And, of course, he already knew why I was here. "I was wondering when you'd ask," he said.

. . .

I've never liked motels because I've never known much good to happen in them. Following Manny up the concrete staircase facing the parking lot, I thought about all the times the two of us had walked up similarly ugly staircases, wondering if we were about to get shot or shoot someone, wondering what the hell awful thing could be going on behind that row of doors. This time I had at least some idea what awful thing had happened.

"So why *did* it take you three weeks?" Manny asked. "I expected you to be over here the day after the funeral."

"It's a good question," I said. "It deserves a good answer."

"You haven't been a cop in a long time." Manny stopped before the door. "I put myself at risk when I let you pretend you are."

"I thought once we were cops, we were always cops. Did I remember that wrong?"

"You know what I mean," Manny said. "And let's hope you remembered that wrong."

"Listen," I said, "if SAPD says it was a pure and simple overdose, who am I to argue? I spent every day of the past three weeks telling myself that it wasn't my business. My business was to remember my friend the way he was. We had a memorial, right? Do we really need an investigation, too? That was my thinking, anyway."

"That's the way I see it." Manny made no move toward the

door. "I looked into it because I figured you wanted me to. I didn't see anything but—"

"—a junkie who ODed?" I said. "I gotta run out the string, Manny. I'm sorry, but I want to know everything."

"I'll help you until I can't help you anymore." Manny had borrowed a key from the manager. He unlocked the door and led me in.

It was exactly the kind of room where you don't want your friends to die. It smelled awful, and there was never going to be any good way to air it out. The carpet was stained and ground nearly to dust except for a man-sized section that had been cut down through the flooring. Bright plywood told me exactly where Terry had died, his body leaking toward the ground floor.

The law had forced the motel to dispose of all human waste, but apparently, it hadn't forced them to replace the carpet.

I walked in first, and Manny followed me. Neither of us spoke for a long time. There was a queen-size bed on one end of the room, a round dinette on the other, a TV on a cabinet, a short hallway to the bathroom, a closet, lamps, an unwholesomely bright bedspread, no dents in the drywall that I could see. The stains on the floor were disgusting but not out of the ordinary. They probably had nothing to do with Terry's last night.

"Report for overdose," Manny started in. "No response, dead for about two days, based on lividity. I tried to get you the paperwork, but I couldn't. I read it all very carefully, though."

"Tox report?"

"Heroin and methamphetamine," he said. "Speedballs. Nothing unusual. Acute intoxication of heroin."

I took a moment to process that word: "intoxication." We

were talking like cops, but that was the extent of my calm. "Was there alcohol in the room?"

Manny shook his head. "The rig was in his arm. Did he have some kind of tattoo?"

I tapped my left forearm. "The Chinese characters for prosperity to cover up some vein damage from the old days."

"That's where he shot up," Manny said. "Into the tattoo. He was right-handed?"

"Yeah," I said. "Check-in?"

"He paid cash," Manny said. "The clerk remembers him. Again, nothing unusual. He checked in under his own name. Clerk didn't see anyone else."

"No trauma on the body?" I asked. "Bruising? Petechial hemorrhaging? Evidence of asphyxiation?"

"No," Manny said. "None of that."

"Did he fall when he died?"

"Without any bruises," Manny said, "I'd guess that he slid when he died."

Taking it all in, I recognized that this was mostly what I'd been avoiding: an accurate picture of his death. Drugs didn't just kill you; they made you look like an idiot.

"They must have found the Mercedes about ten minutes before it was stripped?" I asked.

Manny stroked his goatee and then returned his hands to his hips. "This is a better neighborhood than it used to be. The car was there for two days without a scratch on it."

"Who noticed the car? The manager?"

"You think someone here called in the car?" Manny frowned. "You think these people have time for that? You've been in Laguna too long."

"How'd they find him, then? All we were told was that it took two days."

"Someone called 911 a couple days late. Didn't do *pendejo* much good, but it probably saved the fucking Mercedes."

Off my look, Manny backed down a little. He loved me, but he wasn't going to waste his heart on some asshole attorney who couldn't even shoot dope in his own town.

It was significant information he'd given me: it's one thing to call 911 when someone is in trouble; it's another thing to call 911 two days late. That detail probably told a story about more than one person, maybe even a community of people. Someone certainly had time to think about it, to decide how much he wanted to be involved. That detail stood for a lot of information about Terry's death that I really fucking wanted to know.

"Maybe someone feeling guilty way after the fact?" Manny said.

"Maybe," I said. I made myself look at the plywood where Terry had died.

"Or maybe the person who made the call," Manny said, "wasn't the one who was actually here when it happened."

"Whoever it was," I said, "I need to find the guy."

"Gal," Manny said. "Probably Mexican. She spoke Spanish for the first part of the tape."

I turned away from the bright plywood. "I want them to put some new carpet in here. I'm not going to be able to sleep thinking about that cutout. You think we can lean on the manager?"

"We can pretend we're cops," Manny said. "It's probably some code violation, anyway."

I had a box of Arturo Fuentes for Manny when I said goodbye. And a birthday gift for him that I'd put behind my truck seat two months ago and forgotten to send: a first edition of Pierre Teilhard de Chardin's *The Phenomenon of Man,* which MP had suggested. Manny nearly danced a Mexican jig in the parking lot. What kind of cop gets excited about Jesuit anthropologists? Manny was a good guy, though. I needed his friendship more than he needed mine. If he'd known how much I was hurting—how much I wanted to crush my heart in my fist—he wouldn't have let me drive home alone.

. . .

On the surface, Terry's death wasn't so extraordinary. But it bothered me that the circumstances of his death weren't anything special to Manny and weren't supposed to seem special to me. Terry was a junkie, and this was how junkies died. Failing to hook Claire Monaco back into his drama, he'd probably found another woman to spend his last night on earth with him, and apparently she spoke Spanish. I wasn't sure what that meant for Claire's "electrician named like a dog" yet.

According to Manny, the 911 had come from a pay phone on Flower Street near the Civic Center. I assumed the caller was a prostitute. Hookers and heroin overdoses went together like, well, hookers and heroin overdoses. I drew a grid between the motel and the pay phone and slowed my truck to talk with every loitering woman I passed, asking about the silver Mercedes. After promising I wasn't a cop, I showed a picture of Terry from the program for his memorial. I folded back the part that talked about his fifteen years of service to A.A.

On the street behind Saddleback Inn, I caught up with a Latin American woman wearing Gloria Vanderbilt jeans and a backpack ornamented with tiny stuffed animals. Her location gave me a shudder—I had spent prom night at Saddleback Inn, and now it was a crackhole with some amazingly articulate ornamental iron and a swimming pool plugged with concrete. I was just about to head home—no, she didn't recognize him, no, she didn't remember his silver Mercedes—when she bent closer into my passenger window. She smiled. "Where'd *you* go?"

"Pardon me?" I had the awful feeling that I knew her. That's one of the great things about blackout drinking: you never know what new story you'll hear about yourself. You thought you weren't the kind of cop who slept with hookers, but maybe you just didn't remember.

"You're the cop who fucked up Balthazar."

I was perversely relieved that she knew me by bad reputation only.

"Where you been? You didn't go to jail, that's for fucking sure. You with the sheriffs now?"

"I had to find a new way to make money," I said. "They wouldn't let me be a cop anymore."

"That's good," she said. She slapped the side of my shiny black truck and walked quickly away. I turned my head to see the SAPD cruiser that had abruptly ended our conversation. He flashed his lights and goosed his siren. In a minute, I'd be looking at the badge of a twenty-five-year-old who wouldn't know nearly as much about me as the hooker had. Resting my hands on the top of the steering wheel, I waited for permission to show him my retirement badge.

4

EVEN IN MY WORST DAYS, I'd always had one good thing in my life. I had something that Wade didn't have, that Betsy and Jeep didn't have. Something that Terry had wanted so badly that he'd tried to take it from Claire Monaco.

I had a child.

She lived in Anaheim Hills with her mother. She was the reason I never ate my gun. The reason I wasn't in jail. Ultimately, she was probably the reason I wasn't drinking. It was hard to talk that way in A.A.—the cranky old-timers would tell you that it wasn't enough, that alcoholism was stronger than the bonds of family, that the vision of your adored tomboy daughter wasn't enough to keep you on the wagon. They were right, of course. But they were also wrong.

I called her Crash, but almost no one else did. Her real name was Alison, after that Elvis Costello song. My ex-wife, Jean Trask, when she used to like me, would call her Crash sometimes, too. When she was a little girl, Crash loved arranging Matchbox cars into vast, noisy conflicts: car chases, multicar pileups, that kind of thing. Her desire to stage vivid confrontations hung on in our shared love of fireworks. "Fireworks" is a nice way to put it: "explosives" would be more accurate. On our favorite annual road trip to Nevada, we bought a truckload and then set them off all at once in the desert.

I used to pray that she didn't become a cop. I needed to remember to pray for that again.

She'd been holding up pretty well despite the fact that her parents had been fighting over her all over again for about a year. I'd woken up one morning near my seventh A.A. anniversary realizing that it wasn't okay with me that I had no legal connection to my own daughter. I had been in the middle of a divorce when the DA was deciding whether or not to charge me with attempted murder *and* it was the bad end of my drinking. So it had made some kind of sense to give up custody. But I wasn't that man anymore. The trouble was that I couldn't convince my ex-wife. Now we were about a month away from the mother of all court hearings. My sister, Betsy, had helped me assemble a dossier testifying to my new standing as a solid citizen—statements from pretty much everyone I knew as well as magazine articles about my design work and every financial statement I'd ever filed. It was an impressive display that my sister was confident would do the trick if the judge was reasonable at all.

At the end of Jeffrey Road was a fire trail that ran through private land high enough so that on a good day, you could see the Channel Islands. Sometimes there was an old security guard who tried to run you off, but that afternoon we were lucky. I hadn't originally planned to take my lunchtime trip to Santa Ana, so I hadn't envisioned this bike ride as an antidote to Santa Ana, but it was working well. By the time I'd pulled the bikes from the truck, it seemed like Crash was already beating my ass up the hill. The switchbacks that reached up for the ridge were as lush as anything in Orange County: scrub, cactus, and mustard so vivid that it seemed to dim the rest of the vegetation. The snow that stuck to Saddleback Mountain looked close enough to touch.

We didn't talk for the first mile or so because we were both pretending it was easy for me to keep up with her. When we reached a plateau, Crash broke the silence. "You have something for me this weekend?"

"You don't want to know," I said.

"That big?"

"That loud. But if you tell any of your pyro friends, I'm going to jail."

If the state of California had just started granting learner's permits at thirteen, Crash would have smiled a little wider. I experienced a nagging thought that, God help me, I'd had every day since she was born. This time, I said it out loud. "Do you think I'm a bad father?"

Crash smiled. "No, I think you're an out-of-shape, breathing-too-heavy father. Why do you ask such stupid questions?"

"I feel like a goof with this helmet," I said. "Isn't there some way I can get you to wear one without having to wear one myself?"

She stood on her pedals and cranked ahead of me a few yards.

"Why did your mother need the afternoon off?" I shouted after her.

"She has a date," Crash said.

"With John Sewell?"

"Yeah."

"Since when did your mom start taking off weekday afternoons?"

"Since John asked her to the groundbreaking of the new bazillion-dollar Civic Center. Mom always goes where the rich people go."

"Are you being a smart-ass about your mother?"

"No. If I were an investment banker, I'd follow the rich people, too. Besides, she goes wherever John goes. He's her guy."

"He ever say anything to you about an electrician with a name like a dog?"

"Huh?"

"Never mind," I said. "You think they'll get married?" I wondered what effect her marriage would have on our custody battle.

"Why?" Crash said. "You jealous?"

"I barely know the guy," I said. "I think it's nice that you like him, though."

"You think it's nice that I like him? Why are you talking like a father from a TV show? Yeah, they're going to get married. Yeah, I like him. But you don't even like my coaches. You're telling me that you're going to be totally cool with a stepfather?"

"Unless you call him 'Dad,'" I said. "And then I'll have to kill you both."

Crash rode close to the edge of the road. We were getting

higher and the drop-off was steep. "Tell me what's wrong with you," she said, "or I'm going to throw myself over the cliff."

My stomach churned. There was a part of Crash, I knew, that believed she could do it. So much for escaping the insanity of her parents.

"I've been feeling sad about my friend Terry."

Crash had insisted on coming to the memorial service because that's the kind of girl she is, but we'd never really talked about his death.

"He was like my big brother," I said. "And my father and friend all rolled into one."

We slowed to a stop in the middle of the fire trail. It blew my mind that Saddleback Mountain was no longer wreathed in smog. I'd been looking up at that smog my whole life.

"I know what he was," Crash said. She looked up at Saddleback before she looked back at me. "What's it feel like?"

"I guess I feel lost," I said. Like a dinghy in an ocean that just got emptied by a meteor. "No one has ever died on you, have they?"

"Your dad? Mom's dad?"

"You don't remember them, do you?"

"Not really," she said, "but I know what you mean. I felt that way when you got divorced."

"You remember that?"

She glanced at me like I was an idiot, a glance I recognized from her mother.

"Remember when Terry and I used to take you to the movies?" I said, eager to change the subject. "What was that movie we saw so many times?"

"Terry never talked that much around me. I liked him, but I was never sure if he liked me."

"I didn't notice. Was that weird?"

"Not weird," Crash said. "Maybe confusing."

We started riding again, turning away from Saddleback toward Santiago Canyon Road. Thinking about Terry, I remembered a definition of "cool" that I'd once heard: loneliness seen from the outside in. Terry had always been pretty cool.

"He was jealous," I shouted, my calves burning to keep up. "He wanted kids more than anything, but he didn't know how to make that happen."

"Why didn't he ask somebody to marry him?" Crash said as I caught up with her.

"You think it's that easy?"

"Absolutely," Crash said. "Don't you?"

I wanted to say I didn't think it was that easy. But then I realized we weren't talking about Terry anymore. My thirteen-year-old daughter smiled and started pedaling hard again.

5

STORIES ABOUT TERRY MAKE HIM seem like some sort of tough but loving drill instructor. He was that, but he was also a deeply strange man whose life baffled him as much as anyone.

One time he took me to an A.A. convention in Palm Springs. He was speaking at the banquet, and I think he told me about it ten minutes before we drove away in his Cadillac. He knew I didn't have anything better to do. After we'd been in the hotel for about a half a day, moving from room to room listening to charismatic A.A. speakers, sitting before good-natured A.A. panels, I'd had enough. I couldn't handle the volume of the place. Everyone was vibrating at a frequency that made me want jump from my skin. I went back to our room, took a long shower, and then lay on the bed in my shorts planning to hitchhike home.

Terry returned in crisply pressed linen pants and a blue

Hawaiian shirt that didn't have any wrinkles, either. He leaned against the wall beside the bathroom. "You want to get away from here at any cost," he said. "Failing that, you want to kill yourself. You're thinking about stealing my car right now."

I just stared at him. *Yes, yes, yes,* I thought. *So fucking what?*

"If I were you"—he stood up straight—"that's exactly what I'd do. Go ahead and steal my car. Get the fuck out while you can."

He smiled. And then he left the room.

. . .

When I took Crash home, there was a full-tilt autobahn-eating Mercedes in my ex-wife's driveway, the G-series, the expensive kind. Jean's date wasn't over yet. I'd get the chance to talk with John Sewell sooner than I'd thought. When I took off my seat belt, Crash gave me a wide-eyed look: it was rare that I wanted to see my ex-wife.

I walked in with Crash, armed only with the vague cover story of speaking with my ex-wife about starting a college fund, an idea that had suggested itself after this morning's abrasion with the very uncollegiate Troy Padilla. I sometimes dreamed up these arbitrary conversations with Jean, hoping that if I distracted her from our custody battle, maybe it would go away.

Jean and "her guy," John Sewell, were on the patio, drinking the same expensive ginger ales that I stocked myself. Crash wisely ducked into her bedroom.

As he stretched out his hand, I remembered how much I had wanted to like John Sewell that time when we invited him fishing with us off Dana Point; I was guardedly encouraged when Crash brought his name home one weekend. He was about my size and shape, maybe five years older, going gray, and he had a jaw that belonged in a shaving commercial. He wore a navy suit without a tie, but I knew the tie was around here somewhere. He was the kind of man who held your hand for exactly the right amount of time as he looked squarely into your eyes.

I gave Jean an awkward kiss on the cheek, which is what people like us do to pretend we're not people like us. It had been years since we'd screamed at each other, but that didn't mean we were friends. Jean was wearing a tailored jeans jacket over a salmon-colored shirt and a butt-framing pair of slacks. She was a compact but lovely woman, and she should have married the kind of country-club geek she went to USC with, the kind her father always pushed her toward. The kind of guy who grew up to look exactly like John Sewell.

"We shouldn't be talking," Jean Trask said. "You're suing me."

"I'd be happy *not* to sue you," I said, "if you'd agree to share custody of our daughter."

"It's a good thing, then," she said, "that it's not my job to make you happy."

Her response was so sharp that I almost laughed. "This is ridiculous, Jean. If I lost your trust eight years ago, I've more than—"

"You gave away your rights in this situation," she said. "It would be easier on everyone if you would just accept that."

I looked at Sewell, wondering how far ahead of me he was. The conversation had gone to shit almost immediately, and yet his expression seemed remote, maybe even bemused.

"This is not unreasonable, Jean. I've consented to drug tests.

I've consented to home visits. For the past eight years, I've lived an exemplary life. What do you want me to do that I haven't done?"

"I want you to drop the lawsuit. You have everything you need. I don't deny you access to Alison; she even has a room at your house. What we're arguing over is a technicality."

"You think it's a technicality," I said, "that I have no legal status in her life? You could move her to another state without even telling me."

"You should have thought of that, Randy, when you destroyed our reputation on the front page of every paper in Southern California."

Jean Trask had shed my last name as quickly as a prisoner sheds his orange jumpsuit. Her maiden name had always sounded like military discipline to me. I couldn't remember what it felt like to love her.

Sewell cut us both off at the pass, which I suspected was his specialty. He did it in an interesting way, too: he cleared his throat, looked at the room around us, and then launched into something entirely different. It wasn't denial so much as a weird dominance. He'd decided that the conversation should be over, so he declared it over.

"Randy," he began, "Alison says that project in Capistrano is something to see. How did she put it—Frank Lloyd Wright in skateboard shoes? I'm not sure what that means, but I was impressed by her enthusiasm." Sewell's default mode was to conciliate. I remembered that about him. Or rather, I remembered what Terry had said about him: *Guy can't even take a bathroom break until he's sure everything's in order.*

I wish I were better defended against this kind of compliment, but I'm not. Convince me that my daughter loves me a tenth as much as I love her, and I'm your bitch.

One of Jean's former boyfriends had written me a poem about his "yearning" for us to be good friends. Another asked if I wanted to do a sweat lodge with him sometime. So I liked the idea of John Sewell. He was cordial, and he acted like a man. All I really wanted was a safe place for my daughter to live when she couldn't live with me. An end to my alimony wouldn't hurt, either.

John suggested to Jean that maybe I would like a ginger ale, too, and she left the room with such fury that you could hear the fabric of her slacks whipping against itself. In an instant, John and I were alone together.

"Can I ask you a question, John?"

"I don't see why not."

"You ever meet an electrician named after a dog? Maybe someone who worked for you?"

Sewell smiled kindly and shook his head. "I don't think so, Randy. Why?"

"You don't even want to know," I said.

Sewell looked thoughtfully into my eyes. "I was sorry to hear about Terry. I missed the memorial. I was in Sacramento working on—"

I interrupted him. "We were good friends to him while he was alive, right?"

"That's right," Sewell said. "Although now I wish we had spent more time fishing. Was that a pretty regular outing for you guys?"

"For a while," I said. "Then we got busy."

"That's too bad," Sewell said. "I thought of you being out there every weekend, Terry planning everyone's lives."

"What was his plan for you, John? I can't remember."

"I was going to be a senator. And if I remember correctly, you were going to run a huge development corporation."

"How's that working out for us?"

Jean arrived with my ginger ale. "John's got too much integrity to be a senator. He's going to be a judge."

"Should I be congratulating him now?" I asked her. "Did I miss an announcement?"

"Yes," she said, "you should be congratulating him now."

"It's not official," John interjected, "but it's in the pipeline."

"They're going to give him Judge Fogarty's bench," Jean said. "Now that the old bastard has finally done the right thing."

John looked down modestly. "It came at a good time," he said. "I was looking for new challenges." His statement of intent was flavorless, but I didn't begrudge him: Jean had enough *picante* for both of them.

"Fogarty resigned?" I said.

"He should have resigned years ago," Jean said.

"I think judge *is* better than senator," I said. "Congratulations."

"And I'm pretty sure," Sewell said, "that being a builder who's regularly featured in design magazines beats running a development company."

"That may be true," I said, "but you just came a lot closer to fulfilling Terry's predictions than I have. You ready to give up lawyering?"

"Happily," he said.

Although I didn't necessarily want to end Jean's discomfort

with our mutual admiration, I decided to employ my college-fund conversational gambit. Things had already gone way south with Jean, but I figured maybe I could endear myself to the soon-to-be Honorable John Sewell.

As it happened, Crash walked back into the room in time to hear her mother laugh. "Who is this college fund for? You? That youngster you live with? Alison has less than four years until graduation. What did you think I would do, wait for someone to die and will it to me?"

Sewell smiled in a neutral way. A thought occurred to me that must have already occurred to a smart man like him: this was a discussion we should have been having in private.

"That's great," I said. "How much do you need from me?"

"You're already contributing," Jean said. "I'm putting in your alimony. It's not like I need it."

Humiliation from my ex-wife wasn't anything new, but it was particularly painful in front of her boyfriend. I considered my options. With Crash standing beside her mother, I didn't have any. I could have asked Jean for a steak knife in order to commit ritual suicide, I guess.

"Can I make a suggestion?" Sewell said.

For a second, we both looked at him as though we couldn't imagine how he had materialized in our lives. I managed a nod. Jean barely moved.

"The way things are going with the market these days," he said, "it makes sense for both of you to have college funds. One of you could have a 529, and the other could start a trust in Alison's name. Listen, if you want to talk sometime, Randy, I can give you some suggestions. I do okay with this kind of thing."

Jean wasn't happy to watch Sewell pull me from the fire. She gathered up the empty bottles, and my own not-empty bottle, and took them to the kitchen. Crash followed her mother, probably to make sure she didn't return with that steak knife.

"She hates you." Sewell said it like he was telling me my truck needed new tires.

"I didn't notice it while we were married," I said, "because there was so much disgust, too."

"I'm going to make her hate you less." Sewell stood up, which I took as a signal that I should start heading to the door. "It's no way to start *our* marriage. I'm good at this kind of thing, too."

Leaving without saying goodbye to Jean was an excellent plan. I could call Crash from my truck. Shaking John Sewell's hand, I felt grateful for his attempts to make my life easier. And that wasn't even the worst mistake I made that night.

6

TURNING UP CHAPMAN TOWARD the toll road, I took a moment to enjoy one of the last pieces of open farmland in this part of Orange County. Thousand-foot peaks brooded over both sides of a box canyon that bottomed out into a lake. It was getting near dusk, and I almost didn't mind being myself for a few moments.

On the way toward Laguna, though, my cell phone rang. The caller ID said MVP Entertainment, which didn't sound like anyone who wanted me to build them a home, so I answered it.

"Randy, it's Claire Monaco. I want to straighten a few things out."

Call waiting cut in. It was MP. Considering our talk this morning, and the fact that I'd recently been seen soliciting prostitutes in Santa Ana, I figured I'd better take it: "Hold on a second, Claire. Hi, sweetheart."

"Claire Monaco just called."

"Oh, okay," I said. "Did you, uh, give her my cell number?"

"No," MP said. "I told her I would ask you to call her. Which is what I'm doing now. Do you *have* her cell number?"

"Yeah. I think so. I was talking to her this morning about Terry, in fact. She's trying to help me figure out what happened."

There was a long beat of silence before MP spoke. "Do you know what she did last week?"

"Something awful?"

"She came to the Saturday-afternoon women's meeting at Saint Ann's, and when it was her turn to share, she made amends—in front of everyone—to Sherry. She wanted to apologize for sleeping with Jack the week before. She said she felt really bad about hurting another sober woman. 'A sister' is what she called her."

I thought about this while I swung my truck around on the cloverleaf between the Santa Ana Freeway and the Newport Freeway. A low-wattage energy-saving lightbulb appeared above my head. "Sherry hadn't known about it until that moment?"

"That's correct."

"Aren't you supposed to keep that stuff to yourself?" I said. "I mean, it being a closed meeting and all?"

"Sherry's going to divorce Jack," MP said. "If it were me, I would have cut off his balls."

Apparently, advanced yoga training was more ethically complicated than I had imagined. Maybe I shouldn't have laughed. MP hung up.

When I clicked back over to Claire, she said, "I think you've got some bad ideas about me, Randy. Was that MP on the other line?"

Why, besides causing trouble, would Claire call my home when she already had my cell number?

"Is it possible," I said, "to have *good* ideas about you?"

"This is what I'm talking about," Claire said. "What you just said."

"Tell me something," I said. "Have you made any 911 calls in Spanish lately?"

"I don't know what you're talking about, but if it has something to do with Terry's death, I was out of his life a long time before any of that shit went down. You know that better than anyone. You know exactly when I broke things off."

"Thanks for calling, Claire. Take it easy." I started to hang up.

"I was trying to apologize for being an asshole," she shouted. "Can you just—"

"Okay." Calling yourself an asshole was always good for another minute of my time.

"I shouldn't have brought MP into our conversation this morning."

It sounded like an authentic apology. "I'm sorry, too, Claire. I like you. You're trouble, but I like you."

It took her a moment to fill the silence that followed my admission. "I like you, too, Randy."

Claire hung up. She didn't ask for anything. She didn't feed me another line about an electrician named after a dog. She didn't try to hurt me. Either this was a new strategy to destroy men's lives or she'd actually apologized. When she started coming to meetings a few years ago, there had been a moment when she got it—she knew why she was there—but that moment passed, and she became the kind of A.A. you needed to watch out for: someone who will take you down quicker than you can lift her up. Claire still had volunteers, though. For one short, bad moment a couple of years before he died, Terry had been one of them.

. . .

Every alcoholic has one thing that cuts to the marrow. The thing that he wants but can't quite achieve, the thing that he's always on the cusp of, the "until I get this, I am nothing." For some of us, it's professional success. For some, it's a good marriage. For Terry, it was children.

Terry wanted kids more than anything.

His own father had been an Irish Catholic bank president with eight kids. Terry could no way ever hope to become a bank president—he'd been arrested for everything from a teenage armed robbery to kiting checks right before he got sober, and the fact that he'd been able to join the bar was an A.A. miracle—but he always believed he should have kids. He just never found the right mother.

That deal with Claire Monaco, his attempt to extort her son from her, was at the extreme end of a long line of attempts to put together a relationship that would produce kids. His choices weren't always awful, but they were always off by enough that we had to wonder if Terry wanted what he said he wanted. He went out with fifty-year-old empty-nesters. He went out with psychotically driven career women—the kind who couldn't stop long enough to fill a gas tank, let alone get pregnant. He went out with social-climbing party girls making their way through A.A. as though nothing needed to change about their shallow lives except their consumption of alcohol. Those girlfriends were the hardest for us to take. There was a certain kind of female narcissism that Terry was blind to. I don't know how many times we tried to tell him: *She's only using you, dude. She doesn't even see you.* When that kind of girlfriend moved on for a nicer home and car, Terry was always surprised.

He told me once that he and his wife tried to have children, pushing themselves through fertility treatments and in vitro right to the door of adoption, but his drug addiction destroyed the marriage before that could happen. All he ever told us about his ex-wife was that she'd been a psychiatric social worker when they met, and now she was a high school teacher somewhere in the Bay Area.

If you knew anything about Terry, you knew he wanted to have kids. Wade and I, his real children, thought it was funny how hard he worked at it. It was the one area of his life where we could count on him being out to lunch, almost completely unconscious of the disconnect between his ambition and his actions. He tried Big Brothers for a while, but he got in trouble for spending too much money on the kids. He made himself available for babysitting whenever some single mother in A.A. needed it, but he wasn't much good at that, either. It was like he was trying to be some twenty-first-century version of a 1950s father—a version of parenthood that somehow didn't involve much parenting.

I came to visit him one evening when he was looking after Claire Monaco's four-year-old son, Alexander. This was before their difficulties. It was nine P.M. on a Wednesday, and they were watching *Black Hawk Down*. Alexander's eyes were glossy with the candy that had been opened all around the two of them: heroic quantities of Twizzlers and peanut-butter cups and foil-covered chocolate eggs. Terry waved and smiled at me as I entered the living room. Alexander never broke his gaze from the TV.

"Have you guys eaten anything?" I asked.

"Sure," Terry said, his eyes returned to the screen.

"I mean besides this crap. Something with protein in it?"

Terry shook his head. A Somalian guerrilla died horribly on the wide screen, and Alexander pushed himself farther into Terry's shoulder.

I ordered pizza, and I began trying to be aware of whenever Terry was babysitting.

He regarded me sometimes as an expert on children, but in that funny way of people who have no idea what your expertise is.

"What if the kid doesn't like you?" he asked once.

"What the hell are you talking about?"

We had been skin diving among the kelp forests off Emerald Cove, something that Terry had spent the whole morning outfitting himself for at Laguna Sea Sports, thanks to Wade's employee discount, but which we never did again.

We were climbing up the rocky shelf of the beach. I sat down and began idly popping the bulbs of washed-up kelp plants.

"I mean . . ." he said. "You know what I mean."

"Like, the kid won't be amused by you? What are we talking about? An infant or a teenager?"

"I'm talking every age. I'm talking whatever age."

I tossed a big gross mess of kelp back toward the water. Why I'd even picked it up, I wasn't sure. It felt good to be the one who was giving Terry advice.

"It's beside the point, I guess is all I can say. You spend a lot of time cleaning them up when they're babies, making sure they stay alive, and they love you the way someone loves an airplane that's keeping them in the sky. Mostly, you don't have time to ask those questions. And when they're older, it's beside the point, because it would be like asking them whether they like their own arm or leg. You're so much a part of them. I don't even care if my daughter likes me. I just care whether she allows me to participate in her life, and if she ever stopped doing that, I'd have to camp out on her doorstep until she changed her mind."

"That sounds good," Terry said. He was looking at the ocean when he said it, and I couldn't see his eyes.

. . .

It was about six months after my babysitting intervention, in that same condo, the last one that Terry owned. It was sort of art deco with picture windows overlooking the ocean and two car-ports under each unit. Efficient but not unbeautiful. Architec-turally, it seemed to recognize that it lived on a bluff above Pacific Coast Highway, and it never aspired to be more wonder-ful than that.

As I parked beneath his apartment, I was aware that Terry's obsession with starting a family was getting out of hand. People told me about his difficult relationship with Claire, how some-times they seemed like a couple and sometimes it seemed like Terry wanted to be Alexander's father. We hadn't seen each other in over a month. I was getting busy with work, but I hadn't met MP yet. I was going to lots of meetings, so I noticed he was MIA—he'd retreated from the wagging tongues—but I didn't think much of it until I tried to reach him and he didn't return my calls.

Terry appeared at his front door in an unbuttoned white dress shirt and a pair of board shorts. He smiled when he saw me but didn't say anything, only opened the door. I sat down, pulled my cell phone from my pocket, and tossed it on the coffee table.

"They must think I'm in bad shape," Terry said, "to send you."

I forced a laugh. "Who is 'they,' Terry? Why does there have to be a plot for me to come visit you?" But there was plenty of truth to what he was saying.

"Because there is," Terry said. "Maybe it's just you and Wade. But I'm familiar with the scenario." I didn't like the look of that smile. It was his "fuck you" smile.

"Forget about Wade and anyone else," I said. "This is you and me talking."

"I'm trying to save this beautiful kid," Terry said, "from a mother who might kill him in the process of killing herself." He pointed toward the cabinet that held the wide-screen television. Above it—I hadn't noticed—was a photo of Alexander.

"He seems like a great little boy," I said stupidly.

"You want to say the word, Randy? You think I'm blackmailing Claire Monaco?"

The reason he thought he couldn't go to meetings in Laguna anymore: when Claire Monaco ran afoul of Judge Fogarty, Terry offered to help her out financially in exchange for custody of the kid. Folks had opinions about this. How could they not?

I shrugged, another admission of powerlessness.

"What am I supposed to do?" Terry said. "Watch the opportunity pass me by? Sit here while this kid's life is trashed?"

"You don't know that his life will be trashed."

"That's what assholes always say when they want to excuse their complacence. 'I don't know.' And while we're at it, Randy, where the fuck have *you* been? You come over to my house like a visiting dignitary. You're going to patronize *me*? Where were you when nobody in A.A. would even spit on me? Where were you when I pulled my head out and made the fucking dean's list at law school every fucking semester that I was there?"

It was a big moment for me. For the first time, maybe the only time, he was letting me into the hell of his own addiction. This was the real thing. Since I'd met him, I'd seen Terry acting six different kinds of crazy, but I'd never seen him acting like such a *victim*. He was alone. In his mind, at least, he was completely alone, and he seemed at that moment like a man who had been designed for the relief that only heroin or massive amounts of booze could provide. If you want to know the truth, it was kind of glorious, in a fucked-up way.

"You weren't here for any of that," Terry continued. "And you're not going to be here for this kid. This is *my* deal."

What the hell could I do? I couldn't imagine any good outcome for either of us. I'd try again later.

As often happens, though, my dilemma got worse before it got better.

Someone slammed Terry's front door three times, hard and deliberately. And then I heard a woman's voice shrieking at him to open the door.

Of course it was Claire.

Terry leaped toward the front door, but I moved quickly to stand in front of him. The next words that came out of my mouth were probably the most mysterious and effective words I've ever spoken. All the more mysterious because I barely understood what I was saying. And because of the man who I was speaking them to.

I held up my index finger in front of his face, the way someone from another century might correct an unruly child. "I'm not angry with you. Angry with you is the last thing that I am. But I'm going outside to talk with this woman, and you're *not* to interfere. If you leave this room while I'm chatting with her, I will drop you where you stand. And then I *still* won't be angry with you."

For reasons that I might not fathom even when I'm sitting at God's knee and He's whispering in my ear, Terry nodded and sat back down on the couch.

Claire had been standing so close to Terry's door that she jumped back when I opened it. She was a lot skinnier back then; those were the days of crack pipes and precious little eating. Even after she got her bearings back, she moved with the anxious, staticky jerks of a cartoon cat. She radiated disease. Being with her in those days—even to say hello on your way into a meeting—was like being in the presence of some wily version of death. No wonder most people treated her like Shiva, destroyer of worlds.

I put my hand on her back and led her toward the carports underneath the apartments. There was another line of units higher on the hill, and it wasn't a particularly private place, but Terry couldn't see us, and I didn't mind that everyone else could. If things went south, it wouldn't hurt to have witnesses.

"What are you, his press agent?" Claire said.

"Don't bother trying to make me angry, Claire. I've been worked on by experts."

"He's trying to take my fucking child away, Randy."

"Running over here is going to help you *how,* Claire? You want to get arrested for assault? This is your plan for making sure he doesn't take Alexander away?"

She looked at me earnestly and, I thought, soberly. It was maybe occurring to her that I didn't have Terry's back on this particular enterprise.

"Why are you even here?" I said. "You act like Terry has some power over you, like he can take your kid away. Unless I'm missing something, he can't. You'd have to *give* him custody. He's not the child's father, right?"

"No, he's not."

"Then what the hell are you doing here?"

Something was forming in her brain, some calculation of her self-interest. It wasn't a surrender to the truth so much as a surrender to the facts. I was about to understand her situation perfectly.

"I need him to give me some money," she said.

Even I wasn't quite ready for that one. She needed money to get out of her present troubles, and she was tempted to give her son to Terry in exchange, or at least trick him into thinking she might.

It was stunning to me that I could feel sorry for her, but I did. It took me a moment to speak. "He can't be the last house on the block, Claire. You've gotta have someplace else to go."

"It's a fucking miracle my mother still talks to me. But she doesn't have any money."

I thought about that. When I realized where I was headed, I took a deep breath. You go through life thinking that the moment of greatest danger will look like the moment of greatest danger, but that isn't it at all. The moment of greatest danger mostly looks like the moment of greatest *understanding.* That's so true they should teach it in school.

"How much do you need, Claire?"

"What do you mean?"

"I mean how much money can I give you right now that will make it possible for you to never darken Terry's door again? Enough money to dig yourself out."

"Ten grand would be a good start," she said, "but what I really need is twenty."

I pulled a check from my wallet and wrote it out for twenty-five thousand. "There are two conditions," I said. "You have to stay away from Terry, and if anyone asks you, you didn't get the money from me. Can you do those two things?"

"Yeah," she said.

"I'm not kidding," I said. "You can't tell anyone, and if you talk to Terry again, I will devote a month of my life to bringing down hell on your head. You got it?"

She got it. So well that a year and a half later, when I met her in the café with Wade that morning, she didn't risk mentioning the money. But she had talked to Terry the night he died. I wouldn't hold that against her, but I did hold it against myself that I hadn't talked to him, too.

7

HAD TERRY BEEN WITH A PROSTITUTE that night? Another junkie? Would it be easier to forgive a woman who had run from the scene than a man? Was it someone he'd met in A.A.? That was how people often slipped: in pairs. One junkie trying to talk another junkie out of copping. The disease, however, was a champion debater, and often the Good Samaritan ended up copping, too.

With the darkness settling into the hills, I headed back home. Approaching the day-labor station in Laguna Canyon— a stucco box on the side of the hill, a bathroom and shelter from the rain—I had to wonder how much work my guys were losing because I had no projects to put them on. Yegua was too polite to mention it, but the undocumented economy must have noticed my absence. What happened to the *gabacho* with the F-350 who paid us too much?

I was about to duck down another gopher hole of remorse when I saw Troy Padilla ambling pathetically along the other side of Laguna Canyon Road. The guys at the day-labor station made walking look dignified, but Troy couldn't pull it off. He must have been on his way to a meeting at the Coastal Club. I locked up my wheels and pulled a U-turn across the median. A Range Rover honked. A VW Phaeton honked at the Range Rover. My grille arrived at the spot where Troy had been staring into the gravel ahead of him.

Troy backed away. He looked pathetic doing that, too.

I threw myself out of my truck. "I'm not going to hurt you," I shouted. "Relax."

"Relax" was not one of Troy's menu options. Which was probably my fault.

"Just stay the fuck away from me," he said.

"I'm sorry," I said. "I want to apologize."

"You want to make amends to me?" Troy said.

Fucking A.A. jargon. "No, I don't want to make amends—I've come to apologize. I don't think you were with Terry at the end, and I was wrong to—"

"Make me piss my pants?"

I looked down. "That's not how I was going to say it."

"It's all right," Troy said. "It wasn't all you. I was sharing just now with my friend. I think I was channeling some earlier trauma. Kind of a post-traumatic stress reaction."

I laughed. "I'm pretty sure you were channeling a *pre*-traumatic stress reaction. I was going to kick your ass."

"Maybe that's what triggered it," Troy said. "I have a family history of violence. It was a good thing, though. This was a bottom for me."

More A.A. jargon.

"I threaten Wade," he continued. "You threaten me. I piss my pants. It's a cycle of violence. It doesn't stop unless someone stops it. I've gotta be the guy who stops it. You know what I'm saying?"

To shut him up, I nodded. "You want me to drive you to the meeting?"

Troy stared at me. He could probably write a term paper about his violent family history, but he couldn't decide whether he wanted a ride.

"Get in," I said.

. . .

As Troy opened the passenger door, a young woman emerged from the bushes behind Canyon Auto. She adjusted her jeans as though she'd just relieved herself. Odd enough, but Troy waved and shouted at her that he was catching a ride to the Coastal Club.

"I can drive her, too," I said.

"Emma's not going to the club," Troy said.

"What's she doing, then—embarking on a trek across the continent?"

When she reached my passenger window, I recognized Pierced Navel from this morning at the recovery home. Older than I had thought but no more than twenty. Tonight she wore a grungy button-down and Vans slip-ons. Her dirty-blond hair was an almost fashionable bird's nest. Beneath the tough-girl facade, though, she was blank-canvas pretty, like a fashion model. I imagined she could be as beautiful or bland as she wanted. Still, something about her was very not right. If Claire Monaco's troubles had transformed her face and body into a kind of brassy costume, this girl's troubles had made her transparent. Somehow she reminded me of Claire but without any of Claire's defenses. I figured I'd better apologize to her, too, but Troy, ever helpful, beat me to it. "Randy's probably going to want to make amends, Emma."

Standing behind Troy, resting her chin on his shoulder, she opened her eyes wide, a cartoon of smart-ass expectation.

"I'm sorry about scaring you this morning," I said. "You want a ride?"

"Nothing scares me," Emma said. "And I don't fucking care about your *amends.*"

"That's fair enough. Get in, Emma."

Like Troy, Emma had no effective defense against clear instructions. She pushed Troy in and took the window seat. She propped her back against the door to face us both. "You know what job I want? I want to be a sniper. Maybe have a license to kill."

"A fine ambition," I said.

"Don't fucking patronize me," Emma said. "I'm talking about killing people, maybe even you. And I'm not the only one—it's a big career path for high school seniors."

"*I got it,* Emma. Just be sure I don't kill you first. I'm as angry as you but with eight years of sobriety. That's eight years of cunning."

Emma briefly chewed on that before she said, "How come you're not a cop anymore? *That's* a license to kill."

"You know all that stuff they ask you to write down in your fourth step?"

Emma nodded warily as we entered the Coastal Club parking lot.

I smiled at her. "That's why I'm not a cop anymore."

She laughed and turned back toward the windshield. Her laugh was sharp and loud: it woke me up and squared my shoulders. When I slowed down for the creek bridge between parking lots, Emma opened the door and jumped out. I stopped to make sure she hadn't broken her ankle. That was when she turned around and gave me the finger, high up, like she wanted the whole world to see. She shouted, "I'm smarter than you. Don't forget that. You forget that, and bad things will happen."

"Okay," I said to Troy, "who the hell is she?"

"You don't recognize her?" Troy said. "She's a reality-TV star. She was on that show *Treatment Center*."

"Do I look like a guy who watches *Treatment Center*?"

"Yes, you do," Troy said. "That's pretty much exactly your demographic."

"She your girlfriend?"

Troy sharpened his eyes on me. "What do you mean?"

"You don't know what I mean?"

"No," he said. "She's not my girlfriend."

"Tell me who she is."

"She was raised in a family of Jehovah's Witnesses, but she's also this epic addict. She got kicked off that show for being too drunk and promiscuous, and you gotta understand that the point of that show is being too drunk and promiscuous."

"Where the hell is she going?" I asked Troy.

"Recon."

"Recon?"

"She's always on a mission. She walks. She observes. She covers as much of the South County as she can, forcing it to yield its secrets. Boots on the ground, Emma says, rifle in her hand—thank God she doesn't have the rifle yet. She's too wired to meditate or pray—I think it's her spiritual program. She's been sober a few weeks this way."

"This is the sniper thing?" I said.

"This is the sniper thing."

God help me, I liked her.

. . .

In my first year of talking to Terry, it often seemed like he was going out of his way to avoid discussing the most pressing problems in my life. For example, if I wanted to talk about my pending conviction for aggravated assault. If I wanted to talk about the fact that my wife was not only divorcing me but also keeping sole custody of our daughter. If I wanted to talk about how I was going to make money now that the city of Santa Ana was no longer going to pay me.

If we were anywhere near an A.A. meeting—which was often the case—or even anywhere near other A.A. members, Terry would point to whoever had less time in the program than I did—and even after a little while, there were many—and he would say, "You're not the patient here today." It was how Terry directed us toward A.A.'s "primary purpose"—to carry the message to the alcoholic who still suffers. It was his way of reminding me that we weren't always here to talk about *me*. Terry wouldn't tolerate self-pity. Helping others was the only way to help yourself. I sometimes had a hard time keeping that in mind, but it always saved my life.

. . .

My truck idled outside the Coastal Club. Troy didn't take the hint. I was not going to the meeting. I was dropping him off. But first he had to finish telling me how weird it was that when your dad's in the Mafia, you don't think there's anything weird about your dad being in the Mafia.

"The weirdness of the experience," Troy said, "disappears right into the weirdness of the experience."

Troy's pseudo-intellectualizing made me nostalgic for the straightforward if psychotic Emma. Insane and pretty used to be one of my favorite combinations. I married insane and pretty.

Troy finally seemed to be wrapping up his spiel on the notion that maybe criminals should have their own recovery programs, too (he was reaching for the door handle), when my friend Wade poked his head through the window.

"Park the truck," Wade said.

"No."

"I think you'd be happier."

"Like you?" I said.

"If you don't want to participate," Wade said, "why do you drive newcomers to the club?"

"He was wandering down Laguna Canyon Road," I said. "Someone was going to run him over. And . . . hold up a goddamn minute . . . weren't you two in a smackdown this morning?"

"We're good," Wade said. "Aren't we good, Troy?"

"We're good. *Love and service,* dude."

"Are you sponsoring this guy?" I asked Wade.

"No." And then Wade smiled. "Oh, man. I just got a download. *You* should be his sponsor."

Troy and I looked at each other. We silently agreed this was not a good idea.

"You're probably the only guy around here who's not impressed by his family," Wade continued, "with that badass cop background of yours."

"His father's probably a pharmacist," I said. "Dangerous people don't talk about being dangerous."

"Don't I get to have an opinion on this?" Troy asked.

Wade stepped away from my truck, which didn't mean the discussion was over. Wade never let go of anything that didn't have claw marks on it.

He stood beside my door, smiling at me, knowing he was about to pull his trump card. "You're not the patient here today."

Fuck you, I thought, but I pulled into a parking space.

8

FRANK GILLESPIE GREETED WADE and me outside the meeting room. Long before my time, he was a popular conference speaker known as California Frank. With his sparse gray hair, brown teeth, and early-stage emphysema, he could have been a time traveler from the gold rush.

"Welcome to the meeting. Is this your first time with us?" he asked me.

"Screw yourself, Frank. Have you met our latest science experiment—Troy?"

"Science experiment?" Frank said.

"Wade and I are bringing him to meetings to see if they cure his alcoholism," I said. "If they do, we're going to try it ourselves."

Frank shook Troy's hand. "You must be in bad shape, hanging around with these two. I'll say a prayer. Maybe a few."

The Coastal Club's meeting room was large and airy, with sliding glass doors along the north and south walls. There was no smoking anywhere inside the building. Not since the day it was built.

We got coffee and took seats around the end of a long table near the back wall. The Knife in the Head Men's Stag was named after a founder of the meeting who had once been so drunk that he got stabbed in the head and didn't notice. A "stag" was a meeting for men only. Terry and Wade and I used to be regulars here. One of the abiding rituals of the meeting used to be this old-timer from Oklahoma who'd tell any newcomer who had risked sharing his pain or confusion: "It doesn't sound to me like you're done drinking, son. You'd better get back out there and do it right."

One night that newcomer had been me. I'd wanted to shoot the hillbilly bastard in both kneecaps. With ten minutes of time for reflection between each of the shots.

After a few years, we had followed Terry to another men's stag at an Episcopal Church downtown. Terry called it the Fluffy Sweater Men's Stag. Every fall, half the meeting tied expensive sweaters around their necks. The rants were more tasteful. Wade and I used to bounce back and forth between the two meetings. Even in the days when we were all hanging together every night, there was no strict discipline about meetings: if Wade and I went to Knife in the Head and Terry went to Fluffy Sweater, we'd still all meet together at Jean Claude's later.

As the meeting started, I realized that I couldn't remember the last time I'd been to a meeting here.

After several readings from The Big Book, the chairperson, a skinny twentysomething with sun-bleached hair, announced the topic. "Why don't we talk about *acceptance*?"

Surfer boy picked a tall guy named T-Bone, a former session guitarist who now operated a window-cleaning business with a fleet of five trucks. T-Bone told us his name and that he was an alcoholic.

"HI, T-BONE!" I had to admit it felt good to hear that call-and-response; it felt like home.

T-Bone stood up. "I'm a drunk, so my thinking is never going to be anything but fucked. This"—he pointed to his head—"is broken. It won't ever be fixed. I can't even enjoy a blade of grass without forming an opinion. I imagine trouble and conspiracy everywhere. So when I pray, I ask God to help me accept the world exactly the way it is. I don't like it when sober people shoot drugs and die. But who am I to say? Maybe that's their right. You reap what you sow. A.A. is not for people who *need* it, it's for people who *want* it."

Around the room, guys nodded or grumbled their assent. Then everyone clapped. Of course, he looked directly at me when he said "shoot drugs and die." A few others did, too. I could have told myself that I hadn't been to meetings in a while, so no one could know about my search for Terry's last companion, but I knew Laguna A.A. better than that: the rumor mill was definitely churning. If anything, my absence was making it churn louder.

I almost missed the kid calling on me. Something about "hearing from someone we haven't heard from in a while."

Fuck. I sat up straighter in my folding chair. The entire meeting turned to look at me. "My name is Randy Chalmers, and I'm an alcoholic."

The wave of "HI, RANDY" felt good washing over me. For a long moment, I just stared, with nothing to say.

"Sometimes I hate A.A. so much," I began. "I've been to meetings with most of you, and if there were any real justice, all of us would be twisting in the wind. Terry Elias isn't dead because he sinned, and no one here is still breathing because he's a saint. If anyone has worked out a system for who's going to stay sober, I'm wondering why the fuck he didn't tell me that my best friend was going to OD. There aren't five of you who worked harder at this thing than Terry did. Terry taught me I was powerless over alcohol, but I didn't need to grovel before anyone. Not anyone. And that includes God. And every man at this meeting."

They took a moment to be sure I had finished. Wade gave me a thumbs-up as everyone started to clap. That's what they do in Southern California A.A.: when you finish, they clap. Whether they like you or not. Sometimes *because* they don't like you.

My "share" became the informal topic for the rest of the evening. It was either insane or the best thing anyone had ever said, but no one was neutral. A shaved-head hipster who was rebuilding his copywriting career after five years of vodka and crack used his five minutes to assure me, as politely as possible, that I'd be drunk soon if I kept talking this way and avoiding meetings. Relatively speaking, the guy was a newcomer. The last time I'd heard him talk, he was counting days and not quite so sure of himself.

When the meeting ended, Wade and Troy stepped ahead of

me like bodyguards as we exited the club. They seemed to be scanning the horizon for evidence of any angry approach. But I had to admit it cheered me to feel that I was once again part of a pack. As I left the clubhouse, everyone shook my hand, even the bald hipster who had promised I would drink. Troy and he exchanged wary nods.

"What's his story?" I asked when we walked away.

"He's the manager of my recovery home."

"Did you piss him off?"

"I don't think so."

"So how come he shook my hand but ignored you?"

Troy shrugged. "He's surly with me because I'm one of his charges. Him and Colin Alvarez, that's the way they roll."

After a few more well-meaning guys shook my hand, I found T-Bone standing at the end of the gauntlet.

"Terry was a good guy," T-Bone said. "I don't want you to think I was sitting in judgment. Like I haven't done worse shit. We just miss you around here."

It sounded like T-Bone was talking about more than a heroin overdose. "What 'worse shit' do you mean?"

T-Bone quickly let go of my hand.

"I'm not angry," I said. "I'm just asking. Is there some gossip that I'm not aware of?"

"The last thing I want to do"—T-Bone rubbed his hand over his mouth—"is spread rumors that I wish I hadn't heard in the first place."

"Which is why I'd rather hear it from you."

"It's A.A. bullshit, Randy. That doesn't make it true."

"T-Bone," I said, "just tell me."

We walked off from the crowd. T-Bone put his hand on my

shoulder and spoke close to my ear. "I heard Terry had developed a taste for thirteenth stepping."

A thirteenth step is when you seduce a newcomer. Also known, for good reason, as "cripple fucking." Most folks in A.A. regard this as the height of scumbag behavior, and Terry was one of them. I always thought it was part of his desire to be a father: nothing drove him farther around the bend than a compulsive thirteenth stepper, particularly a guy who preyed on newcomer women. I'd talked him out of violence on a couple of occasions.

"Claire Monaco?" I said hopefully. "She was hardly new. And their thing wasn't sexual. Trust me. It might have been better if it had been."

"Not Claire," T-Bone said. "Some of the girls in the recovery homes were—what's the word I'm looking for—active? We heard that Terry was involved with more than one of them."

"What does 'active' mean?"

"They were making movies, amateur porn, posting it on the Internet. The rumor was that Terry had fooled around with that."

"Amateur porn? Jesus, T-Bone."

"What I heard," T-Bone said carefully. "Doesn't mean it's true. What I heard."

"This was happening at the recovery homes?" I said.

"A rumor," T-Bone said.

What the hell was Terry doing hanging out at the recovery homes, anyway? I wondered about Emma, too—she was exactly the kind of rudderless girl you didn't want around that kind of weirdness.

Up the sidewalk, Wade was lurking. My new friend Troy was lost for a moment somewhere in the crowd. I caught Wade's eye, and he looked away. I said, "Couldn't that be backlash after the thing with Claire? People were saying all sorts of crazy things about him."

"Yeah," T-Bone said, straightening up. "That's probably exactly what it was."

Like me, T-Bone was smarter than he was supposed to be. It didn't bother him to be mistaken for a washed-up musician. Like me, he hid behind his failure. The truth was, he made more money now than he had working for the Eagles. And he was happier. I liked him because he had become, in sobriety, an honest man.

"But you don't think so," I said. "You had a feeling the rumors were true."

He took his hand off my shoulder. He looked down before he looked me in the eyes. "That's correct."

. . .

Just before we reached the truck, as I prepared to ask Wade, A.A.'s premier gossipmonger, calmly, why I'd never heard about Terry's thirteenth stepping from him, my cell phone rang. It was my home number, and I worried it was MP with more bad news. She was making love, maybe, to a better man than me. *Just wanted to share how much fun it is to bang someone besides a bitter ex-cop.*

I decided not to answer.

Troy was explaining why they should change the name of the Knife in the Head Men's Stag.

"Don't you think it invites a certain personality profile," Troy asked, "if you've got so much violence right there in the name? Maybe it's just my background, but—"

"Shut the fuck up about your background"—I *didn't* grab Troy by his shirt—"I don't want to hear any more shit about how you grew up in the Mafia. Okay?" As I hauled myself into the driver's seat, my home number called me again, and this time I pushed talk.

It was Yegua. "The *cholo* is here, parked out front."

9

I PUNCHED IT TO GET BACK to Bluebird Canyon, hoping to catch said *cholo* before he took off again. I told Wade that Yegua had seen the guy parked by my house and that I thought it might have something to do with Terry.

Wade said, "Dude, you think you're being *watched*?"

"I start asking questions about Terry," I said. "And now there's some guy parked in front of my house. Don't tell me I'm paranoid."

"Whatever," Wade said.

"Don't fucking *whatever* me, Wade. Pornography? Thirteenth stepping? I didn't even know Terry hung out at those houses, and now I'm hearing that it was some kind of fuck festival over there?"

"What are you talking about?" Wade said.

"T-Bone said Terry was a thirteenth stepper. He said he was hanging with girls at the houses who were doing amateur porn."

"It's news to me, too."

"Bullshit, Wade. There's nothing around this town that's news to you. When a bird falls from a tree *outside* an A.A. meeting, you hear about it. You want me to believe you didn't hear about this?"

"I didn't hear about this," Wade said evenly.

I turned back to Troy, figuring he was the one I really should have been interrogating. "You're living in one of those houses. You didn't know about this, either?"

"I knew about it, but I also didn't know about it."

"Explain that to me, please."

"It makes sense of some things that I heard."

As much as I wanted to know what that meant, just as we came up Bluebird Canyon, I spotted a battered old Suburban across the street from my house. The driver seemed pretty convinced of his invisibility until I passed my driveway and pulled up beside him. I leaned on my steering wheel and stared through Wade's window. No more than thirty, the guy looked like a refugee from 1969, with his unkempt beard and authentically dirty long hair. He might have been handsome, in that old-fashioned Protestant-surfer-Jesus way, but his attitude was too grim for that. He stared back at me with sharp, angry eyes.

He didn't confront me the way I thought he might. Nor did he cower. Those sharp, angry eyes just kept it up. How's a stalker supposed to look at you anyway? Defiantly? This guy seemed pissed off, all right, but he was also contained.

But when I rolled down Wade's window to speak with him, he suddenly slammed his Suburban into gear and pounded a

U-turn around my truck in the opposite direction. Maybe he didn't want to play the staring game anymore.

I gave him a moment to make it up the road. Then I followed him.

It was twilight as we wound our way through the switchbacks into the hills.

"Why are we following this guy?" Wade asked.

"*We're* not following this guy," I said. "*I'm* following this guy. You're my unfortunate passengers."

"Did he *do* something to you?" Wade asked.

"He's been parking across the street from my house," I said. "I told you that."

"You're going to beat up some guy whose only crime is parking down the street from your house? Don't get all Patriot Act on me, dude."

The ancient Suburban's brake lights flashed ahead of us. I slowed down.

"Am I allowed to talk now?" Troy said.

"Are you going to say anything that will piss me off?" I said.

"Is there anything that *won't* piss you off?"

"Good job, Troy. You've answered your own question."

We turned up Oro into the hills as the Suburban slowed down and turned in to a driveway. The house was a boxy one-story that had been tarted up with solar panels on the roof, a stainless-steel garage door, and a Zen rock garden.

I turned off my headlights and parked far enough down the road where my truck wouldn't be seen. Something told me that he didn't live here: he wasn't the solar panel/Zen garden type of guy.

Confirming my hunch, Surfer Jesus knocked on the front

door, then waited. When the door opened, I recognized the face.

"That's Colin Alvarez," I said. "Why is this dude going to see Colin Alvarez? The guy who's been stalking me just drove to a recovery house?"

"I don't think that's a recovery house," Troy said. "I think that's Colin's own house."

At this, Wade dove into my glove compartment for a pen and a piece of paper. He started to write.

"What are you doing?" I asked.

"Taking the guy's license plate," Wade said. "Weren't you a cop once?"

I was still counting the coincidences as Surfer Jesus spoke with Colin on the front porch. It seemed like a polite conversation, though Colin wasn't inviting him inside. Eventually, he gave the guy a pat on the shoulder, and Surfer Jesus nodded and walked back to his car. It would have been so easy to intercept him on the way back down the driveway, but I had his license plate, and I was already more pissed off at Colin Alvarez for being the destination than I was at Surfer Jesus for driving there.

I stepped out onto the street and turned back toward my companions. "Don't even think about getting out of this vehicle while I'm up there."

The door before me was tomato red and as solid as hands could fabricate. I wanted to bounce it off its hinges and take it home. After firebombing everything else.

I knocked hard on the door, which was almost immediately answered by Colin Alvarez. He was clearly surprised to see me. About an inch or two taller than I was but not much heavier, he practiced some kind of fashionable martial art. I'd never liked Colin, but fortunately, he'd never liked me, either.

He said, "You started an interesting discussion at Knife in the Head tonight."

"You have a video link to the Coastal Club?" That bald hipster who worked for him must have been on the phone with the boss before we even left the parking lot. Colin hadn't asked me why I was standing on his porch. "Why was that asshole posted in front of my house?"

"I don't know what you're talking about, Randy, but I wish you would take down your tone."

"The fucker who was just here, Colin. Why was he watching my house?"

"Mutt?" he said. "Mutt was watching your house?"

That was the sound of Claire's story clicking into place. "Let me guess, Colin. Mutt wouldn't happen to be an electrician, would he?"

Colin looked genuinely confused, which wasn't usually the way he looked. I didn't trust him. I asked again why the fuck this guy was watching my house.

"I barely know the guy, Randy. He's looking for a place to live. I was going to help him find a place at one of my houses, but—"

"But what? Do newcomers usually stop by your Zen palace in the middle of the night looking for a bed? Why don't you cut the bullshit?"

"Because that's the truth, Randy."

Some might argue that this would have been a good time to give Colin the benefit of the doubt, regroup, pursue some other avenues toward what the hell was or wasn't going on. But if my intention had been to think strategically, that bird was about to fly south with a lot of other good ideas I had ignored recently.

"It *is* a nice house," I said. "How many newcomers do you need to extort in order to cover the mortgage?"

Colin's gaze became tight and fixed. Apparently, I wasn't "taking down" my tone.

"You stroll into meetings when you feel like it," Colin said. "People see your big truck and they know about your wonderful new life. But where are you going to be when these newcomers are drunk in a ditch? I help people on a level that you can't even comprehend. I get that you're unsettled by Terry's death, and you're on a bit of a dry drunk. But you should calm the fuck down."

From down the street, I heard my truck door opening. We both looked to see Wade standing near the end of Colin's driveway, his arms crossed. Troy waited inside the truck, out of sight.

If Colin wasn't scared of me, he *really* wasn't scared of Wade. He got up into my face. "I want you and your crew to get the fuck off my property. Unless you feel like beating another Mexican? How long has it been, man?"

Wade's shoes slapped up the driveway.

A regular Gandhi, I held up my hands, and I calmly backed away. Fortunately, Colin seemed to have his own anger management issues: he followed me onto the driveway and came a little too close to my face with the sharp end of his index finger. I caught his arm and yanked it back up behind him, driving him down into the concrete. If I'd still been a cop, I could have cuffed him. Instead, I bent his arm right to the edge of popping out his shoulder. By the time he got himself up, I was pushing Wade back into the truck.

10

MY HEAD HURT WITH TRYING to understand whatever I'd just stumbled into. The electrician named after a dog, it turned out, was more than a figment of Claire's imagination. His name was Mutt, he'd been prowling around my house, and he reported to Colin Alvarez. If Mutt had been with Terry when he died, how did that connect to Alvarez? And why was Alvarez checking up on me? I'd also learned that Colin had some weird things going on in his recovery houses—amateur pornography, for one. Somewhere in the middle of this was my sponsor, Terry, dead in that motel room in Santa Ana.

We headed back to the Coastal Club, where Wade had left his car.

"What did you mean," I asked Troy, "when you said that this

amateur-pornography rumor made sense out of some things you'd heard? What did you hear?"

"There's a guy," Troy said. "A guy I don't like. He used to hang out at the house."

"Does this guy have a name?"

"Busansky," Troy said. "Simon Busansky."

Never heard of him. "And why do I care about this guy you don't like?"

"Because he's a pornographer. And a scumbag."

"He's in A.A.?"

"No."

"Then why was he hanging out at a recovery house?" I asked.

"I don't know."

"Why do they call these places recovery houses," I asked, "when there's so little recovery?"

"It's not all like that," Troy said. "But yeah, it's sort of like that. I think that when a lot of people are getting better, maybe sometimes it attracts a lot of people who aren't getting better."

"Did Terry know him?"

"I heard that they were friends. I didn't want to believe it, though. Simon's already messed with one person I like."

"Who did he mess with?"

"Emma."

"The sniper?"

"You know how you asked me if she was my girlfriend? Actually, she was *his* girlfriend. But this guy . . . he'd make her do things. I've got a bad feeling that this porn they're talking about has something to do with my friend Emma."

It was my first moment of truly liking Troy. It had to happen sooner or later. He said "my friend" like he was drawing a line around her and you'd better not cross it. I checked Wade to see if he'd caught Troy's brave inflection, but he was turned away from me, looking out the window.

I slapped his arm to bring him back to us. "You know this guy? The scumbag Busansky?"

"No," Wade said. "I don't think so. Terry was definitely becoming friendly with Colin, though. He maybe wrote some contracts for him. He was around the houses sometimes, hanging out with the newcomers, like always. That's how he met Troy."

Which told me nothing that I didn't already know. Which made me wonder why Wade had bothered to say it.

When we got back to the Coastal Club, Wade closed the door behind him and walked back to his own car. I assumed that he wouldn't be joining us for the "meeting after the meeting."

As we pulled out of the parking lot, I asked Troy if he'd eaten anything recently.

"What do you mean?"

"I mean how long has it been since you put food into your body?"

Troy looked at his hands as though the answer might be hidden there. "I can't remember."

Newcomers were always going psychotic with low blood sugar. "Sometimes you think you want to commit suicide," Terry used to say, "when what you really want is a bacon cheeseburger."

I took Troy to Wahoo's Fish Taco, where I ate a basket of mahimahi tacos and Troy ate two baskets. Afterward, we strolled the boardwalk. I smoked a cigar. Being around Troy was surprisingly low-maintenance. He talked about himself exclusively, and mostly he answered his own questions. Up to a point.

"How do you save for retirement?" he asked. This was as we passed the art deco lifeguard station that appears in most Laguna Beach postcards.

"How do *I* save for retirement?" I said. "Are you asking me specifically or in general?"

"Both," Troy said.

"I make a lot of money," I said. "But I spend most of it. I guess I figure I'll keep moving into nicer houses, and that'll be my retirement."

Troy stopped walking. He tapped the filter on his Camel Light with his thumb. I took a hit off my cigar and wished I still smoked cigarettes.

"Why are you looking at me like that?" I said.

"Because that's not going to work," Troy said. "You can't save for retirement like that. Did you miss the part where home values dropped something like thirty percent?"

"If you know the answer," I said, "why did you ask the fucking question?"

"I *don't* know the answer," Troy said. "But I guess I know what's not the answer."

That was enough foreplay for me, so I asked him again what had happened that last night with Terry.

"Is that why you bought me fish tacos?" Troy asked. "To ask me a bunch of cop questions?"

"I just want to know."

"Do you know what the topic at the online A.A. meeting was today? It came from The Big Book. It was so good that I printed it up."

Troy actually turned out his pants pockets before he found a piece of paper. It didn't surprise me that there was no cash or keys to impede his search. "Here it is." Troy silently read his piece of paper to himself, nodded, then looked off toward Japan.

I took exactly two puffs from my cigar before I couldn't stand it anymore. "What was the fucking quote?"

"Oh." Troy once again hoisted the piece of paper. "'Sometimes they hurt us, seemingly without provocation, but we invariably find that at some time in the past we have made decisions based on self which later placed us in a position to be hurt.' Isn't that awesome?"

"From Chapter Five," I said. "And what does that mean to you, Troy?"

"Terry told me the same thing: it's an inside job. I spent most of today asking myself why you would want to hit me, and then I read this—I must have done something that put me in a position to be hit."

"Maybe I'm just homicidal. Did you consider that?"

"I've gotta do a fifth step. You wanna do my fifth step with me? At first I thought Wade was insane, but now I think it's a good idea."

Taking Troy's fifth step, a process in which he read to me his "moral inventory"—a catalog of his resentments, fears, and misbehavior—didn't necessarily mean that I was his sponsor. But that's what it meant to most people in A.A. If you trusted someone enough to share with him your inventory, he might as well be your sponsor.

"You want *me* to be your sponsor? This morning I almost beat you."

"My dad hit me once, too," Troy said. "In many ways, I admire him more than anyone."

"Just hold that thought," I said, "and tell me, at least, how you met Terry."

"If you'll consider being my sponsor, I'll tell you anything you want to know."

"Have you even done your fourth step, Troy?"

"I'm working on it," he said. "I'll do it right away."

"Slow down," I said. "Tell me how you met Terry."

"How does anyone meet him?" Troy said. "He was hanging around my recovery house, saying lots of inappropriate shit that was actually quite appropriate."

"Like what?"

Troy raised an eyebrow. "Like the stuff that you say? Like telling someone that they'd never be able to forgive their parents until they stopped taking money from them, like telling somebody else that an orgasm was a commitment. You want me to go on?"

"No." I laughed. "I get the gist. But why was he there? Was he there on business?"

"I figured it was just what sober guys did, went and visited the newer sober guys. It seemed like he was friends with Colin. Like what Wade said, he did lawyer stuff for him. But mostly, it seemed like he was there to talk to me."

"You?"

"And guys like me," Troy said. "He'd tease me, but you know, I always felt special. You know what I mean?"

"I know what you mean."

Troy dropped his Camel Light and crushed it. As he sat down

on one of the wooden benches along the boardwalk, I took another hit off my cigar and *really* wished I still smoked cigarettes. Putting my foot on the bench beside Troy, I watched my smoke drift up the hill toward Las Brisas where once, many years before, I had watched O. J. Simpson put two beautiful women into a limousine and then return to the bar with them exactly forty-five minutes later.

"Did he talk to the girls, too?" I asked.

"You're asking me if he fucked them?" Troy said.

I didn't say anything.

"I never saw that, Randy. If it happened, I never saw it."

"How about that last night?" I said. "Will you tell me about that now?"

"Will you be my sponsor?"

"Tell me about that last night," I said, "and then we'll talk about it."

"I went outside for a smoke," Troy said, "and he was parked across the street, which was kind of creepy. You know what I mean? He wasn't on the phone or anything. He was just watching our house. Terry never seemed like a sitting-in-the-car kind of guy. Usually, it was like he had his door open before the car even stopped. When he saw me, he got out, and we started talking."

"What did you talk about?"

"Same as always. What it was like when he first got sober, how hard it was. Nothing he didn't talk about at meetings, but I've thought about this part of the night more than any other. He talked about how everyone had been sick of him, how they'd wanted him to die and get it over with. And then he asked me if

I wanted to hang out. It was like he needed me more than I needed him, and I didn't like that."

"So why'd you go?"

"Because, you know, it was a privilege, too. Like we were going to be friends, and I wanted that at the same time I didn't want that."

"I know what you mean."

"Do you?"

"Of course I do," I said. "This is me, remember? Where'd you go?"

"We went to Santa Anita, the race track? He said he was going to show me where he hung out before he got sober. He took me to this spot under the bleachers where his old bookie was, and he told me what this chump would be wearing and exactly what he would say to us. He was right, too. This is fifteen years later we're talking about."

It wasn't fifteen years later. Terry had taken me on the same trip seven years ago, and I had been equally impressed. The bookie had said, *Eh, Whitey, how's your pretty wife?* Even when I went, Terry hadn't had a pretty wife in a long time.

"I was with him a couple of hours," Troy continued. "The whole time he pretended that we weren't looking for heroin. We were only taking a tour of all his old copping spots. I thought we were getting to be friends. Isn't that fucked up?"

"And then what?"

"And then nothing," Troy said. "We were supposed to look at some more places he used to cop, but he got pissed at me. I wasn't up for any more Santa Ana. I talk big, but heroin scares the shit out of me. He started freaking out like, 'You think I'm going to cop? You think after fifteen years of sobriety I'm going shoot drugs with an asshole like you?' He told me I was a pussy because I'd only snorted it. He said that I had to be a recovering IV drug user to ride with him, and he kicked me out onto Orange-thorpe near that TGIF. I thought he was kidding, but then he drove away."

This wasn't any Terry that I'd ever known. If it was true, not only had he abandoned Troy to his demons, he'd probably taught the demons a few tricks.

Troy paused to carefully fold the piece of paper with the quote on it. Then he stuffed it in his back pocket.

As he did this, I realized that the bench he was sitting on was the one that had been dedicated to DUI Dave, Terry's own spon-sor, whom I had never met. Terry had told me that Dave used the cuffs of his pants as ashtrays and that Terry had never known him to enter a building without smoking a cigarette outside first. A small brass plaque gave the date of his sobriety and the date of his death. Terry had paid for the plaque himself. If Troy had noticed, he might have said there were no coincidences, and then I would have had to drown him.

"I can't stand the idea that a TGIF in Fullerton might be my last drink," Troy said. "And don't tell me that I can go drink right now. I *know* that. Will you be my sponsor?"

There was a time when I would sponsor anyone. The sicker and more annoying, the better. I thought it was my sacred duty to A.A. Sponsorship was also supposed to be the final step toward freedom from alcohol—the twelfth step, in fact—but I didn't know if I believed that anymore. My own sponsor had been on some kind of fucked-up twelfth-step call the night he slipped and died.

"Terry was protecting you," I said. "He must have known where he was headed, and he didn't want you along for the ride."

"Are you even listening to me? I want you to be my sponsor."

"If you did a fifth step with me—and there's no way you ever will—I'd make you tell everyone *everything*."

"Is that what Terry did with you?"

"No," I said. "That would be your special humiliation."

"Just be my sponsor."

"Tell me more about that night. He called Claire for sex?"

"I figured he was looking for an alternative to copping. You remember how he would flip out his phone and start dialing while you were still talking to him?"

I smiled.

"I like Claire and all," Troy said. "I mean, from what I see at meetings, I think she's trying, but Terry didn't call her for any good reason."

"What'd he say?"

"He wondered if they could talk. He asked her how her son was doing. The call ended pretty quickly after that."

Visiting Claire was a marginally better idea than visiting Santa Ana, but not by much. I blew more smoke toward Las Brisas.

"That's everything," Troy said. "Just be my sponsor."

I took my foot off the bench. "Let's forget about the fact that I almost beat the shit out of you this morning. How insane it is that you're even talking to me. Because I'm going to tell you that I don't like you, Troy. I don't like your attitude. Also, I don't like your face. I don't like your fake beefed-up body, and when you're around me, I feel a little bit nauseated the entire time. Not like

I'm going to puke, exactly, but like I'll never be able to eat food again. I also can't promise that I won't beat the shit out of you. You upset me so much, in fact, that it's probable."

Troy looked at me, then stood up. I relaxed my legs for the punch I was certain was coming. He was entitled to it. "Still want me to be your sponsor?" I asked.

"You have no idea."

11

I'D BEEN WANTING TO TALK to Wade alone since I left him at the Coastal Club. There was something that bothered me about the way he'd gone quiet while Troy and I talked.

MP was asleep by the time I got home after dropping off Troy. I was back on my deck, smoking another cigar. It was near midnight. I called Wade. He picked up on the fourth ring. "That house where Colin Alvarez lives?" he said. "I've been to that house."

. . .

About a year before Terry died, we lost track of Wade for a while. It wasn't as though we stopped seeing him, either.

The way you lose most people in A.A. is they stop going to meetings, but Wade never slacked on attendance. Wade *was*

A.A. He'd always been a pretty good salesman—of scuba lessons, of stereo equipment, of time shares—but his greatest profession would always be meetings.

One day, though, I noticed that he wasn't around so much anymore. Terry and I became edgy with each other almost immediately. We were both what my sister Betsy would describe disparagingly as "alpha males." Wade, however, was something like an alpha male minus. He anchored us in A.A., but also provided a buffer between us. Without him, Terry bossed me around in ways that I didn't need to be bossed around: he'd buy me tickets to basketball games he knew I didn't want to attend, take me to dinner at Sinatraesque cigar bars that made me uncomfortable.

We talked to Wade about his absence, but that was like pushing rope. He agreed that he should be around more—*you're right, you're right, I know you're right*—and nothing changed.

He also seemed to have more discretionary income than usual. He would ski at Whistler, let's say, rather than Tahoe. And he started to develop the kind of expensive interests that he could never quite pull off before. He suddenly had all this old-school high-end hi-fi equipment, for example, and on the rare times we did see him, he would try to get us to listen to LPs with him.

Then one day Wade drifted back into our lives. It started with a phone call. I was only then starting to carry a cell phone. Sometimes, when it rang, I would stare at it.

"Hello."

"It's Wade."

"Hi, Wade. How'd you get this number?"

"Is there something wrong with me calling you at this number?" His voice got higher. "Am I not supposed to call you?"

"Chill out," I said. "I'm just shocked when it rings. Sometimes it seems like a toy I carry to pretend I have a job."

"You have a job," Wade said. "You have a good job."

"Anyway," I said.

"I'm calling to tell you that I've been growing pot under my house."

You get that in A.A. a lot: people saying what no one has ever said to you before. Once, after a meeting, a guy told me that he fucked his German shepherd. Just like that. No one ever told me that kind of thing when I was a cop.

"Should we be chatting about this on a cell phone?" I asked.

We met at Jean Claude's, something I didn't do for the guy who fucked his dog. Wade explained that he'd made over two hundred grand that year growing hydroponic marijuana under his house. He didn't touch the stuff. All he did was run the risk. Guys came and set it up. Guys came and took it away in trash bags.

At first I didn't see what the problem was. "No shit?"

"I don't want to lie about this anymore," Wade said. "Every time I go to a meeting, I feel like a freak."

And then he cried. Guys like Wade and me, there comes a time in our lives when the only thing we have is A.A. For some of us, that time comes more than once. That day at Jean Claude's bakery and café, Wade felt like he'd betrayed his only true family. I felt privileged to be his friend while he passed this spiritual kidney stone, but I called Terry so he could be there, too. I wanted Wade to know that we were in this together; I also didn't want Terry to miss Wade's low point. That's another thing you can't explain to a civilian: how beautiful that lack of hope can be. I put my hand in the middle of Wade's back as Terry hugged him. I told Wade that I loved him. Terry said, "If you're done being a lowlife scumbag criminal now, maybe we can get on with our lives?" Sensing that something was up, Jean Claude spotted us our chai lattés. We all started talking again every day.

Wade's confession was sparked by the fact he was about to get busted. With Terry's legal help, he soon made a deal to avoid jail. Wade traded away most of what he'd earned—his drug-related assets—in exchange for a pass on the criminal charges. He'd probably exchanged some information, too, but I hadn't asked.

These so-called "asset forfeiture" programs had begun even before I became a cop, and I'd been around to watch them grow. What most people didn't realize was that the cops didn't have to convict you in order to take your possessions. If they found illegal drugs in your car or house, your car or house now potentially belonged to law enforcement, whether or not you even got tried. They didn't always exercise this right, but the right was always there. The abuses, though, were legendary: one drug cop I knew had such a thing for Jaguar XK-Es that the drug dealers in his jurisdiction stopped buying them. They found that they got busted less frequently in a Mercedes.

Of course, cops becoming more interested in cash and property than convictions had some problematic implications. If a suspect or his lawyers made it easier for the police to get to his bank accounts, might the cops be that much more inclined to give him a pass on the prison sentence? Or: what if the suspect made it easier for the cops to figure out how to take *other* people's bank accounts? Maybe then they would let him keep more of his own assets? To some agencies, this way of doing business just made good sense. I never liked it much myself—it sounded more like horse trading than justice.

But I wasn't a cop anymore when Wade found himself in the soup. And so I was just glad that my friend didn't have to go to jail.

. . .

"Simon Busansky owned that house," Wade said to me over the phone. "That house was one of the places they grew and processed the pot."

Simon Busansky: pornographer, boyfriend to crazy Emma, guy who freaked Troy out.

"I thought you didn't know who Simon Busansky was," I said.

Wade was quiet for a moment before he said, "I didn't know him well. I don't have strong opinions about him like Troy. He was just a guy who was near the top of the pot-growing food chain."

"You explicitly told me that you didn't know him."

"Yeah," Wade said.

"So you lied to me. What you're saying is you lied to me."

"I lied to you."

"Why did you lie to me?"

"I walk around my life pretending that shit didn't happen," Wade said. "It's weird to be reminded of it, especially like this. Terry was the one who totally saved my ass that time."

"But you don't know anything about Busansky?"

"I didn't know that he was a pornographer," Wade said.

"How did he avoid going to jail?"

"I assume he made a deal with them, too. I'm sure he lost everything. I gotta figure he lost that house."

"How do you figure Colin now owns that house?" I said. "That can't be a coincidence."

"Not sure, man."

"And why the fuck is Busansky hanging around Colin's recovery houses? That doesn't seem right to me. There's no way Terry could be involved in this, is there?"

"I hope not."

"How about fucking newcomers?" I said. "You still think he wasn't fucking newcomers?"

"No way, man. *That* I'm sure about."

"I need to find this guy Busansky. Can you help me?"

"Dude, it freaked me out to be anywhere near that house. I gotta steer clear of this, you understand?"

Uh-huh.

Before he hung up, Wade told me again how sorry he was for holding out on me. The funny thing was that I felt like he was still holding out on me.

. . .

When I went back into my house, I did what I sometimes do: stand at the threshold of our bedroom and watch MP sleep. She didn't move. The soft gray light from the window crossed her back. She was twelve years younger than I was, but maybe that wasn't the only reason she slept peacefully while I did not.

She'd found her way into A.A. the same as anyone—on a wave of more or less crushing despair—and yet I knew my sins were a lot worse than hers. Why did I inflict my bad dreams on someone who didn't have any? That's what I thought about on that threshold between our bedroom and the rest of the house. When we first slept together, I would wake up from nightmares to find her happily reading a book. It took me the better part of six months to realize that it was my nightmares that had made her book necessary.

As my eyes got used to the light, I started to get interested in her bare back above the covers, in her neck and the way it flared around her shoulders into the softness above her breasts. Although I couldn't see it from here, I imagined her skin, the way it smelled and tasted, as though no poison had ever poured through it. I knew that wasn't the truth, but it always seemed that way.

I realized she was lying in bed staring at me. She didn't say anything, but she looked at me as though the events of the morning were on her mind and she was trying like hell to hold them against me, but there was something about the softness of our bedroom and both of us needing not to talk about what had happened. I pushed off my shoes and undressed before I even entered the bedroom. It seemed right to walk through the doorway in nothing but my skin.

12

WHEN I REACHED FOR MY CELL PHONE the next morning, MP was nestled beside me. But when I told her I was calling Manny, she moved away quietly, then headed for the bathroom, without a glance in my direction.

"You know any drug cops down here in Laguna?" I asked Manny. I had to speak with someone who could give me the scoop on whatever asset forfeiture deal might have led to Simon Busansky selling his house to Colin Alvarez.

"There's a funny guy named Sean I met once. A surfer. We met at some kind of DEA junket in Palm Springs, and he was ready to give me a surfing lesson in the pool. He's still Laguna PD, but I think he's on some liaison with the DEA, too."

After taking a second to think about cops who were surfers, I remembered that I knew the guy myself, though he hadn't been

DEA when I used to run into him. Sean Wakefield came around A.A. a few years ago. He'd been going to secret meetings for police, but they weren't working. When someone pushed him in my direction, I advised him to join the general population, and that worked for a while.

I called Sean's cell, and as his voice mail picked up, I happened to be looking out my window at the Pacific. I reached for my binoculars. It wasn't a great set of waves, but it wasn't bad enough to keep a guy like Sean away. By the time I got down to Brook Street, he was peeling off his wetsuit at the top of the stairs.

Sean's almost-cherry seventies El Camino was parked—illegally—at the bottom of the cul-de-sac. He sat down on his tailgate, and I gave him a latté from the Orange Inn. Sean had grown up in Atlanta, and he had some of that big, stupid southern sheriff thing going on. As he pulled on a T-shirt, I could see that he was in even better shape than he used to be. If he was drinking, it wasn't beer.

"What's this?" Sean said. "The sponsor patrol?"

"Was I your sponsor?"

"I never asked you to be, but . . . yeah."

"That relationship works better when both parties know about it," I said.

Sean tossed his wet suit into the truck and wrapped a towel around his shorts. "I heard about Terry." He sipped some coffee. "Sorry."

Over Sean's shoulder, the ocean was gray like you never see unless you live in a beach town. Greasy gray like the bottom of a dead fish. Terry had been the one who pushed Sean in my direction. *Say hello to Sean. Sean's the patient today.*

"Actually," I said, "that's why I'm here. I'm trying to figure out what his last few weeks were like. I might also have some information for you, you know, as a cop."

"You're not here to drag me back to meetings?" Sean smiled. "I'm disappointed."

"What the hell do I care, Sean? If I thought I could get away with what you seem to be getting away with, I'd start surfing, too. And I fucking hate surfing."

Sean took a last look at the sea as he stepped into his flip-flops. "A few times I thought about calling you."

I told him about the guy I knew only as Mutt and gave him the license plate of the Suburban. I didn't mention Simon Busansky's name. I didn't mention Colin Alvarez by name, either, though I did give him Colin's address. Did that address ring any bells from his DEA work? I reminded myself that it could be a dangerous game, sharing information with someone who was hooked in to a federal agency.

"Yeah, I know this address," Sean said. "This is old news, though. Didn't Colin Alvarez buy that house?"

"Who?"

"Oh, don't play games with me, Randy. He was the other guy they said I should have asked to be my sponsor. What are you up to? Is it some kind of A.A. girlfight? I thought that thing with Wade was ancient history. I bet you're curious about Simon Busansky, too."

"You know about Wade?" I said. "You know about Simon Busansky?"

"I know about everything," Sean said. "Hanging out with the DEA guys is like being plugged in to the Matrix."

I took back the piece of paper and wrote down the address of

Troy's recovery home. "How about this address? You know if Colin bought this house from Simon, too?"

"This one I don't know," Sean said. "But I can find out. What does any of it have to do with Terry?"

"Can I leave out that part for now?"

"As long as it doesn't hurt me," he said. "Or make me look stupid."

"I promise to do neither," I said.

Sean smiled as he got into his El Camino.

. . .

I stopped by Jean Claude's café, which is usually where I head when I'm waiting for things to happen. There was a lull between pastry purchases, so I got the full attention of the man himself. Because I've never been good at hiding my feelings from Frenchmen, my concern about Wade was the first thing that came out of my mouth when Jean Claude sat down at my table. Last night's confession didn't feel complete. It didn't make sense, Wade not wanting to know more about Busansky. If Busansky had anything to do with Terry's death, Wade should have wanted to know everything about Busansky.

"I'm worried that a friend of mine is lying to me," I said. "And I don't know how to make him stop."

"Everyone lies," Jean Claude said. "I usually let them alone. If I know they're not telling the truth, well, that's a kind of truth, too."

"I hate it when you sound like a fucking sage European."

"I mean it," he said. "If you know he's lying to you, maybe that's all you need to know."

Huh. That sounded weirdly useful. I was about to apologize

to Jean Claude for saying that I hated anything about him when my phone rang with a blocked number.

"Do you want to fuck me?" a young woman's voice asked. It was Emma, Troy's recon buddy.

"How'd you get my number?"

"I'm very smart," she said. "Please answer the question."

"No," I said. "But trust me, that's a good thing."

"Will you do me a favor?"

"If I can."

"Tell me that you want to fuck me," she said. "Then I won't want you to."

"I'm not going to say that, Emma."

"Just say yes, then."

"Yes?"

"There you go," she said. "I asked you the question in my mind, and you answered affirmatively."

"Can I ask you a question now?"

"No. I gotta go. But I'm watching you. Even when I'm not watching you." She was gone before I could ask her about Simon Busansky. The very next time I had a weird exchange with her, I would have to remember to ask. As I put away my phone, I noticed, too, that I didn't like the idea of her being out there, wherever the hell she was, alone.

. . .

When I got back to Bluebird Canyon, MP's car was gone. It had been replaced by Jeep's meticulously restored James Bondish Aston Martin. She had keys to my house, and she used them often.

She had already pulled two cigars from the humidor and

taken her spot on the deck in the Adirondack nearer to the side of the hill. I stood beside her and looked out over Laguna. The swells were getting choppy, and the surfers would be pissed off, but there was a nice breeze here in the hills. And Terry was dead and I still couldn't explain it. Jeep tossed me one of my own Arturo Fuentes. "Give her some time," she said.

It took me a moment to realize she was talking about Betsy, not MP. "Have you tried to broker a deal?"

"No brokering on this one. I have to stay out of it."

"Are all dykes as chickenshit as you?"

"I'm sad she stopped talking to you," Jeep said, "but I'll be suicidal if she stops talking to me."

"I've wrung my brain out like a rag. What the fuck did I do?"

"It doesn't help when you have to explain why beating up a guy named Padilla *wasn't* a racist act."

"First of all, I've got to figure out if this guy *is* Mexican. I keep forgetting to ask."

"I think you're missing my point," Jeep said.

I drew so deeply from the cigar that I almost inhaled. Unceremoniously, I changed the subject. "Do you think there's such a thing as a normal person?" I said. "I mean, do you think there are people who walk around without all this baggage?"

Jeep didn't answer for a minute, just smoked her cigar. Only one of the things I liked about my business partner was that she enjoyed a cigar or two before noon.

"Why do you want to know?" she finally said.

"This guy who it looks like Jean's going to marry," I said. "John Sewell? There's a directness about him that confuses the shit out of me. It's like he doesn't feel any conflict about what he wants. And he doesn't have to ask himself every morning whether he's good enough to meet the world. I have no idea what that would be like."

"Again," Jeep said, "why do you want to know?"

I looked at her. "Jean doesn't have a high opinion of my parenting skills, and I'm not sure I disagree. This whole thing with Terry has made me wonder about things. On my best days, I'm kind of a mess. And I worry about Crash."

Jeep pointed her cigar at me. "If you're wondering whether this guy Sewell would make a better father than you, that's bullshit. Maybe he'll be a good friend to her, but that doesn't mean a thing about who *you* are to her. There's nobody on this planet capable of being a better father to that child. And if there is somebody, I'd like to meet him."

I went inside to brew some coffee. Then I heard the churning engine of the FedEx truck. At my front door, I greeted Max, a big guy with jug ears who had been a champion kayaker in Uzbekistan. He smiled as I signed. The envelope was from Manny.

As soon as I felt it, I knew what it had to be: the recording of the 911 call.

Manny's handwriting on the FedEx envelope reminded me that we'd been partners for eight years. I knew his handwriting as well as my own. I'd been partners with Jeep for five years; I knew her handwriting pretty well, too. I couldn't, for the life of me, remember what Terry's handwriting looked like.

I walked back out to the deck. "I think I'm ready to work again."

"Just like that?" Jeep asked. "We don't have to run an intervention or anything?"

"As much as that might be fun," I said, "no. But tell me what you think about this: what if I used some of my pseudo-criminal connections in A.A. to find properties around town that were kind of sketchy? Maybe they had a pot farm in the basement or they were running prostitutes out of the bedrooms, and they needed help cleaning things up. Maybe we'd even get a discount for this consideration. Oh yeah, and then we'd turn them into recovery houses."

"It doesn't sound like you're ready to go back to work yet," Jeep said.

"I'm just talking," I said. "Generating ideas."

"You think that's what Colin Alvarez did with those recovery houses he started?" Jeep said. "And is there even anything wrong with that?"

"Maybe. Do you think that's doable?"

"And *why* were you thinking about this?"

I didn't want to answer.

"Does it have something to do with Terry?" she said.

"I hope not," I said. "Right now I'm just making shit up."

I slapped the FedEx envelope against my thigh. My twenty-five-dollar cigar suddenly tasted like a dog turd, so I tossed it over the side of the deck.

. . .

After Jeep left, I pulled the CD from the FedEx envelope. It glowed in my hand for a full minute before I walked it out of my house toward my truck on the driveway.

I got in, closed the windows, turned on the engine, pushed in the disk, and went for a drive.

—911 operator. Please state the nature of your emergency.

—He's dead in a hotel room downtown. *El padre de mi*

hijo. He was freaking out at the hospital. *¡Y el recién nacido queda sin padre!* I haven't seen him since then. And then . . . this . . . idiot man . . . he didn't even call the ambulance.

—Where is this emergency taking place, ma'am? Would you be more comfortable speaking in Spanish? I need you to focus and tell me where this is happening.

—English is fine, I'm sorry. It's not happening. It already happened. He's gone. He's dead of heroin.

—*Where* did this happen, ma'am? You need to tell me *where* this happened.

—Down on Jewel Street. It's the motel down there. I need somebody to find him. I can't go there myself. I need someone to find him.

The caller hung up.

After listening to the tape five more times, I was certain I would recognize her voice if I ever heard it again. A high voice, a little girlie even. She was a woman, though, not a girl.

Everyone teased me about my Spanish, but I knew what *el padre de mi hijo* meant. And *el recién nacido* felt like a slap in the face. My throat got tight and dry with all I hadn't known about the people I loved. Apparently, Terry's biggest dream had come true a few days before he died. My best friend had a son, a newborn, who was now without a father.

. . .

As luck would have it, that was the next time I saw Colin Alvarez: right after I finished listening to the 911 recording for the fifth time. I was driving slowly through the oldest shopping district in Laguna—although every neighborhood was a shopping district now—when I saw him getting into his BMW wagon across the street from the Swedish bakery.

When Colin saw me, I held up my hand, to keep him where he was while I parked in a metered space a few spots down. The baldy hipster was with him. I made a note to get his real name so that I could stop making things worse by thinking of him as "the baldy hipster." That I got the last open space available in Laguna Beach that morning must have been part of God's plan. I don't know why I stopped. Repeated listening to the 911 tape seemed to be underscoring the idea that I didn't have a fucking clue what was going on around me, and this seemed like a good opportunity to apologize for what had been essentially an un-provoked assault. Did that mean that I was ready to call up Sean and tell him to leave off his search for connections between Colin Alvarez and former pot farms? I wasn't yet that spiritual.

"I'm an asshole," I called out as I approached them on foot.

"I'm not arguing." Colin touched his shoulder, which probably hurt like hell.

"Why don't you stay away from us?" Baldy Hipster said.

"It's cool, Joachin."

Joachin? How did I miss "My name is Joachin, and I'm an alcoholic"?

"The precise kind of asshole I am is this," I said. "I was all freaked out about Terry's OD, and I had a lot of questions I couldn't answer, so I followed that guy over to your house and—"

"Got all up in my face," Colin said. "I'm not good with that. Got a few anger issues myself. Probably could have handled my end of things better, too."

Joachin looked ready to start in again, but Colin gave him a look, and he backed off, like *You're the boss.* Despite my reputation as a tough guy, I can't remember anyone ever quite backing down like that for me.

"Well," I said, "I'm sorry."

"So you think this Mutt Kelly guy was following you around, huh?" Colin stepped up onto the curb and then immediately back off of it. I think he was trying not to be taller than me—which he was—and I had to credit him for this weird bit of thoughtfulness. The sidewalk was busy with skinny women carrying large bags. Both of us were looking down at the concrete as we talked. Colin looked up at me. "Do you know the guy?"

"No," I said. "I don't. How do *you* know the guy?"

"I told you. He wants a place in one of the recovery homes. I've got no problem with scholarships when I can afford them, but I'm not sure how serious he is."

I looked at Colin, really looked at him. He seemed to be looking at me, too.

"Go ahead," Colin said. "Ask me anything you want."

"What do you mean?"

"You came to my house to ask me some questions. I got that. And I'll answer any questions I can."

"What was your relationship with Simon Busansky?"

"He sold me my houses."

"Did you know that Busansky was growing pot under most of those houses?"

Colin smiled. "I said that I would answer some questions. I'm not going to lay out my life story, though, and hope that you can make some trouble from it. I got to be friends with Simon, and I had a sense of how he made money. Was that a condition of the sale? No. Was I participating in his business? No, I wasn't. Simon never told me what he was doing, because he's not stupid. Maybe I guessed, sitting around the backyard bullshitting with him."

"Why was Simon still hanging out with you after you closed the deal?"

"I guess I thought I could help him," Colin said. "After a while, it became clear that I couldn't."

"Did Terry ever do any work for you?"

"He wrote a couple of contracts, checked out some deals for me. Me and a lot of other people in A.A., right? I bet you used him for your own stuff."

"That's right," I said. "Let me ask you something else. Did you hear that Mutt was with Terry the night he died?"

I couldn't see anything in Colin's eyes except what you might expect: the attention that such a dramatic revelation deserved.

"Terry was with someone?" he asked.

"You didn't hear that?"

"No," Colin said. "What makes you think it was Mutt Kelly?"

"Claire Monaco talked to Terry a couple of times during the evening. He told her he was doing a twelfth-step call on Mutt."

I didn't say anything more, just watched his eyes. He smiled. "That seems like a good match, actually."

"I thought you didn't know him."

"I know him enough to know that Terry would have been good for him."

"Maybe he wasn't so good for Terry," I said.

"I've got nothing to hide, Randy. And I'd rather that you and I were friends."

"What about the pornography?"

Colin's eyes flashed angry, which I guess I understood. Or at least in the context of this conversation, I didn't feel like holding it against him.

"I'm sorry if I sound like a cop," I said. "I know how far you're extending yourself in my direction, and I appreciate it. I gotta ask because I just heard about it. It's another cluster in this clusterfuck, and I want to find out what it had to do with Terry. I heard that Simon Busansky used to make porn movies and that he might have made some in your houses. Did he ever mention that while you were bullshitting in the backyard?"

Colin looked off down Forest Avenue. He looked back at Joachin, who seemed to be chewing his teeth. When he met my eyes again, he was less angry. "I'm checking into that, too. I just heard about it myself. I'm embarrassed that it seems to have happened on my watch, but I don't know anything else. Can I get back to you?"

"Fair enough," I said. "I'm sorry about your shoulder, by the way."

"No, you're not." He smiled.

"How do you figure? You don't think I'm capable of remorse?"

"It was my bad," Colin said. "I came after you, and you were entitled to everything that happened after that. Enjoy the moment of guilt-free violence. I don't think you're going to get another one."

I didn't know what that meant, and it sort of sounded like a threat, but I figured he was entitled to that, too.

13

YOU'D THINK I'D BE ALL MR. SPIRITUAL after making amends to
Colin Alvarez and finding out my dead best friend had a son, but
no, not really. Because the first thing I did once I got home was
put on a blue Armani blazer that no cop with the possible excep-
tion of William Bratton would ever wear. I slipped my retirement badge and ID into the breast pocket and practiced a couple
of times pulling it out while covering the word "retired" right
there in the middle. If I were going for veracity, I would have
strapped on my gun, too, but I was a little too proud of the fact
that for eight years it hadn't left the lock box at my shop. The
buttoned sport coat, I told myself, should do the trick. I printed
up a list of hospitals in the areas of both the 911 call and the
motel where Terry had died. Impersonating an active police of-

ficer was a federal crime, but I couldn't ask Manny or Sean for help. This one was mine.

Twenty years ago, you could find out almost anything by flashing a badge. After Rodney King and O.J., even uniformed police officers weren't as authoritative as they used to be.

Imagining who could be most easily bullied, I started with the hospital receptionists. But the receptionists had been apprised of California state law.

"Thought you'd save yourself some time?" said the redhead at Western Medical Center whose smock was covered with dancing Grateful Dead bears. "You know you need a subpoena for that information."

It was maddening, as anyone at the right hospital with a computer could have told me: Had Terry been here? Who gave birth to his child? Where did she live?

It was way past lunchtime, and I was getting cranky with my lack of progress. After three hospitals and one compliment to my tailor, I was about to take off my sport coat when I found myself standing next to a smoker outside the revolving doors of St. Joseph's. A skinny white guy in a green smock, he sucked so fiercely that his ash grew at a visible rate.

"You're not a cop," he said.

I smiled, kept my mouth shut. His real audience had been the attractive young African-American woman wearing a denim cowboy shirt. There were several more smokers near the revolving door. Everyone got a good look at me and my Armani jacket. I cranked up my smiling but malevolent stare. Only then I noticed what my police training had initially missed: the plastic wristband that identified him as a patient. My A.A. training, at least, kicked in: the furious smoking suggested inpatient detox.

I shoved into his face the picture of Terry from the memorial. The crowd of smokers drew away. "Have you seen this man? What's *your* name?"

Between glances at my hard eyes, he checked the picture. The woman in the cowboy shirt shook her head, daintily placed her cigarette in the ashtray beside the revolving door, then went inside. Deprived of his muse, the cigarette addict's nerves twisted tighter. Pulling out a notepad, I danced toward the not completely unlikely possibility that this guy and Terry had found each other at some point. He shook his head.

"I asked *you* what *your* name was," I said.

Another voice spoke up behind me. "Can I help you?"

This man, too, was dressed in scrubs, but he was too healthy-looking for a detoxing addict. Maybe a nurse, probably a doctor. Clean teeth, bright skin—he looked me in the eye.

Cigarette Addict beat it back to the rehab, where people wouldn't shove pictures in his face.

"Are you trying to hurt him or help him?" The guy pointed with an unlit cigarette toward Terry's photo.

"He's dead. I'm looking into what happened. May I ask your name?"

As he lit up, we stepped onto a grassy median between the parking lot and the emergency-vehicle lane, away from the other smokers.

"If you stop trying to intimidate me, I'll try to help you, but I'm not going to tell you my name." He smoked, but not desperately.

I nodded.

"You were a friend of his?"

I nodded again.

"Is that a yes?" he said. "You wouldn't have taken that answer from the poor kid you were browbeating."

"That was a yes."

"What kind of cop are you? I don't need your name, but I like to know who I'm talking to."

"I'm not a cop. At least not in a long time." I pulled out my retirement badge, pointed to the word "retired" on the ID. "He was my friend."

After a long moment, the man said, "The mother had a hard labor, and he didn't take it well. He started cussing out the nurses. He asked the attending where he'd learned how to butcher pregnant women. They got him to calm down for a little while, but then it got worse: he started punching his thighs, as hard as he could. I worried that he was delusional or detoxing, so I pulled him outside to chat."

"To diagnose him, you mean?"

"No, I mean to chat. I asked if he was taking drugs. He laughed, said he was fifteen years clean. Talking about it, he started to chill out. I bought him a cup of coffee. Are you his business partner?"

"No. Did he talk about a business partner?"

"I guess that's good. He said his business partner was a nightmare, and he hoped he hadn't figured it out too late."

"Did he say this man's name?"

"Nope. At first he wouldn't even talk about his girlfriend. Later, he told me that he loved her more than any woman he'd ever known."

"When was this?" I asked. "What day?"

"It must have been, yeah, May ninth, a Sunday, around four P.M., because I got off at six."

"You sure about that date?"

"I'm good with dates."

"You must have been a really good listener, too."

That didn't come out the way I had planned, and the doctor—or whoever he was—crouched down to grind his ash into the curb below us. He'd had enough of my shit. He didn't toss the cigarette, though; he would put it in the ashtray beside the door like a good citizen.

"He needed to talk. That's all I have for you."

We stood back to let an EMS truck pass. It had become a bright afternoon. The sky was stark blue, and it gave the hospital above us a hard edge. I suddenly wished I weren't such an asshole. It was a familiar wish.

"Don't take this the wrong way," I said, "but it sounds like you have some experience with guys like my friend."

He looked at me and took time before he answered. "My boyfriend was addicted to Vicodin, but he's been clean in Narcotics Anonymous for three years. My ex-wife was a cocaine addict. My dad was a vicious drunk. I have three brothers and one sister, and each of them explains to me—unsolicited, at least three times a year—why they *don't* have a drinking problem."

I asked my last questions into the grass. "How did it end? Was the baby okay? Was my friend okay once the baby was delivered?"

"My shift was over, and I went back home. At that point, mother and baby were fine. When I checked in the next day, I heard that the father had lost it again, and the attending had prescribed him some Valium. Wouldn't have been my call. I found out later, though, that your friend refused the Valium. It's weird, but I was proud of him."

"You helped him," I said.

He checked for sarcasm and didn't find any. As I shook his hand, I asked him if he might see his way clear to helping me find the mother. He took a deep breath and sighed. "I can do that," he said. "I believe your intentions are good."

I laughed. "Best not to get into my intentions," I said. "But they're good as far as she's concerned. I want to do what I can for her and the little boy."

"Do you think it's weird," he asked, "that I can remember her name right now?"

"Why would I think that's weird?"

"I don't usually take this kind of interest," he said, "but I had it in my mind to call your friend sometime, see how he was doing. What happened? How did he die?"

"Heroin overdose," I said. "Less than two days after you talked to him."

"Jesus."

We looked at each other for a moment, long enough for me to see a weariness in his eyes that I might have missed. Maybe he was seeing the same weariness in mine. I shook his hand again and thanked him for reaching out to a stranger in trouble.

"Who are we talking about now?" he said. "You?"

14

CATALINA ACUÑA WAS THE MANAGER of an apartment building on Flower Street that was currently for sale. The address was five blocks from where the 911 call had been made. It was a two-story stucco building with a row of carports under the second story. The carports were behind a security gate.

I'd made plans for a late lunch with MP, which I'd forgotten until the first time she called me, at two-fifteen. I let the call bounce to voice mail. I was going to text her back, but by two-thirty, I'd already let her second call bounce to voice mail. I spent that whole time staring at the building where I thought I might find Terry's son.

Ms. Acuña's apartment building was down the street from an elementary school. When the kids started walking past my truck at three, wearing gray slacks and white shirts, plaid skirts and white blouses, I figured I had to do something. I got out and opened the toolbox behind my cab. When that felt stupid, I screwed up my courage to cross the street. That was when my phone rang again. It wasn't MP this time. It was Sean calling with an address and a name: Thomas, aka "Mutt," Kelly.

I'm a coward. I prefer physical pain to emotional pain. I returned to my truck and drove back toward Laguna. God forgive me, but confronting the guy who had been with Terry that last night was infinitely less terrifying than meeting the woman and child whom Terry had left behind.

. . .

Mutt Kelly's address was in Canyon Acres. If there was a wrong side of the tracks in Laguna Beach—and no one in the rest of the United States would argue there was—Canyon Acres would be it. Somehow my righteous anger that had been brewing for Mutt Kelly got conflated with the anger I felt at bad architecture. I not only wanted to throttle the guy who'd been parked in front of my house, I wanted to burn down his neighborhood, too. I found exactly the shitty little bungalow I had imagined: a two-bedroom rental that was standing only because someone was too stupid or lazy to tear it down. It would have had vinyl siding, but the city of Laguna Beach confiscates that stuff at the border.

I knocked hard on the door. As he opened it, Mutt Kelly didn't seem to recognize me. He almost looked like he wanted to know how he could help me, though he didn't say it like that.

"What the fuck do you want?"

"I want to know why you've been jerking off in front of my house," I said. Then I kicked the door open into his forearm. It made a popping noise as it dislodged the sawed-off baseball bat he'd been hiding: the kind of half-assed weapon that a teenager stashes under the seat of his ten-year-old SUV.

Mutt's arm wasn't broken, but it must have hurt like hell. He backed up, holding it, until he tripped on a Formica coffee table. On the couch behind the table, I saw a leather jacket with the initials "A.C.M.C." "M.C." stood for "motorcycle club," which often meant "gang," which brought back plenty of bad memories from my tenure as a police officer in Santa Ana. Now I was really mad.

"Actually," I said, "I don't care why you've been jerking off in front of my house. I'm here to beat the shit out of you. When you wake up from your coma, we'll talk. While you're sleeping, I'm going to kill everyone you know."

He kept backing up and I kept walking toward him, getting into the groove.

"I didn't do anything to your asshole friend Terry," Mutt shouted. "You can't blame me for that."

Had I said anything about my "asshole friend Terry"?

The next thing Mutt saw was his Formica coffee table—an American piece of furniture if ever there was one—as it slammed into his good arm and took a nice chunk out of the drywall behind him.

Once he'd bounced off the wall, Mutt rallied himself into some kind of half-assed boxer's stance. I got into my own half-assed boxer's stance and feinted a few punches, which he avoided pretty easily. He suddenly didn't look so ridiculous. When he caught the side of my head with a left hook, I decided it was time to let my rage find its form. I threw my right shoulder into his chest and launched him into the wall. He was tougher than I had thought, but he wasn't going to be tougher than me.

At some point, Officer Sean Wakefield entered the house. As I threw myself toward the job of pounding Mutt Kelly's face into a pulp, Sean announced himself in that voice you learn your first month on patrol. He called my name like he was dragging me by the collar back out of a room. He was in uniform, too, which meant more to me than I would have imagined. Standing there, his hands on his hips, he might as well have been modeling a sweatshirt that said IMPULSE CONTROL across the front. If I had thought I was in charge of my own actions, Sean had arrived to tell me I was wrong. Throughout my assault on Mutt Kelly, I had been shouting. Which was news to me until Sean entered the house and I started to hear myself.

"Were you with him?" I continued to shout. "Did you get him the fucking dope?".

"Randy!" Sean commanded from behind me.

"I didn't do anything," Mutt yelled at Sean as much as me. "I hung out with him sometimes. And *that's fucking it.*"

"*Randy!*" Sean barked even louder this time. "I need you to back the fuck up and come outside with me."

Mutt Kelly put his hands down as I backed away. He had been tougher than I thought, but he looked relieved that the fight was over. Then Sean actually grabbed me by the collar and backed me out of the house.

. . .

Terry and I used to talk about that sweet moment of repose after you've almost destroyed your life. That's exactly how I felt when Sean returned to the cruiser where he'd parked my ass ten minutes earlier. Jackson Browne sang softly from the laptop mounted between us. While I'd been marinating in the car, Sean had convinced Mutt that the episode would not repeat itself, and Mutt had agreed to forget about it. I was already incredibly calm, which was S.O.P. after I'd done something really stupid. When Sean had shown up, I had been about to do what I'd never done even as a bad cop: beat a confession out of a suspect. Sean knew it, which was probably why he had asked Jackson to wait with me.

"Does your supervisor know that you have an iPod hooked up to your computer?" I asked when Sean got back in the car. "Does your supervisor know that you listen to Jackson Browne?"

Sean shook his head, took a deep breath. "This morning"— he checked something on his laptop but made no move to turn down the music—"I kept thinking you were going to say something, but you didn't. And now I can't help wondering if I should go back to meetings."

"You came here because you want to go to a meeting?" I said.

"No." Sean smiled. "I came here because as soon as I hung up the phone, I had an awful feeling you were going to come over here to beat that guy up. But I'm thinking about going to a meeting, too."

"He was just getting his boxing lesson."

"Which is lucky for you, because if he had filed a complaint, I would have had to arrest you. Now that I'm also trying to get sober again, I would have had to tell someone about our conversation at Brook Street, too. Rigorous honesty, right?"

"Maybe," I said. "But you would have talked to me first."

"And then I would have had to tell somebody. You can't drive around beating the shit out of people."

I watched Sean and realized something profound: he was a cop and I wasn't. I sometimes thought of myself as a cop, but that was me lying to myself again. Sean felt that he owed me something, though it had nothing to do with my being a cop.

"I didn't beat him up," I said. "Write that down somewhere."

"This is the point," Sean said. "I'm not writing *anything* down. Unless you give me no choice. Why didn't you tell me you thought this guy was with Terry that night?"

"Did he tell you whether he was with Terry that last night?"

"He claims he wasn't," Sean said. "Who knows? I don't think he's the guy you want to blame, though. You're trying to make sense of this, and I just don't think it's ever going to make sense."

"Why was this Charlie Manson wannabe parked outside of my house? He's in some outfit with the initials A.C.M.C. Who is that? The Ass Clowns?"

Sean gave me a look.

"You think I'm making this shit up?"

"I think you're angry. Which is understandable, because Terry was your best friend. I think this Mutt Kelly has done a lot of stupid things in his life—his sheet includes car theft and drug dealing—and parking in front of your house so he can steal your computer or catch a peek at your girlfriend wouldn't even make the middle of the list. And A.C.M.C. is a gang called the Aryan Comanches. Even their name is a joke. They're too stupid to understand that it's a contradiction in terms."

"Why did this guy start talking about Terry the moment I walked in the door? I never said anything about Terry."

"He says Terry was trying to help him pull his head out of his ass. Terry did that from time to time, you know. Maybe he had talked to him about you. How many meetings in the last few weeks would this guy have to attend before he heard about the legendary Terry Elias, his tragic death, and his avenging ex-cop sponsee Randy Chalmers? Like, maybe, one?"

"I just don't get it, Sean. I know Terry wasn't perfect, but I don't see him in Santa Ana with a guy like this in the middle of the night."

"Then maybe the guy wasn't there."

Sean looked at me with, what? Pity?

"Look," he said, "will you promise to stop assaulting people within the jurisdiction of Laguna Beach if I tell you what I found out?"

"Yes," I said. "I promise." I needed to wonder at some point what my promises were worth. At some point.

"You were right that Colin Alvarez not only bought his home from Simon Busansky, he also bought that other address you gave me, and three other homes, all of which are now recovery houses. This was just about the time when Busansky made a deal with us. We took a ton of cash from him, but we let him sell his houses."

"Is that a fancy way of saying he became an informant?"

"More or less," Sean said. "He became the go-to guy for understanding marijuana cultivation in the South County. He's a real talker. The DEA guys who know him seem to like him. But there's something else: Terry brokered that deal for Busansky, like he brokered the deal for Wade."

"You're saying this had become a regular business for Terry? Making deals between the growers and the DEA? How come I never heard about it?"

"Maybe he didn't want you to judge him," Sean said, "the way you're judging him right now?"

"But if he was making all this money," I said, "why did he need to borrow fifty grand from me?"

"You loaned Terry fifty grand?"

"Forget about that part," I said. "Do you know where Busansky is? And before you say it, I'm not going to roust him."

"Funny you should ask," Sean said. "Busansky had been in pretty good touch with my DEA guys, schooling them regularly on the ways of shady characters like himself. About a month ago, he dropped off the radar, and they can't find him anywhere. I think they miss him."

"They think he's dead?"

Sean reached into the backseat for his notes. "A history of drinking and drugs, a shitload of connection to marginal criminal activity, solo trips to Mexico every month or so. He's been producing small-time porn forever. Hey, he started out writing for *Hustler*. That was the high point of his life besides his brief career as a hydroponic kingpin. He could be decomposing in a *barranca*. Another OD. More likely, he's just living the same life somewhere else."

So: now I knew why it had taken so long to get anything from Wade. If Terry was connected to whatever was going on in those recovery houses, if he was connected to this clown Simon Busansky and the girls "making movies," it had been Wade's hydroponic adventure that had connected him. Terry had helped Wade out with the pot bust, and in exchange, Wade had introduced him to a new income stream. And maybe set him on the path to something much worse.

15

WHEN WADE DIDN'T PICK UP his phone, I drove by his apartment three times. I checked in to each of his favorite restaurants at least once. I even cruised the parking lot of the Coastal Club. No Wade.

I returned home to change my clothes. Just as I was taking off my federal-law-breaking Armani sport coat, I noticed most of MP's wardrobe stacked and neatly folded along the edge of our bed. My girlfriend did this kind of thing all the time: some people get sober and become Oscar, and others become Felix. When I caught MP attacking the grout in our bathtub one afternoon with an electric toothbrush, I hired Yegua's girlfriend to clean our house. Did I need to know that MP had a system for organizing in which brown sweaters were always closer to the top than navy sweaters? She was probably just reorganizing her closet.

The sight of my kitchen reminded me that I was extraordinarily hungry, and the clock on the microwave told me why: it was nearly seven o'clock, and I hadn't eaten since . . . well, I just hadn't eaten. Time flies when you're obsessed with hydroponic pot farms and amateur pornography and why the fuck your dead friends are involved with either of these things. It was only when I opened a ginger ale that I noticed the juicer was gone. I could explain that, too: sometimes MP and her yoga friends had antioxidant parties.

I sat down in my Eames chair and watched the dusk settle into the canyons behind my house, and I had almost made myself forget about the neatly folded clothes when I heard a car cresting the driveway. I went outside to see MP in a Volvo station wagon with ALL PEOPLE YOGA painted on the side. It was the company car for the studio where MP worked. She switched it off and set the parking brake. She wasn't crying, but she wasn't not crying. I crouched beside her window and touched her shoulder. I didn't have to ask whether she'd heard about last night and Colin Alvarez. I didn't have to ask whether I had remembered to call her back.

"It might just be for a little while," MP said.

"You didn't want to take your own car?" I pointed at her VW Cabrio in the garage.

"That's *your* car. I don't want to think about that stuff."

Refraining from begging her to stay felt like I was swallowing a tape measure. "What *do* you want to think about?"

"Whether I'm helping you by being your girlfriend. Actually, I want to pray about that."

"Jesus, Mary Pat. How can you even ask that question?"

MP stared down into the steering wheel. "If you keep this up, you're going to be back where you started eight years ago."

"If it wasn't for Terry, I wouldn't be where I am right now."

MP turned toward me; the compassion vanished from her face. She slammed her hand against the Volvo dashboard. "Don't fucking lie to me, Randy! This isn't about Terry—this is about you wanting to punish someone!"

My fist clenched, and I would have punched the side panel of the Volvo if I hadn't seen the fear spark in MP's eyes. My hand slowly returned to the window. Her mouth closed and softened before she spoke again.

"If my mother had left my father the first time he hit her," MP said, "one way or another, he never would have hit her again. It's as simple as that."

"You think I could hit you?"

"You need to know that I won't put up with this. In your bones, you need to know."

Doing the kind of calculations that a drunk will sometimes do when he sees the writing on the wall, I figured the likelihood of getting through the next twenty-four hours without another assault. Not likely. Then I added up my love for Mary Pat Donnelly. It was significant, but balanced against the slim possibility that I could find out who or what had killed my sponsor, Terry Elias, it didn't add up. I pinned an asterisk to both these estimates to represent the chance that I might also lose my bid for custody of my daughter. Still, God help me, I stood there.

MP looked at me, waiting for me to plead my case.

"Will you please tell me where you're staying?" I said.

16

WADE HADN'T RETURNED MY CALLS. I wanted to go back and do over my interrogation of Mutt Kelly, but Sean had been pretty explicit on that subject, and I took him at his word. I thought about tracking down Busansky's erstwhile girlfriend, Emma, but decided against it because I knew that eventually, she would come to me. All I had left was Catalina Acuña. I decided that I would visit her in the morning and hope that Wade remembered my phone number between now and then.

When I woke up at two forty-five A.M., wishing that I were alone with anyone but myself, I searched the house for distractions and found nothing but more evidence that MP had prepared to never return. Pictures that had been taken with her camera were gone, while pictures taken with our camera remained. The juicer was gone, and so was her garlic press, but a Pottery Barn storm candle that we'd picked up for evenings on the deck remained. The eyesore beanbag chair that she'd found at the swap meet was gone—the only improvement I could detect. When I found myself checking the CD collection, I knew I had to leave.

MP may have taken her juicer and beanbag chair, but I had an espresso machine and a mini-fridge at my cabinet shop in the canyon. I opened the bay doors at about three-fifteen A.M. and made my own damn double espresso with a little crema on the top. Then I started to sort lumber for a project that I'd been designing in my head all evening.

It was one of the first things I learned in A.A.: just do the next indicated thing.

Sometimes people will say, "Just do the next right thing," but that was too advanced for me. Who knew what the next right thing was? Indicated, I could handle.

I left Wade a voice mail telling him where I'd be when he was ready to talk. Sipping strong coffee and denying for the moment that anything in my life was wrong, I began to build a crib for Terry's son.

. . .

I'd been taking courses at Art Center in Pasadena, one of the best all-around design schools in this galaxy. It was a long drive from Laguna Beach, though. So one morning I just quit. My fear of failing and the length of the drive had a talk, and they decided.

Terry and I were walking away from the seven A.M. meeting at the Catholic grammar school above Pacific Coast Highway.

The flower stand across the parking lot was a gang fight of color. I told Terry of my decision as we reached his car, which in those days was the Caddy.

"I've been thinking about this," I said, "and it makes sense that I stop going to that school."

Terry turned around to face me. The traffic was rushing beside us. Over his shoulder I could see Vic, the one-armed florist, fluffing up a bucket full of crocuses. Terry took a deep breath, and I stood exactly where I was. Maybe even leaned in to him.

"You've been a loser all your life," Terry began through thin lips. "And now, for the first time, you've got a chance to win. There's no way you're going to quit that school. You'll get in that car this afternoon and you'll get your ass up there."

A huge silence grew between us. Vic looked over. Very quietly, I said, "Why?"

"Because if you don't," Terry said, "I'm going to kick your ass."

My smile had no love. "You *can't* kick my ass, Terry. I'm the ex-cop with the impulse control problem, remember?"

Terry didn't back down. His smile had no love, either. "Then one of us will be in the hospital tonight."

He walked away. I laughed to pretend I wasn't scared. He turned back, practically charging at me.

"You think I'm here on this planet to be a fucking lawyer?" Terry shouted. "You think you're here to build houses? You think you avoided jail after that circus in Santa Ana because you're lucky? We're in Alcoholics Anonymous, you fucking prick. We have the power to bring dead people back to life. *That's* why we're here."

"So why am I driving to Pasadena?" I yelled back. "Why

don't I stay here and go to a meeting? Talk to a newcomer? Clean some fucking ashtrays?"

"Because you think too goddamn much." Terry tapped the side of my head, hard. "You need something to do, something that scares you to death. Can you understand that?"

"No."

"Can you do it anyway?"

That afternoon I drove to Pasadena.

. . .

Once upon a time, I wanted to design furniture, too. So far, I hadn't been as successful with that as I had been with home design. I'd spent about six thousand hours and twenty thousand dollars trying to design the first prototype of the first chair in my first line of furniture, and I was as close to the beginning as I was to the end. I enjoyed my shop, though, where I liked to pretend that I was an honest workingman with thick hands and a simple brain.

The crib: I pulled out my laptop, went to Google, and looked through a hundred images for cribs. I finally found a Shaker design that was as simple and unadorned as anything I'd ever seen. It was nothing more than a box with slats for the baby to see through. I made it out of quartersawn oak, I made it well, and I tried mightily to avoid putting anything of myself into it. For a few hours, I felt some peace as I assembled that simple, boxy design. The only time I fucked up was when I stripped a bolt near the drop side (I'd fabricated the fixtures myself) and scraped my knuckles on the wood. Other than that, the time I spent making that crib felt better to me than sleep. But then I did sleep.

. . .

Having conked out with my head on the workbench, I woke up looking straight at my masterpiece. I felt a click down deep in my heart when I recognized how well the crib had come together. It reminded me that my first impulse toward making things had been when Crash was a baby. Silly fabrications were always flowing from my hands. Crash was always asking me for things: *Daddy, make me a flower. Daddy, make me a robot. Daddy, make me a sky that's full of flowers and robots.*

I did what I was told. Maybe that was all I was doing now. It seemed to me then—as it had seemed to me this morning—that I might die if I didn't find a form for my feelings. I made robots and flowers and sky out of my love for Crash. I made a crib out of my love for Terry and his son, whom I hadn't yet met.

Wade showed up at about nine. I turned off the planer and threw my safety visor across the room. I checked my knuckles and they had stopped bleeding. As Wade walked toward me, my project caught his attention. "Why are you building a crib?"

The clamps had pushed some wood glue out of a dowel. I wiped it away with a damp rag. "Commission."

"Someone commissioned you? When did they hope you'd deliver? Just in time for medical school?"

"Make yourself useful," I said. "Drill up some espresso."

After he had made the espresso and steamed some milk, Wade opened a bag of pastries he had brought from Jean Claude's.

"MP moved out," I said.

Wade took out two chocolate croissants and started to chew on one. "She'll come back."

"It's lucky for me that you know so much about women."

Wade's espresso tasted like you'd stuck your head in a bucket of scorpions, and I hadn't known how much I needed a chocolate croissant until I was eating one. For a single second, I was in my happy place.

Wade went and stood by the crib. One of his problems in life was that he couldn't hide his feelings from me for long. He was impressed. He kept looking at it. For another second, that made me as happy as the chocolate croissant.

"What are you charging for this?" Wade asked.

"I'm being an artist this time." *Being an artist* was how Terry described my tendency to underbid.

"It's really beautiful, man. But there's no way this is a commission. Come on, who's it for?"

"Terry's son."

Wade looked genuinely startled, and I guess I knew right then that this was his first time hearing. I finished swallowing the croissant before I told him about the hospital trip and Catalina Acuña.

"Fuck," Wade said. *"Fuck."*

Thinking about that fatherless baby, I was angry again. "You connected Terry to the pot farms. That's how he met Simon Busansky. That's how he found this lovely new business taking money from drug dealers. He got involved with those people because of you. And that's why you've been avoiding me again."

Wade shrugged, turned away from me. He looked up at a wall crowded with tools: drill press, band saw, rotary saw, and more specialized woodworking gimmicks than I would ever use. I couldn't see his face but I kept going: "Working out a deal for you is one thing. Working out a deal for someone like Busansky?

That puts Terry in a totally different league. That's a business. You should have fucking told me. It wasn't the kind of thing he should have been doing."

"Why?" Wade turned around. "Because you would have fixed it? Because you would have done what I couldn't do? Protected Terry from himself? You give yourself a lot of credit, dude."

"Maybe," I said. "Maybe I just don't want to feel like I was excluded."

"You weren't excluded," Wade said. "You excluded yourself."

"I was falling in love. I was building a career. I have to hang out in coffee shops with you two for the rest of my life?"

Wade looked at me. He didn't shrug, he didn't turn away. At that moment, a bicycle bounced up from Laguna Canyon Road into the parking lot that I shared with three other shops. A cute little bicycle bell rang three times. Emma was on the handlebars, and Troy was pedaling. Troy stopped, straddling the bike a few feet from Wade. Emma rang the bell one more time. Then it must have become obvious to them that Wade and I had reached some kind of climax, because neither of them spoke, and the bell didn't ring again.

To his credit, Wade smiled before I did. "Yes," he said, "I was hoping you two would hang out with me at coffee shops for the rest of our lives."

Troy seemed upset to have missed the joke. He shaded his eyes from the sunlight in order to see into my shop. Emma got off the handlebars and, without a moment's hesitation, got up into my truck. She closed the door and then closed her eyes. Locked both doors, too. Troy lifted the front wheel of his bike and let it clatter to the pavement.

I sat down on the worktable that held the crib. Wade sat on the worktable against the wall.

"You want to know what happened to Terry?" On the bench beside him, Wade pushed a pile of sawdust together into a mound. "He got interested. You remember the way Terry got interested? After he steered me out of trouble, he made a study of how the grow-ops worked. I didn't think he was getting involved. I thought it was like, you know, Betsy's model trains."

"Grow-ops?" Troy said. He was on the other side of the shop trying to figure out my planer by sticking his hand into it. "What's a grow-op?"

"It's a hydroponic pot farm," Wade said. "Under your house. That's what they call them in Vancouver. It was a stupid idea to import the concept to California. In Canada, they write you a parking ticket. In the States, well, things are more complicated. If you have a license for medical marijuana, that's one thing. If you don't . . ."

"You get arrested?" Troy asked.

"It's a federal felony," I said. "I thought you were a criminal mastermind."

"Okay," Troy said. "I just thought things were lightening up, at least as far as pot goes."

"It's hard for things to lighten up," I said, "when everyone's still making money from them *not* lightening up. If the cops find one of these illegal grow-ops, and there's money behind it, it's a big payday for them. The drug assets become law enforcement assets. Buys a lot of surveillance equipment and coffee machines and overtime. Back in the day, we would have killed to split something like this with the DEA."

"They don't even have to convict you," Wade added, "in

order to confiscate your related assets. Make it easy for them to get what they want, and you can avoid jail entirely."

"Fucking feds." Troy crouched to inspect the table saw. "It's piracy, is what it is. It's like my dad always says, there's no difference anymore between cops and criminals."

Wade and I looked at each other. Where the hell did we find this guy?

"Anyway," Wade said, "by the time I was back on my feet, Terry seemed to know everyone. I figured, he's a lawyer. Lawyers know criminals, right?"

"Like Simon Busansky?"

"Like Simon Busansky," Wade said.

"Here's what I don't understand," I said. "Why did the DEA let Busansky sell his houses to Colin? Why not just take them?"

"The reason you don't get that," Wade said, "is because you don't have a mind for this shit. It's a *relationship*. Simon probably said something like, 'Hey, you guys could take my houses and a lot of my money. But let me sell a couple of houses off first.'"

"It wasn't Simon who said that, right?"

"No," Wade said. "It was probably Terry."

"And then Terry turns around and puts Busansky together with Colin and, I'm sure, takes a cut off that end, too." I thought of my sponsor's smile in the grocery store at the mention of recovery houses. "And if the DEA lets Busansky do this," I continued, "it means that he's in their debt?"

"That's right," Wade said. "And the wheel keeps turning."

"So you're telling me Terry went into business with Busansky?"

"If you're asking me whether Terry got involved in anything

that was illegal, I don't know. He's over there at the recovery house, talking to newcomers like Troy, sure"—Troy looked up as though surprised to hear his name—"but he's also romancing the idea that maybe he doesn't have to spend so much time talking with newcomers like Troy. Because maybe it's more fun to trade war stories with a guy like Simon Busansky. Simon was swimming around in this world where you could run grow-ops, get busted for them, and have enough money left over to eat nice meals and not get a job."

"Terry wasn't trying to help him get sober?"

"Maybe that's what he was doing. After my own thing, I couldn't hack it. Simon made me uncomfortable. When Simon was around, I wasn't."

"What about Colin?"

"Colin's a Boy Scout," Wade said. "He always thought A.A. was like, I don't know, *Go and sin no more*. Terry hooked him up with Simon in a deal that allowed him to cheaply expand his business or his mission or whatever he thinks it is, but I'm sure he didn't like this shit any more than I did. And there's no way I can buy him knowing about any porn. Colin threw people out of the house if he found a dirty magazine under the bed. Right, Troy?"

Troy nodded. "He says it's demeaning to women."

My hands were throbbing, but so was my spirit. "Terry had just had a fucking baby, Wade. His dreams had come true. Why would he end up in a motel in Santa Ana? *Thirty-six fucking hours after the child was born.* Something must have set him off. This guy at the hospital said Terry was ranting about a business partner. I think that's Busansky. And not even the DEA knows where he is. So how the fuck do we find Busansky?"

All of us at once looked at Emma in my truck. Her eyes were still, eerily, closed. We turned back. "I'm going to get to her in a minute," I said.

"I don't know, Randy," Wade said. "But I think you're missing the big picture here."

"What's the big picture, Wade?"

"This guy." Wade pointed at Troy. *"This guy."*

Troy withdrew his attention from an investigation of the motor beneath the table saw. He seemed to be in the process of memorizing my shop, although I was also sure he heard every word. It took me a moment to recognize what Wade was saying: *Troy is the patient today, dude.*

"Troy's fine," I said.

"I'm not worried about Troy."

"You think I'm going to drink if I don't sponsor Troy?"

"How should I know?" Wade said. "I'm the one who dropped the ball on Terry, remember? All I know is that without this guy, we've got nothing."

As Troy joined us between the worktables, I thought about the two days since I'd met him in that other garage. How did we get from there to here? In our dysfunctional little A.A. family, we'd traded Terry for Troy.

"Tell him," Wade said to Troy.

"Tell him what?" Troy asked.

"Tell him that you're done."

"Done?" I asked. "Done with what?"

"Oh," Troy said. "My fourth step."

What separated the men from the boys in A.A.: the moral inventory. Basically a list of resentments, it also ended up being a list of sins and fears and the chronology of an entire stupid life. A good sign, too, that the kid was serious. The fifth step should be the very next thing, in which you shared that list with another person. People sometimes called it the end of isolation. I myself thought of it as the beginning of my new life.

"You finished the whole funky resentment-list thing?" I asked.

"Yeah," Troy said.

"What about the sexual inventory? Did you write down all the people you hurt by your selfish pursuit of sex?"

"Yeah." Troy laughed and looked at Wade. "It was a short list."

"How about your fears?" I asked. "You write down your fears?"

"Relax, man. Wade wouldn't let me get away with shit. He went through the book page by page. It was old school."

"When are you going to do your fifth step?" I said.

"This is the question," Troy said.

Waiting to do a fifth step after finishing the fourth is a bad idea: like waiting to replace your skin after it's been peeled from your body. Terry had canceled half a day to hear my list of resentments and fears, woes and missteps.

"You should do it with this man." I pointed at Wade.

"I'm not his sponsor," Wade said.

"Then why were you helping him write the inventory?" I said.

"It takes a goddamn village," Wade said.

"I explicitly told him why I wouldn't become his sponsor."

"I know," Wade said. "Because you can't stand the sight of

him, and you're such a badass that you might punch him at any moment. So maybe you feel about him pretty much the way Terry felt about you?"

I looked at Troy. "Is tomorrow morning soon enough?"

Troy pointed at his borrowed bicycle. "Like I've got someplace else to go?"

"I'm still not your sponsor," I said. "This is a one-off, never to be repeated."

"Everyone gets that," Wade said.

As I contemplated a future that included knowing Troy Padilla's darkest secrets, I looked up at Emma. At precisely that moment, she opened her eyes and stared right at me.

I walked around to the passenger side of my truck, which was parked in front of the bay door that opened my shop. Emma popped the locks, and I got in. Then she locked them again. Troy said that Simon had hurt Emma, which was another way of saying they were in a relationship. I guess I already knew that she was here to tell me something. The trick would be getting her to tell me in a language I could understand.

We sat quietly for a minute while Wade and Troy vacillated between watching us from outside the truck and fixing more coffee. I pretended for a moment that I was the kind of good A.A. who practiced meditation. I began to count my breaths, but by the time I got to four, I wished that I had a cigar in my mouth to enhance the process. Still, there was something about sitting next to Emma, feeling her try to contain her restless energy. I had to admit that I already loved her—and Troy—a little bit more than they annoyed me.

"I'm not going to talk to you about him," Emma finally said.

"Then I don't want you to," I said.

"Oh," she said. "You *want* me to."

"Maybe," I said, "but I'm taking that desire and putting it in a box buried deep in my mind, and then I'm going to find out what happened to him whether you help me or not."

She turned to me, smiling.

"Isn't that what a recon marine would do?" I said. "Put those unquenchable desires and unanswerable shames into deep storage? And still complete the mission?"

"Which makes me want to tell you everything. You're a real mind-fucker, aren't you, Officer Chalmers?"

"Not really." I softened my voice. "I know you want to tell me, Emma. You've been circling around it since we met."

"I do," she said. "I really miss him."

"This is Busansky?"

"Simon."

"Was he your boyfriend?"

Emma laughed. "Not that *he* knew it."

"But you loved him?"

"The way that you love a guy who spends half his time trying to convince you to do weird shit on video, yeah."

"You want to tell me about that?"

"It was supposed to make me feel free, but it didn't make me feel free. Recon makes me feel free."

"Did you, ah, do weird shit with my friend Terry, too?"

"Did I fuck him, you mean?"

"Yeah."

"You're not ready for the answer to that question, Officer Chalmers. You gotta walk a few more miles in this marine's boots."

"Tell me anyway."

"I loved Terry," she said. "Not the way I loved Simon."

"Which is your sweet but fucked-up way of telling me you didn't sleep with him." I sure hoped so.

"Maybe," she said.

"Okay, Emma. But if you really care about Simon, you need to answer some questions. And I don't want you to fuck around. Fuck around about everything else, but I want straight answers to these next few questions. Okay?"

She nodded.

"Did you know that Simon sold all those houses to Colin?"

She nodded again.

"When was the last time you saw Simon?"

"About a month ago. He took me to this swingers club in San Diego. He wanted me to—"

"I don't need the details of that right now," I said. "But when he brought you back home, to the house, was that the last time you saw him?"

"Yeah," she said.

"Is it weird for him to be gone this long?"

"He goes to Mexico sometimes, but he'll send me an email just to keep me on the hook, you know? He doesn't want me to wander too far, if you know what I mean."

"What do you think happened to him, Emma?"

"I think he's dead, but I don't know *how* he's dead. Or why he's dead."

"What makes you think he's dead?"

She stared at me frankly, and I knew I was missing something.

"If you had a woman as smart and pretty as me," she said,

"who was willing to do anything that you asked, how long would you disappear?"

I was relieved when she started to cry. This was a girl who needed to cry. I put my hand on her shoulder. If it hadn't been for my bucket seats, I would have hugged her. "Okay," I said.

"Any other questions, Officer Chalmers?"

"Yeah," I said. "Are you ready to settle the fuck down and become a regular A.A. member like the rest of us?"

AFTER WADE TOOK OFF for the scuba shop, Troy and Emma learned how to make espresso the way I liked it. While I finished the crib, I gave them both the kind of meaningless but fun chores that Crash had grown out of: Emma sorted wood, and Troy swept the floor. My life was starting to feel like a clubhouse again, which was not the worst thing.

I told Troy and Emma it was time to help me transport the crib to Santa Ana. Ms. Acuña needed to pick the stain herself.

. . .

My sort-of sponsee Troy was, apparently, technically oriented. As we left the canyon, he explained to me what was so cool about the automatic shutoff on my table saw. Until that moment, I didn't know I *had* an automatic shutoff on my table saw.

I made Emma sit shotgun, so I could grab her if she tried to jump out of the truck. I planned on keeping her close from now on.

On the way to Santa Ana, I asked Emma and Troy the same question Terry asked me eight years ago. "What would you guys do if anything were possible? If God, against all odds, actually loved you the way He/She/It is supposed to love you?"

"Him first," Emma said. "Actually, him only. I don't want to play."

"I'm afraid my dad will hate it," Troy said, "and because you and Wade are becoming surrogates for him, I'm afraid you're going to hate it, too."

"Did you just say 'surrogates'?"

"Yeah. It means—"

"I know what it means, Troy. But it's not a word you should use around me again. And *never* in this truck."

"Okay. Jeez."

Emma laughed. One of the most horrible moments in A.A. is when you decide to make someone else's bullshit your own. That's what Terry did for me at Corky's when he explained how much he *didn't* like me. That's what I was doing for Troy, taking him with me to Santa Ana for no good reason but his company. It was more complicated with Emma, but not by much.

Before Troy could answer the question—*what do you want to be when you grow up?*—he took one last detour through the drama of his "criminal" family: "The culture of blame and revenge was the hardest thing to abandon. Being raised Catholic was tough, too. That Higher Power wasn't—"

I wanted to shoot myself. "Troy," I finally said. "Please shut the fuck up."

Troy looked as though he'd misunderstood. I wasn't fascinated?

"Listen," I said. "We all come to A.A. feeling like punks, talking about how tough we are, pissing in everyone's coffee, but I don't believe you're from a dangerously criminal family. Dangerous just doesn't look like you."

"I never said *I* was dangerous."

"I don't care. Okay? I'm going to hang out with you, I'll even be your sponsor, but I don't want to hear any more shit."

"You'll be my sponsor?"

"And you don't have to be anyone special. You just have to be a still-breathing alcoholic."

Troy's face changed, like he had coughed up a spiritual hairball. "I'll stop talking about it," he said quietly.

. . .

Catalina Acuña was approaching forty, with a sharp nose and bright eyes. Her long hair was like the feathers of a swift black bird. There were strands of gray, too, but I liked them. When I buzzed at the wrought-iron security gate of her stucco apartment building, and she came out to meet me, she said that no one called her Catalina anymore—her name was Cathy. Her accent was less heavy when she wasn't reporting her boyfriend's death.

I pointed to the back of my truck, where Troy was standing like Vanna White beside the crib. Emma was in the truck, having asked if she could skip the whole "heartbreaking single mother rising from the ashes of her life" thing and stay in the car. I couldn't believe I'd managed to get this feral reality-television star to ask for my permission to do anything.

"I had a free day," I said to Cathy, "so I thought I would bring it over."

"Who are you?" Cathy made it sound like her own failure to remember.

"We just need some decisions about paint and stain. I tried to contact Mr. Elias, but his cell phone isn't working." It occurred to me that I would be going to hell for this. But at least I wasn't wearing a blue blazer.

Cathy looked down, closed her eyes, smiled. As she walked toward my truck, I had the pleasure of her first impression.

"Terry ordered this?" Cathy glanced at Troy.

"Designed it, too."

"It's too nice for this place," Cathy said. "Can you keep it until we move?"

Troy nodded as though this were his department. I decided to lie some more.

"There's a bit of, well . . . Mr. Elias didn't pay for the whole thing."

"I owe you some money?"

Making up a number that might tell me something, I said, "Five hundred dollars, ma'am."

A teenage girl who had to be Cathy's daughter pushed through the security gate. She was carrying a big-headed baby boy.

Just the fact of him stunned me. He belonged to Terry like my hand belonged to the end of my arm. The same narrow, permanently skeptical eyes, the same flat Irish nose. It was one of those moments—like the moment Crash was born or the day I met MP—when the wall between my world and all the other worlds became impossibly thin, and I had to admit to myself that I didn't know anything about what was going on.

Cathy turned toward her children. "This is my daughter, Paloma. And my son, Danny."

Holding her baby brother, Paloma spread her feet, a bit dramatically, into a wary, athletic stance. Letting me know that she was prepared to kick my ass if need be, baby or no baby. Not yet as pretty as her mom, Paloma was a solid little tomboy. I liked her very much for not liking me at all.

My heart ached for Crash, my own child of trouble, tougher and smarter than any child was supposed to be, never allowing herself to be fooled by the world. Why hadn't I gone to see my own daughter today?

"Come inside and I'll write you a check." Cathy didn't seem concerned about the money; I definitely could have gone higher. "Paloma can pick the colors."

With Danny still on her shoulder, Paloma gathered up the stain samples and followed us inside.

Stomping my feet on her mat like an honest workingman, I entered a room that hadn't been painted in a decade. The furniture was worn, and not in a way that looked comfortable. Nothing that suggested Cathy's quickness to write a five-hundred-dollar check.

As we sat down on the vinyl couch, Cathy asked if we'd like something to drink. Danny's eyes, blue like his father's, wouldn't stop reminding me of the man who had died of a heroin overdose about a mile away.

Troy was polite enough not to ask for anything, but I smelled coffee. The next learning opportunity came right after Cathy returned with an Anaheim Angels mug. She pulled up her purse from the floor and asked what name she should put on the check. I just went for it.

"Randy Chalmers, please."

I saw how my name stiffened Cathy, but I already liked her too much to continue playing detective. Instead, I turned to Paloma, who still seemed wary as hell. "Are those hands and feet registered as lethal weapons? I hear the Santa Ana Police Department takes a dim view of martial artists who use their skills recklessly."

Paloma's mouth made a surprised "O" until I pointed to a glass bookshelf across the room filled with tournament trophies.

As I squinted to read the words beneath the golden action figures, Paloma said, "Jeet Kune Do. My sensei trained with the man who invented it."

"You don't think I know who Bruce Lee was?" I said. "I saw *Enter the Dragon* sixteen times the summer he died. I hadn't cried like that"—I paused—"for a long time."

At a certain point, Cathy had abandoned writing my check. Paloma hoisted Danny back into her arms.

"Paloma says they killed him," Cathy said.

"He was a threat to the establishment," Paloma said. "He tried to bring the disciplines together."

Typically, Troy had begun sniffing around something that I hadn't yet noticed: a white box in the corner that had, until recently, held a new MacBook Pro. He looked from the box to Paloma. "You got the fifteen-inch? Sweet."

Paloma nodded. I knew enough to know that Paloma's nod had increased the price on an already expensive computer by about six hundred dollars.

Cathy caught my eye. Of course she knew who I was. And now I knew where my fifty thousand dollars had gone. But I was without desire to get it back. Somehow I would extricate myself from my stupid trick and approach her like a friend. What I should have done in the first place. Maybe I would even let her make the first move. Yes, that was it: I would let her make the first move.

Drooling on Paloma's shoulder, Danny made a sharp happy noise as if to approve my decision. Troy asked if he could buy the computer that the MacBook had replaced. Paloma produced a thick IBM laptop. "It's a cheap piece of shit," she said.

Cathy fixed her with eyes terrible enough to back down a black belt. "My boss gave it to us," she explained.

"I'm good with crappy computers," Troy said. "It'll be perfect for me."

Cathy wouldn't take Troy's money, which was fortunate, because he didn't have any. She handed me a check for the imaginary balance on the crib. After Paloma picked the colors and we waved goodbye, Troy and I returned to my truck, where I grabbed a FedEx envelope without disturbing a napping Emma. Who knew she would look so peaceful? I addressed the envelope to Cathy Acuña and placed her check inside. Once the crib was installed, it could happily join the fifty thousand dollars. Of everything that bugged me about the last days of Terry's life, there was nothing bigger than this: why had he felt the need to hide this woman from his friends?

We sat in the truck for a few minutes without speaking. Troy seemed to respect my mood. I was in the process of being vastly humbled by my own life. What could I say about Terry's death if this was what he'd left behind, this lovely little family? What was I doing trying to avenge him when I should be helping the mother of his child? When I'd reached the end of my thinking,

I shoved my door back open and walked toward the apartment building. *Fuck this, I'm going to just talk to her.*

Cathy met me outside the security gate, where I removed the check from the sealed FedEx envelope. I gave it back to her. "You know who I am?" I asked.

"Yes."

"I'm sorry I lied to you."

"It's okay," Cathy said. "I didn't say anything, either."

"How come we've never met?"

"He talked about you a lot," Cathy said. "He was proud of you. Maybe he wasn't so proud of me."

That was ridiculous. I shook my head. "I think maybe he wanted to protect something that was precious to him. I wish he hadn't, but I understand the impulse."

"It was a tough time," Cathy said.

I told her what I knew about the hospital, about Terry freaking out. "Cathy," I said, "what the hell happened?"

"I never saw him again after Danny was born. The doctor said he gave him something to calm down, I think, and he was gone. And then he did what he did the next day."

"He didn't take the Valium," I said. "You should know that. Do you think he was taking anything else? I mean before the end?"

"I don't think so," Cathy said. "I never saw it. Maybe it turned out he didn't want to be a father?"

"I think he wanted it more than anything," I said. "I think he would have been good at it, too."

"Maybe," she said. "Maybe we just want to believe that."

She invited me back into her apartment. Paloma and Danny were quiet somewhere upstairs.

"Here's something else," Cathy said. "I think Terry would want you to have it." She handed me The Big Book, *Alcoholics Anonymous,* third edition. Terry had left it at her house. I recognized his copy immediately, every nick and scratch on the cover. I bet I could have told you which pages the spine was broken at.

"Forgive me for asking," I said. "I know you reported him to 911. How did you find out where he was?"

"I got a call," she said. "He didn't say who he was. Just that he was a friend of Terry's."

"Did you believe him?" I asked. "That he was a friend?"

"I didn't know what to think. I just called 911."

That was my cue to roll off the names. Mutt Kelly, who Claire claimed had been there. Simon Busansky, who seemed to have gone missing about the same time Terry died. Colin Alvarez, just to see. I felt only a little bit guilty when I asked about Troy Padilla, who was waiting for me in the truck. You never knew. But none of these names meant anything to Cathy.

"I think there's something I should tell you," she began again. "Terry left us a lot of money. That's why we're moving, and that's how we're buying nice things. I'm not going to manage this building anymore. I might go back to school."

"I understand."

As much as I wanted to question her about every detail of Terry's last few months, I reminded myself that I'd stepped into a new world. In this world, it was becoming clear to me, I wasn't responsible for just myself and Crash and MP, but also this woman and her children. I knew this like I knew that little Danny's eyes were blue. I was already supporting them, to some extent, with the fifty thousand, but there would need to be more.

"Maybe this is out of bounds," I said, "but fifty thousand dollars isn't a lot of money these days. I can help you come up with a plan."

"Fifty thousand dollars?" Cathy said.

"I know how much money Terry gave you," I said. "I can also give you more."

Cathy shook her head, smiling. "Terry never gave us money. He made us the beneficiaries of his life insurance policy."

Oh.

"But the way he died?" I said. "They paid off?"

"They will," Cathy said. "A million dollars. The man who owns this building? My boss? He's a lawyer, and he says there won't be any problem. He says that Terry committed a crime in shooting the heroin, but that won't invalidate the policy."

"Wow," I said.

"Yes," she said. "It's amazing, isn't it?"

As much as I wanted such a great gift for this lovely family that Terry had left behind, I didn't quite trust what I was hearing. Maybe I wasn't in the mood for a fairy tale.

"Why is your boss so involved? Was he a friend of Terry's?"

"My boss was the one who brought the policy to me. I didn't even know about it. The money first came to him, but he didn't want it, so he passed it down to me."

"Terry's policy paid out to him? Why?"

"He and Terry had done some business together. He said it was because of that. But he doesn't need the money, so he— what did he call it?—he *bounced* it down to me."

I took a moment to breathe. My heart was beating too fast, and I wanted to be careful about what I said next. "You're the secondary beneficiary?"

"That's right," Cathy said.

"I don't want to offend you," I said, "but I have to ask: why would your boss pass up a million dollars? I didn't think anyone was *that* rich."

"I think it's because of Paloma," Cathy said. "I think he wants to make sure she's taken care of."

She smiled cautiously. Was I missing something?

"He and Paloma are close?" I said.

"Not really," Cathy said. "Paloma hates him."

I was still not getting it, and Cathy was trying not to spell it out for me.

"Your boss is Paloma's father?" I said.

"It's a long story. Maybe I'll tell you someday when we're old friends."

"Wow," I said. "But it sounds like this guy is stepping up to the plate. I like to see that in a man. And it sounds like you're close to him."

"Not so much anymore. Once I was. John looks out for us, though."

"John who?"

"John Sewell. He owns this building, but he's going to sell it."

John fucking Sewell. My fishing buddy, my financial adviser, my hope for an end to alimony.

"Because he's going to become a judge," I said. "I know John. I think I might be seeing him later, actually. You want me to say hello for you?"

18

AFTER RETURNING TROY AND EMMA to my house, I called my daughter. I hadn't spoken to her in a while, but I didn't make any plans to see her. Crash knew something was off. When I asked if she knew where her mom was this afternoon, she hesitated before she told me that my ex-wife and her fiancé were at the Newport Bay Yacht Club.

It should have been my first question way back when: who stood to benefit from Terry's death? A million dollars is a lot of benefit, particularly if you can shift that money away from yourself toward a former mistress who is now the mother of your child. John Sewell was suddenly my prime suspect for the business partner Terry had been ranting about while Cathy had their baby. I needed to know what business they had been in. It seemed like the most fun to simply demand that information from Sewell himself. He had offered to help me if I had any questions about money, right?

The Newport Bay Yacht Club. You'd think the gatekeeper to that exclusive Orange County institution would keep out tourists like me, but it goes to show once again what you can accomplish when you're willing to wear your officiously blue Armani blazer. They were halfway through lunch when I arrived. John had some kind of club sandwich with an iced tea, and Jean was picking at a Caesar salad, the kind where each salad spear has been individually groomed. I noticed that she was drinking wine.

In that dining room looking out over the Newport Bay, I could see what California's vast wealth had made possible: an infinite variety of ridiculously expensive Hawaiian shirts. Sewell looked more comfortable in his dark suit and tie, and Jean's white Armani shift made me remember things I wanted to forget.

Reminding myself that a fistfight with my ex-wife's fiancé wouldn't help my custody suit, I slowed down a bit on approach. Jean looked unhappy to see me, but Sewell seemed, if anything, more at ease than the last time we'd pretended to be friends. I stood beside their table, glancing imperiously around until a waiter took the hint and brought me a chair.

"What the hell are you doing here?" Jean said. "Please don't make yourself comfortable."

"John offered to give me some financial advice. Suddenly, I really need it."

Jean turned toward her fiancé with disgust, but Sewell reached over to pat her hand while giving her a look that seemed to reflect calm masculine authority. Was this how you controlled a woman like Jean?

"I'll give you five minutes," Jean said, "while John does whatever the hell he does with people like you. But if you're not gone when I get back, I'll make you go away myself."

She removed her napkin and started away from the table. I sat down beside Sewell.

"Is there something I can do for you?" Sewell asked. "Or did you just want to cause a scene?"

"Does she cut your meat for you?" I asked.

"Pardon me?"

"Once, when we were spending Thanksgiving with Jean's parents, I was talking to her dad about Frank Lloyd Wright—Mr. Trask used to see him walking around Oak Park—and when I turned back to my plate, Jean had cut my turkey."

It took Sewell a second. "No. She doesn't cut my meat."

"Thank God for that. You think Cathy Acuña cut Terry's meat?"

"I don't know where this is headed," Sewell said.

"Let's start over. You know that Terry had a kid with Cathy Acuña."

"Cathy Acuña is an employee of mine. That's the only piece of what you just said that I recognize. She manages some properties for me, a job she's about to quit. I don't know if she's vacated her apartment yet."

"Pregnancy is hard for an employer to miss," I said. "The gals, they slow down a bit. You might have noticed this when she had *your* baby."

Sewell adjusted his plate. "I'm sorry about your unresolved issues with Jean and whatever else is causing these delusions, but I'm going to request you change your tone. Otherwise, I'm going to get angry, too."

He talked about anger like it was a distant planet that our great-grandchildren might visit in a spaceship.

"First things first, then," I said. "You're the beneficiary of a million-dollar life insurance policy that Terry took out before he died. How the hell did you pull that off?"

"A life insurance policy is always a good idea," Sewell said. "I often encouraged Terry to behave in a more professional manner. Buying life insurance was only one of the suggestions I made."

"Which doesn't explain why it paid out to you," I said.

"Terry never thought he would die, and he paid very little for it. I made a few calls, though, and it seems that sometimes even insurance companies can be brought to their senses by the threat of a lawsuit."

"From a superior court judge," I added.

"I'm sure that didn't hurt. Look, I was helping Terry with all his affairs, and we were doing a fair amount of business together. It was his idea to put the policy in my name. He owed me some money at the time."

"Cathy thinks you bounced the money down to her out of the goodness of your heart," I said, "but I'm not feeling it."

"Who cares what you feel?" Sewell said. "I don't need the money, and she does. Terry had her down as the secondary beneficiary. I knew they had recently gotten involved. It's always horrible to hear about a child who won't have a father."

"You're sorry that *Terry's* child won't have a father. What about *your* child?"

"That's a situation that's none of your business. I've always done the right thing when it comes to Cathy and her daughter."

"Your daughter's name is Paloma," I said.

Neither of us said anything for a long moment.

"Listen, Randy, are you accusing me of a crime? If so, I wish you'd start by telling me what the crime was."

"I don't know yet," I said. "Maybe you don't want Cathy talking too much about what you and Terry were up to."

"I have nothing to hide," Sewell said. "And by the way, I know who you must have been asking me about at Jean's house. Mutt Kelly? He did some work for me on my building. I think Terry might have suggested him to me. Do you need to get in touch with him?"

I gave myself a moment to process the fact that Sewell didn't care how I could connect him to Mutt.

"Look," I said. "I have no problem with you dating my ex-wife. Marry her, for all I care. And if your hands got dirty doing business with Terry, you can't imagine my lack of interest. I just want to know what happened to my friend."

"I didn't speak to Terry for six months before he died. After proposing to Jean, that turns out to be the best decision I've made this year. I always got beaten up when I tried to help Terry."

"Have I been beating you up, John?"

"Some would characterize it that way."

"When I start beating you up, John, *everyone* will characterize it that way."

For a second, I could see his anger, that distant planet. Anger, I knew well, equaled stupidity, and I wanted Sewell to drop some IQ points ASAP, to play on my level for a minute. Instead, he picked up his sandwich. Taking the kind of sensible bites you see only on TV commercials, he became his old *I do well with this kind of investment* self.

"I'm telling you this out of respect for your daughter," Sewell said. "Terry was like an apprentice. I wanted to pass on some skills before I was offered the bench. I walked him across from real estate to criminal law. I thought the addiction issues were behind him. At a certain point, I couldn't ignore the deterioration of his behavior."

"You're saying he was shooting heroin six months before he died?"

"I'm saying he was unnecessarily angry—like you are now—and it seemed like a good idea to put some distance between us."

"What the hell were you two doing? I hope you weren't stupid enough to get involved with this homemade pornography."

"I have absolutely no idea what you're talking about," Sewell said. "I have no connection to pornography."

"How about marijuana?" I said. "Are you connected to any hydroponic pot farms?"

Sewell took another bite and began to chew without such precise mincing. He wasn't going to answer any more stupid questions, but he also wasn't calling security.

"I just figured something out," I said. "You're the reason no one has been busted for growing pot in Laguna Beach. You made it more profitable for the DEA *not* to bust them. The DEA confiscates all the related assets without the muss and fuss of criminal charges. You eventually needed a front like Terry so it wouldn't interfere with getting ready for the bench. Terry was your partner."

"There's nothing illegal about anything you're describing," he said.

"But how good does it look for a future judge to be giving hand jobs to a federal agency on behalf of drug dealers?"

Sewell stopped chewing, swallowed. I noticed that he hadn't touched his excellent-looking potato salad. "That's what lawyers do. Keep people out of jail. *Negotiate.* In some ways, though, you're right. I risked sullying my reputation. And apparently, it killed Terry."

"How did it kill him?"

"You can't rub up against that kind of business without some personal cost. Given his history of addiction—"

I smacked the table hard enough to spill some of Sewell's iced tea. Every Hawaiian shirt in the dining room turned toward me. "Don't give me a lecture on substance abuse. *How did it fucking kill him?*"

"Terry told me that the road gets narrower. That the longer you stay away from drugs, the riskier it becomes to ethically compromise yourself. Did I make that up? Isn't that what you A.A. people believe?"

"So who was he rubbing up against?"

"I washed my hands of that business a long time ago. I'm not sending you off to bother any of my former clients."

"Like Simon Busansky? Colin Alvarez?" I said. "What are you hiding? Why are you trying to put me back in my box?"

Sewell shook his head as he stared into me. Another gesture that would go well with the black robe. "I'm not the one who's hiding. It's not my life that's this . . . swamp of resentment and fear."

"My life is not the issue here."

"If you say so, Randy. I'm sure you're also not responsible for Jean being so angry that sometimes she can't look me in the eye. For Alison working so hard to be perfect that I'm afraid her heart will seize. Maybe it's time to start looking at your own behavior.

What do you make, a couple hundred thousand on every house you design? More? I can't get through one conversation with Alison without hearing what a great man you are. Why on earth would you want to prove her wrong? I know that Terry's death put you off balance—that's true for everyone who knew him— but let me be clear: I have no connection whatsoever with pornography or drug dealing or anything else you have in mind. And while it's profoundly none of your affair, I *will* do the right thing by Cathy Acuña and her daughter. But if you continue this pressure, I'm prepared to file charges of harassment."

At that moment, Jean returned to the table, a lot calmer than when she'd left, which was not a good sign.

"Do they teach you that in law school, John? How to wash your hands? You brought my friend into this, and then it seems to me like he was *how* you washed your hands."

"From what I've heard," Sewell said quietly, "neither of us was very close to Terry near the end."

I would have thrown him through a window or at least forced him to eat his potato salad. But with my ex-wife returned to the table, I wanted to be slightly more tactful than that.

I said, "Jean, why don't you get security. We'll see how long it takes to restrain me. I'm thinking maybe five minutes before they get me out of this crowded room full of rich people? Although it might save time if they shot me. You think they'll shoot me?"

"We're about to find out," Jean said.

Hearing the purposeful steps of large men behind me, I turned to find a phalanx of former USC football players. Jean smiled up at them.

The three security guys had about eight hundred pounds between them, most of it in the big Samoan-looking guy who was coming around the table to stand behind Jean. I guessed they would give me about thirty seconds to come to my senses before they carried me there. If it had been just two of them, I might have made a show of it. So long as it was the smaller two.

Sewell said, "My patience is gone, Randy. And frankly, Jean never had any patience to begin with. I like Alison a lot, and I want things to be civil with her father, but this is the last time I'll accept this behavior. You're not my friend, and you've shown no desire to become my friend."

"Don't explain yourself to him," Jean said.

Sewell looked at her, held his hand up slightly, and Jean backed down. "Jean thinks you're pulling the world down around your head because you don't want responsibility for a teenage girl. I argued against that, but I'm starting to wonder. Here I am, trying to settle things between you and Jean. You're the same kind of fool that Terry was, and if you don't stop, you're going to lose everything."

My laughter was forced. "That would have been a better angle before I found out about your insurance scam. Why don't we meet at your office tomorrow morning and you can sign away your rights to that money? You say you want that money to go to Cathy and her children? There's a simple way to guarantee that."

Jean made a move toward the football player behind her, but Sewell again help up his hand. "I'm not creating a legal document out of your fantasies. Cathy will get the money because I gave her my word."

"You think he's trying to take money from that woman?" Jean said to me. "Jesus fucking Christ. You're sick."

Sewell tried the hand trick again. "Sweetheart—"

"Did you know that your daughter cried herself to sleep on Wednesday night?" Jean said. "She loves you too much to say it, but she's afraid you're so upset about fucking Terry that you're going to drink again, and she remembers what that was like."

"I'm not going to drink again, Jean. And you have no idea who this guy is. Go ahead and deny me custody, but don't do it because you think Sewell is a better man. We've always worked together when it comes to Crash."

"No, Randy, we haven't worked together. I've worked for Alison, and you've worked on yourself. Where was your daughter when you were going to A.A. meetings twenty-four hours a day? Did you notice how much she needed you while you sat around whining to strangers? It's the same shit that I grew up with, just dressed in a new vocabulary. I won't let it ruin my next marriage, and I'm sure as hell not going to let it hurt my daughter. By the way, how did you find us, Randy?"

"How did I find you?"

"How did you know we were at the yacht club?" Jean said. "Who did you call so that you could come here to harass my fiancé and get yourself thrown into the street like a criminal? You're an animal to use my daughter against me."

The Samoan-looking guy thought that was a pretty good cue to step forward and invite me to leave.

19

AFTER GETTING THROWN OUT of the yacht club, I spent the afternoon and early evening at Jean Claude's, starting to feel foolish. I was willing to blame John Sewell for genocide and global warming and every crime that incredibly stiff white men had committed since the Civil War, but I couldn't prove he'd done anything that had led to the death of my friend. Jean was right in her own way. However great a father I'd been for the last eight years, it didn't erase the years before that.

At about six o'clock, Jean Claude—who had a pretty good sense of when I required his intervention—came out to sit beside me. He didn't speak for a while, just sipped his espresso. This was how he often drew me out: by sitting companionably beside me while my thoughts formed. The fact was that there had been many times when neither of us spoke, and my French friend seemed as pleased with those meetings as the ones when we talked.

"You think I should give up on finding out what happened to Terry?" I finally asked him.

"Did something happen to Terry?" Jean Claude said. "I thought that he was dead."

"Please don't give me the whole existential bit," I said. "Because I can go to fucking Starbucks."

"As a Frenchman, I'm supposed to think that Americans are fucked up about sex," Jean Claude said. "But you're much more fucked up about death. You'll drop your fear of sex in a heartbeat if it helps you forget your fear of death."

"And your point is what?"

"You want to destroy the entire planet because your best friend left you alone. Because he's dead and he's never going to come back. And he's not going to be an angel in heaven, either. He's not even going to hell. Because there is no hell or heaven."

"Like I said, your point?"

"I'm not in A.A.," Jean Claude said. "I could live a hundred more lifetimes, and I would never be in A.A. If you want me to, I will close the shop right now, put you in my car, and drive you up to L.A., where I will show you ways to hurt yourself that you can't even imagine. We will drink and fuck our way across the state in such an epic fashion that they will write songs about us. And then, after a week or so, we can come back down and resume our boringly productive lives."

I looked at him to see if he was serious. I believed he was. "I love you, too," I said.

Jean Claude stood up from the table and seemed mildly perturbed as he took away my espresso cup. I decided that I would go home.

As I turned up Bluebird Canyon, I got a call from Emma, who was supposed to be back at my house with Troy, trying to figure out a way to organize my files. I had promised them twenty dollars an hour if they could make an improvement. It seemed like a job that Troy could handle and Emma couldn't hurt.

"I'm almost there," I said.

"Well, that's good," Emma said. "Because I'm not."

I pulled over. I would need all my attention to coax her back from Recon. "Where are you?" I said. "I'll come pick you up."

"I've got a night's worth of work ahead. No bivouac for me."

"Are you . . . outside?"

"Define 'outside'?"

"Are you roaming the county on foot," I said, "tempting fate?"

"Yes," she said. "That's *exactly* what I'm doing. I'm giving fate a come-hither look."

"Where the fuck do you go at night? Are you *trying* to get raped?"

"Why? Do *you* want to rape me?"

I laughed.

"That's funny?" she said.

"No," I said. "*You're* funny. You're so used to being the most fucked-up person in any room. But you forget that when you're talking to me, *I'm* the most fucked-up person."

She laughed. "That's why I report to you."

"Are you looking for Simon?" I asked.

"No," she said. "Yes. Maybe. I don't know."

"Because you know I want to help you with that," I said. "I'd like to find him, too."

By now I thought I had a sense of when Emma would hang up, but this time she didn't. I waited without speaking while she continued to not hang up.

"I really *didn't* fuck Terry," she said. "I'm not sure why I want you to know that."

Thank God for small favors. "You want me to know that you loved him," I said, "the way we all did. Because you're starting to realize that we—your pals in A.A.—are the only real friends you have left. Which is why you don't have to roam the countryside at night. You can just come back to my house and hate the fact that you depend on us as much as we hate the fact that we depend on you."

For a minute, she didn't say anything. Then she hung up.

. . .

Why was it so hard to believe that Terry had destroyed his life all on his own, pure and simple? There were still too many things I didn't like, besides John Sewell and his insurance policy. Something about the recovery house scheme didn't sit right with me. And why was this Simon Busansky character missing in action? Why had Mutt Kelly parked outside my house? Who had made that call to Cathy? Who was the business partner who so preoccupied Terry during the birth of the child he'd always wanted? And why, when he had a woman like Cathy to come home to, was he doing anything but coming home to her?

A woman to come home to. I pulled a U-turn in front of my house and headed back toward PCH. It was almost time for MP's Friday-evening yoga class.

I turned in to the shopping center above Pacific Coast High-way and parked in one of the slots. Eventually, MP's borrowed white Volvo parked a few spaces away. She stayed in the car, which I decided meant she wanted me to walk over. But just as I opened my door, she got out and approached my passenger window.

She was wearing her yoga togs and a pair of Chinese slip-ons. I felt a down-low tingle that was half fear and half lust.

"I think I've missed this truck as much as I've missed you," she said.

"Great," I said.

She smiled. She had thin lips that puffed up whenever I kissed her long and hard. She reached through the window and took my hand, which was awkward because there was an empty seat between us.

"This truck is who you are, Randy. Almost everything that happens to you happens in this truck."

"*Almost* everything."

When she got in, she put her hand on my shoulder. "Can I just tell you something? Can I tell you one thing?"

"I want you to come home."

"I know that," she said.

"Then why don't you?"

She looked down. "Can I say what I wanted to say? Maybe it will help."

I nodded.

"I used to wake up in the middle of the night"—MP moved her hand a little farther up my arm—"and feel like my heart had exploded. I'd lie there breathing hard, and I couldn't imagine how I was still alive. I thought that God was punishing me. I mean, at the end of the day, my name *is* Mary Pat Donnelly, and I've got all the baggage that goes with that kind of name. I thought I was going to hell, that I would spend eternity being cut off from the people I love. You don't think it was a big deal, the stuff I did when I was drinking, but this would happen to me every night. Do you want to know how it finally stopped?"

Hoping that she wouldn't let go of my arm, I nodded again.

"Do you really?" The rims of her eyes were watery. "You have to *really* want to know. Because I've never told anyone before."

"I do," I said. "I really want to know."

"The first few times we slept together," MP said, "I was still having those awful nights. And then the last time it happened, I woke up and looked at you sleeping next to me. I saw your back. Your head on the pillow. I listened to your snoring. And you know what I thought?"

"Please," I said. "Tell me."

"I thought, *If a man like this could love me, then God must love me, too.*"

And then she kissed my hand. And then she walked into All People's Yoga.

Here's another thing you learn in A.A.: when the drunk loses the woman he loves, you know you're not at the end of the story. You know it's going to get much worse.

20

IT WAS ANOTHER BAD NIGHT. My girlfriend had moved out. Troy Padilla was now my roommate. We hadn't heard from Emma in hours, and it seemed increasingly likely she was doing something stupid. I suggested Troy make some calls to her friends, but since she didn't have any friends except Troy, that didn't yield much.

Troy turned out be quite the little organizer. He'd gotten most of my home office sorted out before I came home. Then he went to work on both my computer and the computer he'd rescued from Cathy Acuña. He knew what he was doing, and it occurred to me that this might be a way for him to go. "You ever think about going back to school?" I said.

He gave me a sharp look. "What makes you think I haven't

finished school? What makes you think I don't have a Ph.D.? Have you ever asked me? No. You just assumed."

"Do you have a Ph.D.?"

"I dropped out of college after two semesters," he said. "But that's not the point, is it?"

I let it go. We were worried about Emma. Around midnight, we both went to bed—Troy in Crash's room—and I slept for ten hours. The last thing I told him was to wake me up if Emma called. She never did.

. . .

I was sitting with my coffee on Saturday morning, in my bathrobe, using my Eames chair for the first time in what seemed like an eternity, when the doorbell rang. I got up to answer it.

There was something about Jean Trask's confident greeting, the fact that she was smiling, that gave me pause. A woman like my ex-wife doesn't smile unless she's about to kick you in the balls. Or maybe right after.

Jean was holding something behind her back.

"You're too happy," I said.

"You don't want me to be happy?"

"What you call happiness is what other people call Randy getting it up the ass."

"Won't argue with that." She gave me a manila envelope, and I briefly thought there might be pictures inside, maybe eight-by-tens of every stupid thing Randy Chalmers had done in the last seventy-two hours.

But it wasn't photos—it was a restraining order. A duplicate, not the official one, which I could be sure would arrive soon enough.

"Doesn't it defeat the purpose of a restraining order," I said, "for you to be delivering the restraining order yourself?"

"I've made it clear to the court," Jean said, "that your impulse control problem has returned."

"How'd you get it done so fast?"

"Do you really have to ask that?" she said.

"Your boyfriend is a judge," I said.

"It didn't hurt," Jean said, "that you're locally famous for extreme violence." She took back the piece of paper.

"What the fuck, Jean?"

"I don't want my daughter growing up around you. You can spend as much time with her as you want once she's a fully formed adult, but I'm putting an end to this crap right now. If she doesn't become an alcoholic, she'll marry one."

"You think you can prevent that?"

"Not completely, but without your charming example in her face all the time, she'll have a better chance. This piece of paper gives me control, and I will exercise that control. John's a good man, and—"

I had to laugh. "You think Sewell's a better role model than me? I know he's dirty. The way he handled Cathy Acuña? I don't know how he got into the South County courthouse, but that man's some kind of fucking psycho."

"This from a man who's been editorialized as a psycho."

I felt like my intestines were about to slide down my legs into my shoes. "I can prove what kind of man he is. Just give me some time."

"You think I don't know about every element of his career path? You think I didn't know about his Mexican daughter? You think I didn't have him completely checked out before I would contemplate bringing him into my home? Did he steal from anyone? Did he beat anyone nearly to death? He made some money off a corrupt economy that even the police participated in, and he's paying it back now."

"Why are you giving me this in person?" I said. "Do you hate me that much?"

"You can have Alison two afternoons every week, and you're going to agree to that in writing. The visits will be supervised by a therapist until I'm clear that you're not going to try to take her. This is nonnegotiable. If you push me or you continue to harass John, you'll lose that."

"Please don't do this, Jean."

"Please don't do what, Randy? When was the last time you called your daughter except to use her against me? Do you even know where she is now?"

It was a close call, but I had an answer. "It's Saturday morning. She's with her friend in Corona del Mar. They're taking that sailing class together."

"Wrong, but that was a good guess. During your malaise, you missed the change of seasons. She's at softball camp. When you didn't call, I made other arrangements. John drove her."

Jean threw the restraining order at my feet and walked away.

. . .

I don't know how I made it from Laguna Beach to Anaheim Hills in half an hour, but it involved the Ortega Highway, and probably the last man who accomplished this feat lived in a California before actors became governors. John Sewell was about to take my place as the proud parent of a softball player named Alison Chalmers, and nothing seemed more important than finding them before the game started so I could interrupt him in that ambition.

In some weird way, I wasn't that angry. An emotion pursued to the nth degree can become the opposite of itself. The furthest reach of resentment is amusement, for example. Maybe the last frontier of hatred is love.

I had to give it to my ex-wife. It was apparent that she would chew off her arm at the elbow if that would make Crash's life better. I felt empathy for her delusion that she could protect Crash from a disease that had destroyed both our families. Saying that Jean's father had been a vicious drunk and her mother a vicious drunk's wife was like saying that water was wet and the rocks in my head were hard. Why else would she have married an angry drunken cop? And why would she marry a control freak like Sewell, thinking that she could leave all that behind?

At the top of Crown Valley Parkway, though, I reached the end of empathy and decided on another course of action: kill that motherfucker John Sewell.

When I pulled in to the parking lot beside the softball fields, he looked like he'd been waiting for me, wearing an outfit Jean might have picked for him: chino shorts and a powder-blue polo shirt, just the thing for a cardboard-cutout father. A game was under way beyond where he stood. It was the kind of athletic facility that made some folks proud to be American: unblemished grass that had been pumped with enough chemicals to kill a whole species of fish once it ran off to sea, backstops with the steely determined functionality of Third Reich architecture, and about sixty beautiful healthy girls, spread out over four fields, playing softball as though that were more important than anything.

"I was betting that you'd show up," Sewell said.

"Jean thought I'd have gone down in flames by now?"

Sewell shrugged.

The scent of his cologne across the gravel parking lot reminded me that I hadn't shaved in two days. Dropping him right then would have taken less energy than putting out the trash.

"The important thing," Sewell said, "is I knew you would. A man should be the leader of his household. In the course of things, Jean's going to have to calm down. You'll have less trouble from her in the future, I promise."

"What are you going to do? Stuff a sock in her mouth? Duct-tape her wrists and ankles? If you're going to marry her, you stupid fuck, you'd better get a clue that she's smarter and stronger than ten of you."

"No, Randy, I'm going to give her what you couldn't: walls, safety, a context. She's going to be married to me for the rest of her life, and we're going to do great things together. And you—you're going to continue making money and pursuing your art form, and you won't have any more trouble from either of us."

Beyond Sewell, a game seemed to be ending. The girls cheered and slapped high fives. The sunlight behind them raked my eyes, and it seemed like their own radiance had hit me.

"All I have to do is give up custody of my daughter? That's a great fucking deal."

"It's a formality, Randy. You didn't have custody to begin with. It's how we make Jean happy. You'll get to spend as much time with Alison as you want, I promise. Why would I want to prevent that? So that you can become more important to her—

and Jean—than you already are? No, thank you. I'm not trying to take her away from you. I just want to be . . . on your team. By the time she starts to trust me, you'll probably have another family with your girlfriend, and you'll be grateful for the help."

"If Paloma Acuña were my daughter," I said, "they'd need napalm to keep me away from her."

"That's dramatic," Sewell said, "but maybe not helpful."

"I don't know what else is wrong with you," I said. "But I'm going to find out. I have a feeling that if I dig deep enough, I'll find enough racketeering and enterprise corruption to go around."

"What I think you're describing is *business*," Sewell said. "I didn't participate in anything illegal. I gave good advice to men who often ignored my good advice. You need to grow up, Randy. How can you give Alison the opportunity to grow up when you haven't done it yourself?"

"Crash," I said. "Her fucking name is Crash. Stop calling her Alison."

"Crash?" Sewell laughed. "You named your daughter after a car wreck. Can't you see how—"

I hit him without thinking. The fact of it didn't surprise me—I'd been dreaming about it the whole way out—but I was surprised to be once again acting without my own consent. That's the way people talk about taking a drink, as though it's happening to someone else at some gauzy distance. Like your arm is lifting the glass, and your consciousness has nothing to do with it. While the cartilage in his nose crunched under my knuckles—not really a crunch, more like a pop—I wouldn't have noticed if I'd been surrounded by the South Coast Symphony.

But I wasn't surrounded by the South Coast Symphony, I was surrounded by five teenagers in softball uniforms. One of them was my daughter.

They were standing under ten feet away. They must have run up during my tunnel vision. The look on Crash's face told me that she'd missed nothing. I walked toward her as Sewell, hands on knees, bled into the parking lot.

That's another dubious insight that sets recovering alcoholics apart from the general population: no matter how bad you think you feel, you can always feel worse. Losing MP was a chocolate milk shake with whipped cream and sprinkles compared to this.

It was not the first time in my life that I had scared my daughter, but it was the first time since I quit drinking, over half her lifetime ago.

"Honey . . ." Nothing in her eyes encouraged me to finish the sentence. I wanted to die.

Crash shrugged away my hand on her shoulder. "Don't you fucking touch me." She backed away and turned to run, and thank God, her friends ran after her.

21

THAT STYROFOAM ICE CHEST behind the truck seat in my mind
was squeaking like a motherfucker.

As I drove, I reviewed the facts: I had destroyed my relationship with my daughter. I had given my ex-wife the justification
for a restraining order that would make my custody claim im-
possible. And I had dreamed up a criminal conspiracy somehow
responsible for my friend's death that even I didn't believe anymore.

I went home because I didn't have anywhere else to go.

When I parked my truck in front of my house, I was greeted
by two Laguna PD detectives getting out of their Ford Fusion.
They introduced themselves and offered IDs. Cardenas was built
like a fireplug and had a face like a Mayan totem. Clancy was tall
and rangy and Bill Waltonesque. God bless America.

"Your son," Cardenas said, "told us you'd be back soon. We figured we would wait."

"He's not my son," I said.

They both looked at me, maybe expecting I'd feel some responsibility to explain myself further. But I'd left all that bullshit back on the softball field in Anaheim Hills.

"Your boyfriend?" Clancy finally said.

"Can we talk inside?" Cardenas pointed toward my house.

After I'd given myself and Cardenas a glass of water and poured Clancy a cup of coffee from a pot that Troy must have made, we all sat down at my black-walnut-burl dinette. I asked them what they wanted, but I was sure I knew. Judge Sewell must have been quicker on the cell phone than I imagined.

"Where were you last night between two and four in the morning?" Cardenas asked.

"Here. Sleeping. Why do—"

"Can your, ah, boyfriend corroborate that?" Clancy interrupted.

"He's more like a ward," I said. "Like Batman and Robin?"

"Can he corroborate that you were here?" Cardenas asked.

"He was sleeping in another room," I said. "But I think he'd say I was here."

"He'd *say* you were here?" Cardenas wrote something down in his notebook.

"He'll corroborate that I was here," I said.

Cardenas wrote some more in his notebook. Clancy, I noticed, hadn't opened his notebook and never stopped looking at me.

"How would you characterize your relationship with Thomas Kelly?" Clancy asked.

"Who?"

"Mutt Kelly."

Oh shit, I thought. *Is this my day for restraining orders?* "I barely know the guy," I said. "Why do you want to know?"

Cardenas looked at Clancy, and Clancy shrugged.

"And please," I said, "for Christ's sake, stop that."

"Stop what?" Clancy asked with an exaggerated display of bewilderment.

"The meaningful fucking glances," I said. "I'm not impressed. I've pulled the same tricks myself. I'm trying to be courteous, but if you don't tell me what's going on, I'm going to ask you to leave. It's already been a long day for me."

Cardenas did not look at Clancy when he said, "Mr. Thomas, aka 'Mutt,' Kelly was found beaten to death in a parking lot about fifty yards from your cabinet shop. We estimate the time of death between two A.M. and four A.M. He died of blunt force trauma to the head, probably the result of being beaten severely around the face, but it also could have been that he died from trauma to the back of the head when he fell on the concrete as a result of being beaten severely around the face. Either way, we're calling it a homicide."

The news made me nauseated. To distract myself, I looked around at my home, which was better designed and furnished than any dwelling I'd ever occupied. These last few years it had become like an extension of my body, an extension of my soul. I brought clients here, not because it was the best work I'd ever done but because it spoke for me in a way I couldn't speak for myself. The space had an unexpected and serene coherence. More than anything else I'd done, my house stood as a triumph over that earlier, disordered, distinctly unserene life.

And now it all seemed like shit. It embarrassed me. No one deserved a house this nice. Why did I feel that way? Mutt Kelly was nothing to me. But he might have been with Terry that last night, and someone had killed him. Where the two things related? I had to find out.

"You think I killed him?" I asked.

"Did you?" Cardenas asked.

They stared at me, waiting for my answer.

"Sean told you about Thursday afternoon," I said. "Is he jammed up about this?"

Sean Wakefield must have fessed up about my interrupted assault on Mutt Kelly. I wanted to be angry, but he was probably in trouble for not telling them sooner. What he had seen made me a very natural suspect.

"That's not your concern," Cardenas said.

"I made some bad choices on Thursday afternoon," I said. "Sean intervened, and that was the end of it."

"So you're saying you've had no contact with Mr. Kelly after this, ah, intervention?" Cardenas said.

"That's what I'm saying."

"How do you explain the fact that Kelly was carrying your phone number in his pocket at the time of his death?" Clancy said.

I couldn't speak. He had my phone number? There was no scenario I could imagine in which that made sense. But it also deepened my inexplicable sadness over this idiot's death. After a pause that was way too long, I said, "I have no fucking idea."

"How do you explain the condition of your hands?" Clancy said.

We all took a good luck at the scrapes and bruises I'd caused myself by building that crib in the middle of the night.

"Mutt Kelly didn't have a lot of defensive wounds," Cardenas said. "If he was fighting with someone, he was way over-matched."

"Look," I said, "I don't know what I can tell you. I didn't do it. This guy was a biker, wasn't he? Isn't it more likely that he got into some kind of beef with one of his associates?"

"We were thinking it was one of his associates, too," Clancy said. "But maybe not a biker."

Cardenas closed his notebook. "We're going to tell you what we imagine. You had some business with Mutt Kelly. He agreed to meet you near your shop. There was a confrontation, and it didn't go well for Kelly. We're hoping you can fill in the details."

"I can't tell you what happened," I said, "because I wasn't there."

"Please, Mr. Chalmers," Cardenas continued. "You have a story for us? Your side of things? We want to hear it."

"We figured," Clancy said, "that you were probably asking him the same questions you'd tried to ask him on Thursday afternoon."

"I was asking him questions about my friend Terry Elias. About how he died. I thought Kelly might have been with him that night. Kelly said he wasn't. I was pretty upset, hence the poor choices."

"We know about Terry Elias," Clancy said.

"What does that mean?" I said. "You know about Terry Elias?"

"Just assume we know everything," Cardenas said.

"What the fuck else do you think I've done?"

"What happened to you?" Clancy said. "You used to be a cop, and now you're a drug dealer?"

"A drug dealer?" I said. "What are you talking about?"

"We're talking about your friend Terry Elias and the fifty grand you gave him to bring more of this shit into our community."

Clancy was getting pretty worked up, and Cardenas held out a hand to calm him. I wish someone had been there to calm me.

"What the hell are you talking about? Terry wasn't a drug dealer."

"We've found hydroponic pot farms underneath all the houses your friend Terry helped arrange to buy from Simon Busansky," Cardenas continued. "When we cleaned up this mess the first time and let those houses be sold to an A.A. group, you can imagine the last thing we expected was for those pot farms to reappear. Try to feel our profound disappointment with our friend Simon. Unfortunately, we can't find him to express it ourselves."

"Terry couldn't have been that stupid," I said. "He wouldn't have been involved in something like this. I don't know Busansky. I'm sure he's a scumbag. But there's no fucking way my friend Terry was involved in dealing drugs."

Even as I said it, I didn't know what to believe anymore. Was it possible that they could have run a full-scale hydroponics operation under the sleeping heads of a few dozen A.A. newcomers? While Troy and Emma themselves were living in those houses? Did Terry know? Had Terry invested in it? Could he have invested in it with my money?

I did a quick inventory of my actions over the last few days. I found myself looking like a guy who'd lost an investment, shaking every tree he could think of to find out where it had gone.

"Oh, fuck me," I said. "I can see what you're seeing, but that's not what happened."

"Tell us a different story, then." Cardenas spread his hands out across my unnecessarily beautiful walnut tabletop. "Help us understand."

"You think I've been going around rousting these guys because of money?"

"You're going to tell us"—Cardenas laughed—"you gave that shyster fifty grand because he was your friend?"

The way he said it, the confidence of his conviction that I was a sharp operator among other sharp operators, stunned me because the truth was so much the opposite. I stood up. "This has been fun. No one has ever accused me of being a criminal mastermind before. You want to charge me with murder, charge me. Otherwise, get out of my house."

They stood up. Cardenas picked up his notebook.

"Before you leave," I said, "tell me how you have Mutt Kelly involved. What's he got to do with the pot business?"

They smiled at me.

"Okay, never mind," I said. "I'll see you when you get a warrant."

Neither of them moved away from the table. In fact, Clancy leaned forward a bit. "I always wanted to give you the benefit of the doubt"—Clancy slowly pocketed his own notebook—"because I know how easy it is to call someone a racist."

"The thing that gets me," Cardenas chimed in, "is how well

you landed. A lot of guys, they get a settlement like yours, they blow it on a sailboat. Look at you—you built a business. Granted, it's a drug business, but—"

"You think I got a settlement?" I said. "Man, I didn't even get my pension."

Cardenas dramatically gestured to the home around us, like *Are you fucking kidding me?*

"I work," I said. "This all comes from work."

"We work, too," Clancy said. "But we don't have houses like this. Hell, we don't even live in Laguna."

"You guys want to turn this into some kind of class war?" I said. "That's your tactic for getting me to confess? I was a cop, and then I couldn't be a cop anymore. You want to learn how to build houses when you retire, I'll fucking teach you."

"Who knew," Cardenas said, "that beating up beaners could be such an awesome career move?"

I can't say what poor choices I was about to make next, because we were interrupted by my sister, Betsy, and I didn't get the chance to find out. She didn't knock. She walked right in. Talking on her phone, she stood at the edge of my living room, beside the couch. She was wearing lizard cowboy boots, black Wrangler jeans, and a green suede jacket over a T-shirt that all by itself cost more than anything in either of their wardrobes. The cops were trying not to stare.

"Yes, it does," Betsy said. "It looks like everything's quite cordial at the moment." The last part was somehow addressed both to me and to whoever she was on the line with.

"Yes," I replied. "Quite cordial."

"What are their names?" she said into her phone. Then, to the detectives: "What are your names?"

When they hesitated, I answered, "Detectives Cardenas and Clancy."

Betsy repeated their names into her phone. "Yes, sir. I don't think we're going to have any trouble with my brother's civil rights, but I appreciate your concern. I don't have to call you 'sir' anymore? What do you call a terrorism czar, anyway? Mr. Ambassador? No shit? Right. Right. Jeep sends her love, too. Next Friday." Betsy switched off her phone, shrugged. "Former boss."

The boys looked like they'd been smacked by a fistful of quarters. It was the kind of stunt that would have made Betsy such a great detective herself. Mr. Ambassador? Who knew if there was anyone on the other end of the line? But I wasn't betting against it, and neither were Cardenas and Clancy.

"Gentlemen, I'd like you to meet my sister, former Assistant United States Attorney Elizabeth Chalmers."

They walked out my front door as though they'd been dismissed.

. . .

After the cops left and I'd had a chance to explain myself, Betsy started throwing books across the room. Phaedon architecture books, the expensive kind. "Jesus Christ, Randy. How many ways can I say this? You're going to lose access to your own daughter. They're going to charge you with murder."

"Actually," I said, "I'm not as—"

Hearing the bedroom door open, we turned to find Troy standing barefoot in the hallway, a pair of headphones hanging around his neck. "Can I come out now?"

"No," I said. "Go back to your room."

When Troy turned dramatically back to Crash's bedroom, Betsy said, "That's your alibi? A kid who asks your permission to leave a room? Could this be any more pathetic?"

"Why are you even here?" I said. "I thought you weren't talking to me."

"I still have friends in government," she said. "I got a call that this investigation was about to land on you."

"They can't prove any of it. I wasn't involved."

"Would you please pull your head out of your ass?" she said. "These people don't have to convict you to destroy your life."

"I'm innocent. And Terry couldn't have been party to fucking drug dealing. I gotta believe that. Besides, I've got another problem."

Betsy was already scrolling through the numbers on her phone. "These guys are going to arraign you. We needed pricey counsel about a month ago. What other problem?"

"On the softball field, in front of Crash, I broke John Sewell's nose."

It looked like Betsy was going to continue scrolling, but then she threw the phone against the kitchen wall. It didn't do anything satisfying, like shatter. In fact, it bounced all the way back to her cowboy boots. She picked it up and tossed it on the breakfast bar.

"And I don't want pricey counsel," I said. "I want you."

"What is this, a fucking Lifetime movie? I'm not an attorney anymore, and frankly, you disgust me. You hit a man who's going to become Crash's stepfather? A judge?" Betsy put her face in her hands and turned away.

I put one arm around her shoulders and gently turned her back toward me. "I'm not asking for me," I said. "I'm asking for

Crash. Someone needs to look out for her, and maybe you'll have to jettison me in order to do that. You're the only person I trust, and you're the only attorney I know who's smart enough to untangle the mess I've created."

Betsy looked at me sternly for a long time, and then her sternness melted. She picked up her phone from the counter and sat down cross-legged on the tiled kitchen floor. I sat down beside her, and neither of us spoke for a while. She held my hand while my heart pounded and the refrigerator hummed.

My sister often hated me, but she would always help me when I asked her. I needed that kind of person in my life, or I wouldn't survive. Wade, Jeep, Manny—I still had a fortune in friends who would drop everything to help me. But what about me? Who would call me? After what had happened today, would Crash ever call me again? Why didn't Terry call me when he could have? I would have sworn that he could call me, but he didn't.

Mutt Kelly had been found dead with my phone number in his pocket.

22

AT A CERTAIN POINT, Betsy had to embark on her efforts to prevent law enforcement from destroying my life. She made me promise that I wouldn't leave the house until she returned. To get Troy out of my hair, I offered him the keys to MP's Volkswagen and a couple hundred dollars to go fix up his computer.

"I don't feel good about Emma being out there," he said.

"What do you want me to do, Troy?"

"I want you to find her."

"Give me a minute, Troy. Just give me a few minutes."

Troy went back to the bedroom, and I sat down in my Eames chair and commenced to think about why Mutt Kelly might need my help. The longer I sat with it, the more certain I was that he'd wanted to talk to me. At some point, I'd have to deal with the insanity of my assaulting him at his house, but that was later. Right now I needed to know what he'd had to say.

What did I know about Mutt Kelly? I knew that he'd worked for John Sewell. As much as I hated Sewell, I couldn't connect him to this foolishness. Whatever his faults, he wasn't the kind of guy who would think growing weed under recovery houses was a good idea.

Whoever was behind this stupidity—and my heart begged that it wasn't Terry—would need an electrician, and that's what Mutt was. There was nobody more important to the success of a grow-op. All those lamps needed a lot of juice, and it went a long way toward avoiding arrest if you could keep the juice off the grid. In other words, find a way to steal it. A good electrician could probably help you hide your operation from the inhabitants of the recovery houses, too. That was it, I thought—Mutt was the guy who stole the electricity.

I wanted to go somewhere with this information, but where? It wouldn't change anyone's opinion of me or my behavior. The cops thought I was living a lie. I couldn't help imagining Terry, what it must have been like for him to be telling those kids upstairs how to stay sober while he was making money off the pot growing under the floorboards. Was that what happened? Was that the beginning of the road that ended in the motel room in Santa Ana?

I remembered how Troy had described Terry, parked outside the recovery home the night he died. Troy was right: Terry wasn't a sit-in-the-car kind of guy. He was always moving forward. What had stopped him from moving forward that night? Maybe he was stuck between those competing truths—what was going on above the floor and what was going on below it—and he couldn't get to the next thing in his life. The next thing in his life was, of course, his son. The son whom he never saw. Terry told me once that any animal will get depressed if you can keep it from taking action. What kept him from taking action? I had to know.

Not for the first time in my life, I broke a promise to my sister, Betsy. I got in my truck and drove up the hill.

. . .

When I drove my truck past Troy's recovery house, I couldn't find any evidence that the cops were nearby. I could only assume they'd already been here. I slowed at the place on the street where Terry would have parked his car. This gave me a good view of the backside of the house, which was supported by concrete piers over the canyon. It was a good time to be visiting the house: most of its inhabitants would be at the very young and very popular South Coast Hospital Beginners' Meeting.

I parked my truck well down the street and cut across the hillside between two houses a few hundred yards away. I scrambled up toward the back end of the recovery home. Before leaving the truck, I'd thought to grab a carpenter's belt and some work gloves so I didn't look too much like a criminal sneaking up on the house.

There was an access door underneath the concrete piers. It had been freshly painted, and I removed the overused screws that held it in place. Someone had gone to the trouble of building another floor below the house by digging into the hillside and framing a platform. That same someone had been very careful about sealing it off: it took me five minutes to remove the access door.

Once I was inside, I saw that this was no dead-space storage. The subfloor was heavy-duty, much more than would have been necessary for old surfboards and Christmas lights. Just the thing, though, for several hundred five-gallon pots full of dirt and fertilizer. Nothing like that was there now. Maybe the cops took it. There was a lot of loose wire around. Growing marijuana without sunlight required a lot of wire.

It sure looked like a suburban pot farm to me. And it looked like someone had cleared up in a hurry. I tried to locate where the power main would have entered the house, and sure enough, close to the top of the slope, I saw the shiny two-inch galvanized conduit coming up from the ground. There was a large section of loose dirt below the vertical pipe, but the visible section of the conduit was unmarked. It was a felony all by itself to steal electricity, and whoever rigged this would have dug down at least four feet to make sure they could bury the evidence of tampering.

Whoever rigged this. I reminded myself that I knew who rigged this. I had to give it to Mutt Kelly: it took huge balls to tamper with the six hundred amps of unregulated power that was coming into that house. And there was no circuit breaker between the meter and the transformer that serviced the whole block. It was like a fire hose pouring into a straw, and even power-company cowboys with gloves and insulated tools wouldn't do a live-wire bite unless they were in a fiberglass bucket on the end of a manlift. You could get killed even if you didn't make a mistake.

So I approached that mound of dirt very carefully, and that was when things got weird.

Basements are stinky, right? You can't expect to crawl up the ass of someone's house and have it smell like flowers, but as I crouch-walked closer to the conduit, I started to puke before I even recognized why I was puking.

You never forget the smell of a dead body, even when it's making its way up through four feet of dirt. Even as a cop, I never got used to it. This time my understanding was so complete and awful that I stood up and hit my head on the two-by-twelve above me. And then I puked a little more. And then I got out of that fucking basement.

It could have been a dead animal down there, but I knew it wasn't—not with all the care that had been taken to seal the space. There was almost enough dirt to contain the smell, but not quite. I could have dug deeper and found out more, but there was no way I was going back into that basement and no way I was going to dig anywhere near that bite.

Marijuana farming is a victimless crime. Until it isn't anymore.

A moment to breathe fresh air and pull myself together would have been nice, but once I got back outside I understood that the cops hadn't been here yet—if they had they would have checked under the house, too, and they would have already found the body. Sure enough, as I picked myself up to head back to my truck, I heard a huge crash near the front of the house. I imagined what a battering ram would sound like, splintering that hollow-core door off its frame. Bingo. As I cautiously looked around the side of the house, I heard the screeching arrival of about five cars up the driveway. Cops can be such drama queens: can't they brake without shredding their tires?

With all the commotion, there was no way to saunter down the street toward my F-350, so I started to make my way across the canyon. Scrambling down barren hillside on a rocky path that I hoped would find a road, I came upon, of all things, a flock of goats, probably the same ones that had been my entertainment three mornings ago over at my place. Wondering at the denuded landscape that these guys had left behind, I took too long to recognize Sean Wakefield, wearing a Kevlar vest, emerging from the ravine below the goats. I waved hello while the sensibly wary goats spread across the hillside away from us. Sean spoke quietly into a walkie-talkie that he then replaced on his vest. Instinctively, I kept both my hands out where he could see them. Still, I couldn't quite believe it when he drew his gun.

"I'm sorry, Randy," he said. "But I'm going to have to cuff you and walk you back up to whatever you were doing under that house."

"What I was doing under that house," I said, "was puking. There's somebody buried up there, Sean, and I think it might be Simon Busansky. I don't know who killed Mutt, or why Terry is dead, but I think this is where the bad shit started."

"You're not a cop anymore, man. I don't know what you are, but you're not a cop."

"Didn't you guys check out this house when I gave you the address?"

"My DEA guys have been looking into these houses for weeks. They started getting antsy when Simon Busansky stopped coming by for his chats. If anything, your bullshit slowed us down. Once you came to me, we had to hold off the raids until we figured out how you were involved. What's the deal, Randy? You beat the life out of Mutt Kelly off intel that I fucking gave you, and now I'm going to find out that he wasn't the only guy you put in the ground?"

"What the fuck, Sean? You really think I killed Mutt Kelly?"

"The way you showed up at his house was wrong."

"Of course it was wrong," I said. "And you were there to stop it. I heard everything you said, and I never went back. You know who I am. I'm a fuckup, but I'm not that kind of fuckup."

I noticed that Sean hadn't lowered his gun. An unlowered gun is a hard thing to miss. "And if I'd known that there was a dead body under that house," I continued, "why would I be anywhere near the fucking house?"

"I don't know," Sean said. "But you're going to have to explain yourself up the chain of command. Right now I need to redeem myself for letting you go the last time."

"I caused you some trouble, didn't I?"

Sean laughed. I lowered my hands a little and moved a bit closer to him. "Believe it or not," he said, "that fuckup with you doesn't even make the top five for the week. Your reappearance in my life seems to have precipitated a crisis."

Now that I took a good look, his skin had the gray puffiness that comes after an epic bender. "You're hitting it hard," I said. "Good thing we have a solution for that. We'll go to a meeting together."

"First I'm going to arrest you. Assume the position, Randy."

"You really think I'm involved with this mess?"

"I don't know what to think. Assume the position, Randy."

I outweighed Sean by thirty pounds, but that didn't mean he

was soft. Even a soft guy with a gun in his hand is problematic. I couldn't figure any smooth moves besides following instructions. I knelt and clasped my hands behind my head. It was the first time in years that I had knelt for any reason. When I first came to A.A., someone suggested that I pray like this, on my knees, because it demonstrated the proper attitude. I never was much for that type of thing. Kneeling there, though, the rocks pressing into my skin, I did pray. It was an awful prayer, but earnest: *Just let me fucking finish this. Please, God?*

Hearing the gentle sound of Sean's weapon sliding into its holster as he carefully made his way toward me, I opened my eyes to stare at a creosote bush about a yard from my face. Which reminded me of hacking around Cleveland National Forest with the Boy Scouts. I remembered Jimmy Crews, who made Eagle Scout only to die in Operation Desert Storm, explaining the best way to escape a grizzly: run downhill. According to Jimmy, "the grizz" was so top-heavy that he would "fall over his own ass" chasing you.

Somehow that anecdote became a plan for action: the moment the handcuff touched my wrist—maybe the moment before—I would slam my body backward into Sean, my skull connecting with his forehead and sending him down the hill with me tumbling close behind.

Sorry about that, Sean.

But then the handcuff didn't touch my wrist. I waited, probably longer than I needed to, before I turned around to look.

There was nobody there. The goats jeered appreciatively at Sean's mercy from across the canyon.

23

I CAME UP OUT OF THE CANYON a block or so downhill. It was good luck for me that a landscaper I knew named Jorge was putting down sod in front of a great big, achingly-overdesigned-with-way-too-much-glass split-level. I asked him for a ride to Jean Claude's. I figured it was smart to bypass my truck and my house for the time being—no telling how long Sean's goodwill would last, or how soon Cardenas and Clancy would stop being scared of my sister. Of course, I didn't explain any of this to Jorge, who seemed to recognize that I was lying about my truck breaking down, but did me the favor anyway.

I called Yegua on Jean Claude's phone; my own phone was back in the truck. Jean Claude wasn't in that afternoon, which was fine with me: without even knowing what I was into, JC would have straightened his mouth and narrowed his eyes, and

I didn't think I could take his froggy disapproval. Ten minutes later, Yegua and his girlfriend showed up. I told him that I needed a ride to Wade's and asked him to retrieve my truck from Troy's recovery house as discreetly as possible. I guess I could have called Wade, but I was a little embarrassed: I was on the run from the cops. I just wanted to get out of the wind for a while. If Wade wasn't home, I could wait things out with Yegua.

"Bien," he said. *"Bien. Muy bien."* He smiled enthusiastically at his girlfriend as though she, too, needed to be part of his cheerful acceptance of my routinely insane behavior. Juana, a pleasantly overweight thirtysomething with heavily mascaraed eyes and a Rolling Stones T-shirt, smiled with less enthusiasm.

Yegua drove me to Wade's apartment on the beach side of Pacific Coast Highway, north of Taco Bell. It was a converted motel, and Wade had less than four hundred square feet, but there was a window on the ocean, and for him, that was the whole deal. Wade was home, thank God. Troy was there, too, but it was clear from his grimace that he didn't intend to enjoy my company.

"Why is he here?" I asked Wade. "And why is he pissed off at me?"

"Because Emma's been gone since last night," Wade said, "and you've been MIA since this morning."

"Isn't this what she does?" I asked Troy. I wasn't convincing myself, either.

"This is different," Troy said. "She's been watching you running around being the Lone Ranger, and now her self-delusion has gone into the red zone."

He didn't look at me when he said it. I swallowed the five Excedrins that Wade had brought me and told them what I'd unearthed under the house. Before we could get started on what it meant or what the fuck we did next, Wade's cell phone started ringing. He handed it to me. "It's Colin Alvarez," he said.

I took Wade's phone with a big sense that my life was about to change for the even worse.

"You really fucked me," Colin said. "Do you have any idea how much you've fucked me? Every asset that I have in the world has been frozen since this morning. Every place that I could possibly go is being watched by the cops."

"I'm sorry," I said. "I guess it was my idea to start growing pot under recovery houses and then bury my partner."

That shut him up for a moment. "They found Simon?" he finally said.

"I found Simon," I said. So it was Busansky under the house. "What were you idiots thinking? What happened? Were you the one who buried him?"

"I'll tell you about that when I see you. Right now I need your help. I've got a Mexican passport, and I need to get across the border while it's still good to me."

"Fuck you, Colin. I don't know how you managed to suck Terry into this, but if you think I'm going to—"

It was just then that my life got worse than even worse. The phone was jostled, as though Colin were struggling with someone. I heard a voice I recognized say, "Don't you fucking dare touch me, you fake fucking Mexican bastard."

"Colin?" I said carefully. "Why is Emma with you?"

"Why is she with me? Three or four agencies can't fucking find me, but she shows up this afternoon with crazy to spare. Get as much money as you can and get your ass over here, Randy.

Before this girl wears me down to nothing but my desire to shoot her."

He gave me an address and hung up. I gave Wade back his phone.

There were three surfboards leaning in a corner of Wade's apartment—one long board that angled out into the room at nearly forty-five degrees and two short boards that were almost vertical. I threw a folding chair at them all, and the fiberglass made a thunderous clatter as it fell to the floor, sounding like the inside of my head. The tip of one of the short boards broke clean off.

"What the fuck are you doing?" Wade said.

"Thinking." I told them what Colin had said.

"Where are you supposed to meet him?" Wade asked.

I looked at the address scribbled on my palm. "He's got a house in Emerald Bay?"

"I heard about that," Wade said. "His new idea. Colin was going to bring folks down from Hollywood, start a celebrity recovery house. He was going to call it the River Phoenix Recovery Home."

"Are you fucking kidding me?" I glanced at Troy, who was looking wild with this new information, angry at me or himself, I wasn't sure. "How come the feds don't know about this place?"

"I guess his plans got sidetracked," Wade said, "by the dead fucking body under his house. Maybe he doesn't even own it yet. Colin must have killed Mutt, too. At least the cops won't be looking at you anymore, Randy."

"All I'm thinking about is Emma," I said. "I gotta get her out of there."

I grabbed the keys to Wade's BMW. Wade inserted himself between me and the front door. "Take a deep breath," he said. "You keep making the same mistake. You have to chill for a minute."

"Troy's right," I said. "I'm the reason Emma's been wandering the county trying to find Simon. She was imitating me. She bought in to the idea that we could figure this out. I got my rocks off playing detective, and she's the one who's going to pay."

"I'm not signing on to that," Wade said. "You gotta call Manny, at least. You gotta call Manny or someone. You can't do it by yourself."

I had to admire my friend: he was willing to go to the mat, but it wasn't going to be a big mat, and it wouldn't take long to get there. I shoved him hard, maybe even harder than I had intended.

I was about to discover, though, that my cop instincts had slowed to a crawl. How often had Manny and I walked into a domestic disturbance where we knew that the biggest threat in the house wouldn't be the drunken husband but the ready-to-defend-him wife? Or the ten-year-old son who'd found a gun or a baseball bat to protect his family? A dog was a detail you couldn't afford to miss. How many times had I sat at the bar after a shift, smugly telling younger cops: the one thing you don't pay attention to will be the one thing that kills you.

In this case, I didn't pay attention to Troy Padilla. Before I knew it, he had his arms up around me in some crazy maneuver that felt like a full nelson but didn't respond to anything I knew about getting out from one. I flopped around like a fish in a gill net.

"You know what Krav Maga is?" Troy spoke quietly into my ear.

I grunted. "A sort of martial art?"

"A retired Israeli hit man taught me. Let me know when you're ready to calm the fuck down."

"I was expressing frustration." I struggled against his arms. Even I could hear how feeble my excuse sounded.

"Wade and I are tired of your frustration. Isn't that right, Wade?"

"That's right, Troy."

"We love you," Troy said, "but no more frustration."

"If you knew Israeli kung fu"—I gave up and relaxed into the hold—"why didn't you use it when I threw you up against the truck?"

"Back then," Troy said, "I thought you were some kind of A.A. legend. I was intimidated."

"I guess I've cured you of that delusion."

I didn't think I had been about to hurt Wade, but—Troy was right—once you're on that train, you can't say where it stops. Waiting as Troy tried to gauge my spiritual fitness, I didn't notice at first as his hold loosened and then disappeared.

I turned around to face him. "Thank you."

I don't think Troy quite knew how to handle gratitude coming from me. He managed to nod.

Turning back to Wade: "I'm sorry, Wade. I'll replace the surf-board."

"With a better one," Wade said. "First, go find our girl."

24

I CONVINCED WADE TO HOLD OFF on calling Manny until I got the cash Colin needed and headed up there. Just let me separate Emma from the situation, I told him, and then the cavalry would be welcome. I had about ten grand in a safe under the floor of my home office, and I called Yegua to get it for me. As I waited for the money to arrive, I told Troy that he could kick my ass later if he wanted, but he wasn't coming. I wasn't going to put another kid in jeopardy, and Wade seemed willing to babysit Troy.

As I drove north in Wade's BMW, I reminded myself that Colin was desperate enough to kill Emma. He was officially a bad actor and capable of anything. Including the murders of Simon and Mutt. Maybe I was wrong about Simon being the trouble. Maybe it was Colin all along who had been the business partner whom Terry regretted getting involved with.

None of that mattered, except to the extent that it kept me focused on what did matter: getting that twisted little sweetheart out of harm's way.

Hopefully, ten thousand dollars and the promise of some misdirection to help Colin escape to Mexico would do the trick. I was going to tell him whatever he wanted to hear if it helped me separate him from Emma. He wanted me to lie to the cops, I was his man. He wanted Wade's car, he could have that, too.

Ten K. Promise him anything. Get the girl.

The local constabulary, however, were not as stupid as I had hoped. As I drove past the Pavilions supermarket that adjoined Jean Claude's café, I noticed a conspicuous group of windbreakered and clean-cut men and women passing around pieces of paper over the hood of a Crown Victoria. Even as I slowed to get a better look, a Laguna Beach PD squad car joined the party. As I proceeded past the shopping center toward Emerald Bay, there was nothing in my mind but *Fuck, fuck, fuck, fuck, fuck.*

Maybe these guys had been setting up the caravan to arrest all those pot smokers near the basketball courts on main beach, but in this age of decriminalized possession, it seemed more likely that it was a second federal operation based on information gathered at all the other Colin Alvarez houses they had busted today.

Nothing substantial had changed, I reminded myself. Ten K. Promise him anything. Get the girl. But faster.

The wall that separates Emerald Bay from Pacific Coast Highway and the rest of Laguna Beach is cheerful enough, all earth tones and without any barbed wire that I could see. As I drove up beside it I was in many ways still the boy who had grown up ten miles inland and understood—accurately—that the wall was meant to keep me out: from Emerald Bay beaches, from Emerald Bay homes, from Emerald Bay lives.

If more evidence of Colin's insanity were needed, the idea that rich folks living in one of the most controlled neighborhoods in the United States would welcome a houseful of alcoholics and addicts from Hollywood was more than a few fries short of a Happy Meal.

There were some spectacular homes in there, though, and sometimes they required my attention to keep them spectacular. As a result, I thought I knew exactly where Colin's digs were. I figured I had as much as a half hour and as little as five minutes before the cop caravan arrived from the supermarket. There was a little stucco booth at the entrance to Emerald Bay where you told them your business or got turned back, and after I'd told Mike Sullivan (retired LAPD) that I'd come to check some work I'd done on Hector Domenico's house, he waved me through. Once I was inside Emerald Bay proper, I parked immediately and called Colin from Wade's phone.

I could see most of the beach from my spot on the street. Also, the Emerald Bay Clubhouse and fire station. There were plenty of people out on this mild afternoon. A lot fewer, though, on the north end, in the shadow of the cliffs, where I figured Colin's house must be. The sun was glistening off the water, which I told myself to remember as I could be thrown in jail at any moment.

Colin's life was over, one way or the other. He was either on the run to Mexico or he was in jail for a long time. If he'd already killed Simon Busansky and Mutt Kelly—and somehow I wanted to believe he had been responsible for Terry's death, too—he'd kill Emma. She was my priority here. I had to wonder, though, if Colin had help. Had that baldy hipster Joachin signed on for the adventure, too?

When Colin picked up the phone, I said, "I'm in Emerald Bay right now. The cops are assembling a caravan at the shopping center down the street. Let Emma go right now, and I'll be there in two minutes with ten thousand dollars."

"Fuck you, Randy. I'm not giving her up until you get here. Bring me the money."

I checked the rearview mirror and saw a couple of black Crown Vics coming up the narrow road behind my parked BMW. Also a Laguna Beach PD squad car to secure the perimeter behind them. I waited to see another squad car to secure the beach behind the houses, but none was forthcoming. Maybe that mistake would give us the time we needed.

"They're here now, Colin," I said into the phone. "Get that girl out the back onto the fucking beach. Those guys are going to be through your front door in under a minute."

There was nothing between Colin and the battering ram but me. I decided against heading up the beach toward the cliffs on the north end. Too long out in the open when I wasn't dressed for sun and fun. How easy would it be for a Fed to recognize me and wonder what I was doing once again in the middle of their operation? Instead, I drove up toward the remodel I'd done for the former head of the U.S. Olympic Committee. This was the Hector Domenico whose name had gotten me through the front gate. Hector had the last house on the beach before the cliffs.

I did have more business with Hector, which was how I knew that he was in Iraq this week, helping to rebuild their telecom infrastructure. As I parked in the driveway and strolled calmly toward the front door, I could almost feel those Crown Vics whipping past me.

Brute force wasn't my first choice to gain entry. Fortunately, Hector hadn't locked the front door, which made me happy until I realized why: he wasn't in Iraq. He was home, having an afternoon snack with the owner of my favorite café, Jean Claude Vigneron. They were wearing navy blue bathrobes, but Jean Claude's didn't fit as well, because they both seemed to belong to Hector.

I took a moment to notice how the two-seat island we'd placed in the middle of Hector's nearly industrial-sized kitchen was as intimate as we had hoped. The two of them didn't look lonely among all those stainless-steel appliances so much as the appliances looked accessible. Good job, Randy.

"Tomorrow morning," I said, "I'm going to stop by Jean Claude's for a few double espressos, and I'm going to explain everything. In the meantime, you're both going to trust me. Okay?"

Hector was flabbergasted, but as I continued through the house toward the French doors, Jean Claude smiled. He knew me well enough, I'm sure, to encourage Hector to stay indoors. Maybe take cover. They might have been planning that anyway.

Trying to project Hector's wealth and power, I strode onto the beach. If you had to negotiate a hostage release, the north end of Emerald Bay Beach wasn't the worst place. The very rich people who had exclusive access to this half-moon of sand seemed to be mostly near the clubhouse. I didn't yet see any police officers, and there were only two couples on the north end of the beach.

One of the couples turned out to be Colin and Emma. With some difficulty, Colin guided Emma toward me across the sand. She strained fiercely against him, but his fingers dug deeply into her arm. Colin had a gun, covered with a sweater, pushed into her ribs. He looked about a decade older than the last time I'd seen him. He was unshaved, and that didn't suit him. Emma's expression couldn't seem to settle between rage or terror. She was either about to take a bite out of Colin's head, or in about a minute, he would have to carry her.

As I checked the houses beside us and the beach beyond us, I opened a manila envelope for Colin. "Here's ten grand. This is the most I could get on a Saturday evening. Give me the girl."

"Do you have any idea what a pain in the ass she is?"

"Let's do this," I said, "before those nimrods check the beach."

"I asked you a question, Randy. Maybe you could treat me like a human being this one last time."

"I know acutely," I said, "what a pain in the ass she is."

When I was a cop, I'd had maybe ten minutes of training for a hostage situation. My body was nearly liquid with anxiety.

"That's good," Colin said. "I'm feeling the love now. How come you've got so much compassion for a freak like this but none for me?"

"Toss that gun into the ocean, and I'll give you as much compassion as you want."

"You know whose gun this is?" Colin asked. "Hers. She found me at the new house. Then she tried to shoot me without taking the safety off."

Emma said, "Randy, I think this prick killed my boyfriend,

and if he wants me to shut up about it, he's going to have to kill me, too."

"See what I mean?" Colin said.

"He didn't kill Simon," I said. "Simon killed himself. I mean, it was an accident, but it was Simon's fault." The way I was starting to see it, Simon must have been fucking around with the power bite and gotten himself electrocuted. It was the most dangerous part of this marijuana business. He must have been buried right where he died.

If I was right, I figured that I'd see it in Colin's face. He looked grateful, like a falsely accused child who had received the sudden and unexpected understanding of an adult. "How do you know that?" he asked.

"Don't ask."

"What are you talking about?" Emma said.

"Listen," I said, "there's plenty of stupidity to go around. Simon convinced himself that he knew enough about electricity to unhook a six-hundred-amp feed. That was stupid. On top of that, it was stupid to bury Simon next to the bite. It was really stupid of you to pull a gun. So can we all just please, you know, calm the fuck down?"

"What do you mean you buried him?" Emma cried.

Colin dug his fingers deeper into her arm and pushed the gun harder into her ribs. Emma began to weep.

"I mean it," I said. "Let her walk away from here, and you've got my full attention. We'll figure out a way to make this better. Maybe you don't have to run to Mexico. I'm seeing it from your point of view—Simon put you in a tough spot."

"Is Mutt dead?" Colin asked.

"Yeah," I said. "Mutt's dead."

"So you figure that with two murder charges and the reality-TV star here accusing me of kidnapping, I'll be able to have a nice talk with the cops?"

I was plenty terrified already when I began to notice men who weren't dressed for the beach coming around the sides of house. They were in the backyard of Colin's property, and one of them had come around Hector's house. I kept my eyes on Colin as that cop crouched behind a short fence. He had a rifle, too. Had he seen us yet? I had at least five armed men to worry about, give or take a sharpshooter.

"That depends on what happened," I said. "With Mutt, was it self-defense?"

"The guy was boiling over. He helped me clean up this mess with Simon, but it was intense for all of us. And he couldn't hack it after Terry died."

"Just tell me what happened," I said.

"Simon had no business being down there trying to deal with the power, but he was tired of waiting for Mutt. Terry brought Mutt into the deal because we needed someone to hook up the juice, but he didn't show up half the time we needed him. Simon got himself killed because of it. Mutt was the one who found him down there, but he couldn't handle it. I mean, it fucked up Terry and me, too, but Mutt was losing it. Terry was babysitting him all the time, walking him through his guilt, trying to get him clean. And then Terry was gone, and it got so much worse. I had no idea how to keep Mutt in line. When you showed up at my door and said he was sitting outside your house, I knew I had to straighten him out. I was going to talk with him. He hit me, Randy, and I totally lost it. I don't know what happened: it was like the old days. I blacked out. He stopped breathing. I took off."

It was me—I was the one who had pushed Colin over the edge. I delivered Mutt right to the door of Colin's cluelessness. And got Mutt fucking killed. "Terry was involved in this shit from the start?"

"Of course Terry was involved," Colin said. "It was Terry's idea. Him and Simon. The last place the DEA will look! Under a recovery house! I was balancing five different mortgages, and the real estate market was hurting everyone. We were going to make something good out of something not good. Terry kept saying how it's all going to be legal soon anyway, and they both thought they knew the DEA better than the DEA. I needed to keep my houses going. I wanted to help people. But we fucked up. We really fucked up."

"Was Sewell involved?"

"That guy? He's just a suit. I never talked to him again after I bought the houses."

"It's way past time to shut this down, Colin. We'll figure out a way to handle the cops. Together."

"These guys are going to take everything I own, man."

"That's a reason to kill someone? It's a reason to scare the hell out of this girl?"

"Are you disappointed that there was no great criminal conspiracy? Bored now that you know it was stupid people making stupid decisions?"

"I'm pretty far from bored right now, Colin."

We were standing about six feet apart, and the Glock was sort of pointed at Emma and sort of not. Emma had given up the insults and given herself completely to crying. Something had broken inside of her when she heard about Simon, and it wouldn't come back together until I got her away from that damn gun. As I calculated how quickly I could be on top of Colin's right arm, he placed the barrel back against her rib cage. I noticed too that the beach behind Colin was quickly emptying. Uniforms were corralling people toward the clubhouse.

"No," I said. "I'll stand out here in the wind with you as long as you want. We'll let these cops try to figure out how to shoot us. But this is where we both stop making mistakes. Let the girl go."

Colin watched me for a long moment. A bullhorn cracked through the white noise of the waves from the direction of Hector's house: *Mr. Alvarez. This is the Laguna Beach Police Department. Surrender your weapon and lie facedown on the beach.*

He let go of Emma and shoved her toward the sand. She ran toward the houses, where the police rushed forward to sweep her up. My heart rate slowed by half as Colin swung the gun around to point at me.

"What makes you think they care about my well-being?" I asked. "They're probably getting ready to unload on both of us. Tell me the rest of it. What about the videos? Did Terry know about that?"

"That was all Simon," Colin said. "Terry found out about it after Simon died, and he was heartsick, same as me. We didn't sign on to any of that. That was Simon, taking advantage of some kids who couldn't help themselves."

It was small comfort in the larger arena of fucked-upness, but I had to admit that I was relieved. "Let's put this down, Colin. Right now. We can survive this. We've come back from worse."

"Worse than this?"

"You think those assholes have anything scarier than the first month of A.A.?" I said. "You think they've got anything more painful than detox? We've got things that they can never take from us."

The thought seemed to please him. Colin actually smiled. "Tell me why you even care. Is it just Terry?"

"I wished I could have helped Terry," I said. "Maybe helping you will be a consolation prize. Listen, we're standing on this very expensive beach *together.* Everything I touch turns to shit, too. When I want to help people, I hurt them. When I try to hurt people, they end up dead. I didn't bury Simon Busansky and I didn't beat Mutt Kelly, but I'm well acquainted with the hell you're in right now."

And that hell got even hotter as I watched a second cop join the guy with the rifle beside the fence. They seemed to have settled on a course of action. Emma was long gone somewhere behind the houses on the beach, hopefully getting some comfort. I glanced behind Colin and had to admit that as far as I could see there were no people except the ones with guns pointed at us. The cops could end this at any moment and tell any story they wanted about what happened.

"This isn't the life I wanted," Colin said quietly. "I wanted to help people."

"I believe that," I said.

Hearing me say it, Colin seemed to relax. His arm dropped, and the gun pointed down at the sand. Underneath everything, neither of us had become better men in almost a decade of trying. But now we'd done what alcoholics had done since booze was first distilled—shared our story of failure—and maybe that was all that mattered.

Confronted with any kind of bad luck, Terry used to joke: *I had a good run, boys, but apparently the jig is up.* We always laughed, but it wasn't a joke. In our hearts, we knew we were fools for believing we could ever change who we were.

"I could use a cup of coffee," I said. "Can we go somewhere they have coffee?"

I didn't like the way Colin was holding that gun. His grasp seemed a little too determined, like he needed the gun for something.

"You ever clean up that mess in Santa Ana?" Colin asked.

"What do you mean?"

"The beating that propelled you into A.A. on wings of glory?" he said. "Your fifteen minutes of fame?"

"I got sober," I said.

Colin laughed. "You didn't clean it up, did you?" He tossed my ten thousand dollars back at me. He was still holding the gun a little too lovingly. "Get away from me," he said.

I held my ground. "I can help you."

I have a sixth sense for trouble. Mostly, but not always, because I'm the one who causes it. The beach around us was potent with each of our sins. I swear that the gray, churned-up sand wished that it could swallow us and pretend that neither of our stupid lives had ever happened. I could feel those cops, too, on the other end of the beach ready to finish our conversation. It was time.

"It cracks me up," Colin said, moving his finger inside the trigger guard, starting to move the gun up. "You can't figure out why Terry died."

"Why don't you clue me in?" I said.

"There comes a point where there's nothing left to do. You just have to let it—"

There must have been a great end to that sentence. Colin probably figured it would be the last thing he ever said.

But: when they told me to study, I skipped school. When they told me to stay out of trouble, I sought it out. And when they told me how a good cop should behave, I did exactly the opposite. Maybe that was my special disease. I wasn't good at acceptance in any form. And so, before Colin could point his gun at his own head, I scrambled forward the several feet between us and slammed my fist as hard into his face as I possibly could.

25

THE FIRST TIME I TRIED to reach Crash was right after putting Emma into MP's arms.

We'd been taken to the police station on Forest Avenue, where Clancy and Cardenas and DEA agents and attorneys of different varieties mostly looked us over because they had no idea what questions to ask. Colin was in a world of shit, and what had happened on the beach was only a small part of it. Betsy came by and then Manny came by and then Wade called MP. Which was the thing that made the biggest difference to me, because I knew as soon as I saw her that she could help Emma like no one else could. I cried when I realized that, which must have further confused the shit out of my various interrogators. And so right after Manny and Betsy convinced the cops that I could leave for a while with Wade, I convinced the cops that Emma could leave for a while with MP. After that, I started to breathe again, and I called my daughter. But she didn't answer.

Fifteen minutes later, I called her again. And then again five minutes after that. Except when she'd been out of the country with her mother, she'd never taken longer than a half hour to return my calls, not since I'd given her a cell phone three years ago. One time Jean had made me sit her down and tell her not to text-message me from the classroom. The absence of her response was like a gaping bloody hole in my chest. Yeah, sure, maybe she was in the dentist's chair or backpacking in the Sierras, maybe she was taking a practice test for the SAT, but I more or less knew that my daughter was putting a wall between me and her life, and that was about the worst thing I could imagine.

Troy drove my truck and I rode shotgun while Wade leaned forward from the backseat. Wade kept his hand on my shoulder as we drove south. If someone had brought the Preamble, we could have held an A.A. meeting. They took me to dinner at the Penguin because it was the next right thing they knew to do.

The Penguin was an unremarkable, very small breakfasty joint that had been Crash's favorite restaurant right after my divorce from Jean. One morning when she was about five, we ordered pancakes. Crash started crying because they weren't silver-dollar pancakes, the kind Jean made. Too many things had changed too quickly. I grabbed a coffee mug and started punching small pancakes out of the larger ones. *There you go, sweetheart, silver-dollar pancakes.* She stopped crying. At that moment I was the greatest designer in the world.

If Wade had known the same daughter wasn't returning my calls, he would have taken us somewhere else. Eating turned out to be a good move, though. As we sat down, Yegua called to say that my house was being taken apart by the cops—Cardenas and Clancy were having a hard time letting go. I wasn't worried that they would find anything. Since I'd been in business with the totally scrupulous Jeep Mooney, she hadn't even let me cheat on my taxes.

Unfortunately, Wade and Troy had more on their minds than feeding me. Wade thought it would be good if I went ahead and took Troy's fifth step, right then and there.

"Are you fucking kidding me?" I said.

"You told him you would do it," Wade said. "Frankly, I think it's a good idea."

"Frankly?" I said. "Stop acting like some kind of professional A.A. Can't I just this one time take a break?"

"No breaks," Wade said. "You're not the patient here today."

I studied Wade. He nodded like an old-timer—like he was not only wiser than me but more humble about it.

"I'm not judging you," he said. "I'm just being your friend. If my life were at stake, you wouldn't cut me an inch of fucking slack. I love you, Randy."

Wade started to tear up and, goddammit, so did I.

"I cut Terry too much slack," I said. "I should have never let him out of my sight." I was thinking about Mutt Kelly too. He could have been sitting at this table with us. But I wasn't ready to talk about that yet. Some wounds you have to let fester for a while.

"Don't go bogarting all the blame for Terry," Wade said. "Because the wind's blowing through my guts right now, too."

"Okay," I said. "Okay."

I looked up to see Emma standing outside the restaurant,

with her face up between the big letters P and E painted on the window. My heart leaped to see her, but then it did a backflip when I saw MP standing beside her. I was up and out of my seat and out the door before you could say "daily reprieve contingent on the maintenance of our spiritual condition."

Without thinking about it, I threw my arms around MP. But then, wondering if that was kind of selfish, I grabbed Emma and pulled her into the bear hug, too. Maybe it looked like I was going to start crying again, because MP said, "I know, sweetheart, I know."

I held on to MP, but I didn't know what to say to her. I had something to say to Emma, though. "I'm sorry I didn't take better care of you."

"No worries," Emma said. "I'm going to train you. After MP gets done training me."

MP smiled cautiously. "You and I are going to talk. But maybe not today."

"Today," I said, "you've got your hands full."

When I got back to the table, I checked my phone. Crash still hadn't called me back. I looked at Troy. "Let's do it."

. . .

When I did my own fifth step with Terry, I was as insane as I've ever been in my life. Six months of not drinking will do that to you. We shared a pizza at a mall in Laguna Niguel in the late afternoon. He told me he needed to do some shopping before we got down to reading my inventory. He'd been invited to a charity ball by a vascular surgeon he was dating, and he wanted a new tuxedo shirt. I said no problem.

Two hours and four malls later, we hadn't found the right

shirt. Terry was the kind of guy who was fastidious about grooming and clothes. The ruffles on this shirt were too big. The collar on this one was too spread. "Will you look at those cuffs?" he said. "That can't be right." He asked my opinion on each shirt, and I said something like "Looks great to me," but mostly, he wasn't listening. I made up my mind to walk out six or seven times, take the fucking bus back to Laguna if I had to, I didn't want to do this fucking inventory in the first place, before he finally found a shirt at Barneys in South Coast Plaza. It looked a lot like the first shirt we'd seen at Saks in Laguna Niguel.

But as we drove back toward Laguna—he had told me we would do the fifth step in his living room—he started asking me specific questions about my drinking. How bad was it? Had it always been bad? Did I think it would maybe ever get good again? As much as he hadn't been paying attention to me for the last three hours, suddenly, his attention was absolute. I have never been listened to so completely or well. Just after we passed Jeffrey Road in Irvine, he asked me point-blank whether I was an alcoholic.

"Let's just clear that up," Terry said, "before we do anything else. Make sure the foundation is solid."

I could show you the pavement his Cadillac was driving over. I remember the exact spot.

"I mean, really," Terry said. "Are you an alcoholic? Are you powerless over alcohol?"

The most naked question anyone had ever asked me, and I felt like I had to tell the truth.

"I mean, I've got problems with alcohol," I told him, "but I don't know if I can say that. I want to be honest with you. I need help, but I don't know if that makes me an alcoholic."

Saying it, I felt like a dog on a leash. Something was holding me back, but I had no idea what it was or how to unhook myself.

Terry nodded. I still had his absolute attention. "Let me put it another way," he said. "Is there anyone on this whole planet who has a better life when you don't put alcohol into your body?"

It took under a second to make the list: Jean. Betsy. Manny. Who was I kidding? The citizens of Santa Ana. The citizens of California. Cops everywhere . . .

"It's a long list," I said.

"More than one?" Terry said. "Name for me just one."

"Crash," I said. "Crash would have a better life if I didn't put alcohol into my body."

"Crash?" Terry said.

"My daughter, Crash," I said. "Alison."

He nodded again. It felt like my life was hanging in the balance.

"You're an alcoholic," Terry said. He turned and held my eyes. "You don't ever have to wonder about that again."

From that moment, I never did.

. . .

I let Troy drive us toward Aliso Beach. Until today I could count on two fingers the men I had allowed to drive me anywhere in any vehicle during my adult life: one of them was dead of an overdose, and the other was Manny.

Troy looked skeptical as I instructed him to pull off PCH into the neighborhood above Victoria Beach. He parked in a space where we might be able to see a sliver of sunset. Where real estate was this precious, the houses were even tighter than the rest of Laguna.

"We need to pray first." I got out of the truck to look for someplace to kneel. There was a wooden bench above the beach access. Terry and I had prayed beside his couch, but a bench would work just as well.

Troy hesitated at the curb. "We're on the street."

"First of all," I said, "nobody gives a shit what we're doing. Second, do you think praying is the weirdest thing anyone's done on this bench?"

Troy slowly got to his knees. We said the Serenity Prayer together, the way Terry and I had, and then I asked God to help us grow toward Him, to become better members of A.A., and to become better friends. I said this last part because Terry had said it with me.

Troy quickly got back into my truck. He had about fifteen pages in front of him: laser-printed, infinitely less dog-eared and more orderly than my own. He wouldn't meet my eyes.

"Okay," I said. "Start reading."

. . .

By the time Terry had driven me back from South Coast Plaza, the air in Laguna was cool and clear. A good afternoon to doze near the beach but not a good afternoon to sunbathe.

Then we got down to business, Terry sitting in a rocking chair and me sitting on his couch. It must have been the same old shit. I've heard a few fifth steps since, and nobody reinvents the alcoholic wheel. Every so often there's a guy who starred in gay porn movies, or guarded the president of a South American country, but usually it's the same litany of resentments and rationalizations and fears. He did this to me and therefore I can't have that. She said that to me and therefore I feel this. Dad lied. Mom left. We twist our lives into the shape of our anger.

Terry asked questions to make sure he understood. This was your first girlfriend? How old were you? Had Jean filed the papers yet? For the most part, though, he nodded and said, "There you go again, clamoring for justice."

Which was funny, because I was a cop, but it was also true: I was always looking for some wrong to be righted. It had been that way since before I could talk.

Clamoring for justice again, Randy? Is that it?

When I shared the shameful parts of my sexual inventory, Terry sometimes shared an incident of his own or a dark thought he still entertained.

I came into the deal thinking I was the biggest scumbag in the world. I left thinking maybe Terry was.

But I felt better.

. . .

Troy had lied, cheated, stolen. He didn't like the world the way he'd found it, so he'd tried to bend it to his will. He hated his parents for not helping him with this project. For the same reason, he hated every woman who'd loved him.

Someone had once described it to me as driving a car with concrete tires and insisting that the world be paved with rubber.

Troy's sexual inventory was pretty bland. He'd slept with a half-dozen women, the kind of sweet girls who get mixed up with idiots like Troy. He was their project. I told him about Jean Trask, how I was her project.

By the time Troy finished his resentment list, sex inventory, and list of fears, we'd been talking for a couple of hours. My coffee was gone.

"Anything else you want to tell me? This is the time to get it out. Not just sex but anything." I wanted to make certain there were no monsters under the bed. In an alcoholic, festering secrets can kill.

Troy thought about it. He was still at a place where thinking took tremendous effort. "I'm worried about one thing I left out."

"This is like a confessional. It's not going beyond the cab of this truck," I said. Aching to go to Jean Claude's for another cup of coffee, I checked my glove box for any fugitive Excedrin extra strength. The massive headache that had been postponed by The Penguin was getting back on schedule. "Unless it's funny, and then I'm going to tell everyone."

"You know how you're always saying that I should shut up about my father being in the Mafia?"

"Yeah," I said. "But I think my exact words were 'Shut the fuck up about your father being in the Mafia.' I'm sorry about that, Troy. I've been a little edgy lately. I could have been kinder. I want to be kinder from now on."

"I've got a couple things to tell you," Troy said. "I'm not from New Jersey—I'm from Seattle. I'm sorry I lied about that. But I think I know why I talk about him so much, why I've made him into such a . . ."

"Legendary figure?"

"Yeah, that. I guess I want to believe that he's such a badass because it makes me feel better about what happened."

I waited.

"The last time I lived at home," Troy continued, "about two

years ago, we got into a fight. I honestly don't like what he does for a living. I got mad about something, and I said that if he were a real man, he'd find a different line of work."

I nodded. Troy stared down Victoria Street toward a scoop of the Pacific Ocean that was worth about 150K to my client Bill Trembly, who happened to live beside it.

"He agreed with me. He fucking agreed with me, Randy. That's what I couldn't take." Troy started crying, something I'd seen him do before, but this time I was glad for it. I moved my hand to the seat behind him.

Troy continued, "I hit him in the face. He didn't defend himself. It was like he wanted it. He just stood there. I hit him again, too."

From where we sat, I should have been able to see more of the ocean. A great big eucalyptus tree blocked my view. I thought about mentioning that to Bill Trembly, who could add even more to the value of his house with a smaller tree. Fuck eucalyptus trees anyway.

Troy said it again: "He wanted me to do it."

"Can I tell you something," I said, "that I've never told anyone but Terry? I think maybe it will help."

So I told him.

. . .

I saved it for last. I didn't know if I was going to share it at all. Around the time I came into A.A., a young man in San Diego had been successfully prosecuted for murder based on testimony from another A.A. member. In a blackout, he'd killed a couple living in his parents' old house. When his sponsor was forced to testify, it was ruled that there was no privilege between members of a self-help group.

"I tried to kill that guy," I said. "If Manny hadn't shown up, I'm sure I would have. I was drunk, but no more than a lot of times."

Terry knew what I was talking about. He just listened.

"In my head, I was thinking he was a worthless fucking drug dealer. He'd run away from me, and he'd punched me, and I'd had all I could take. I started whaling on him, first with my nightstick, and when my nightstick broke, I punched him until my hands were bleeding. I was completely insane. I didn't care what happened to either of us. I wanted to die, but I wanted to kill that motherfucker first."

I looked at Terry. It felt like ten minutes passed while I waited for him to speak.

"What was his name?" Terry finally asked.

"Balthazar. Balthazar Bustamante."

Terry shrugged. "You're lucky the guy lived." That was all he said for a long time.

I've never been in a purgatory worse than that moment. Terry stared off out his window, and I stared at Terry. I was feeling more fucked than ever when he turned back toward me, smiling. Then he said something else. You have to understand, that's how Terry was. Just when you couldn't believe that he would pull it out, he pulled it out.

"How big do you figure God is?" Terry asked.

"Jesus, Terry, I don't know."

"You figure He's bigger than you and me?"

"I hope so."

"You think He's bigger than Orange County?"

"Sure."

"How about almost killing a man? You think He's bigger than that?"

My brain was pea-sized back then, but I thought I could see where we were going. I nodded wearily. Reading the menu, I thought I'd eaten the meal. Holding the hammer, I thought I was living inside the house.

"It's like this," Terry said. "There's a part in The Big Book where it says, 'Either God is everything or else He is nothing. God either is, or He isn't.' And then it asks us to make a choice. Everything or nothing? God or no God? A solution or the hell that you know by heart? What's your choice, Randy? How big do you want God to be?"

I'd read The Big Book twice, but I didn't remember that. It was in a chapter called "We Agnostics," which I looked up as soon as I got home.

"What's it going to be, Randy? This is where you get to say."

"I'm voting for a very big God," I said. "Because I fucking need one."

There were no white lights, and I didn't fall off a horse, but I think someone heard me.

After that, Terry told me that he loved me, that we would be friends for the rest of our lives because of what we'd just done together. I had a hard time believing that, too.

"One more thing," Terry said.

"What's that?"

"You're going to have to make amends to that Mexican guy," he said. "Face-to-face."

"You think?" I asked.

"Only if you want to live."

. . .

I never did—surprise, surprise—make amends to that Mexican guy. About seven years ago, Manny found his address for me, but Manny also told me that I didn't need to meet him, that it would cause more harm than good. Manny meant well, but he wasn't an alcoholic. Colin Alvarez had been right: it was unfinished business, and I had never felt completely free of Santa Ana because of it. I had never stopped seeing myself as that bad cop.

Of course, my failure to make amends didn't stop me from telling Troy that he would have to make amends to his father.

Troy just nodded.

"Did he ever do anything nice for you?" I asked.

"He did nice things for me all the time," Troy said. "That's not the point."

"That's exactly the point. He loved you the best he could, and you've got to let him off the hook. Are you still taking money from him?"

"What do you mean?"

"I mean, do assets that were in his account show up in your account a few days later for reasons that have nothing to do with you selling him a product or rendering him a service?"

"His office sends me a check every month."

"That's gotta stop, too. You're going to get a job. Either that or go to school. Now let's get some more coffee."

I felt a bit hypocritical, having no immediate intention of making amends to Balthazar Bustamante, but that's one of the cool things about A.A.: it is possible to walk another person toward "the sunshine of the spirit" while still keeping your own head firmly implanted up your ass.

The uncool thing about A.A. is that there are other people in it.

"You going to make amends to that guy in Santa Ana?" Troy said.

"What makes you think I haven't?"

Troy looked at me.

"Get out of my truck," I said. "It's my turn to drive. If you're fast, you can get to the other side before I lock the doors."

Troy stepped cautiously into the street. When he met me by the tailgate, he seemed totally unprepared for the hug that I gave him. I even kissed him on the neck. "I love you," I said. "Doing this thing we just did means I love you." They were the same words Terry had said to me, and probably the same words that DUI Dave had said to Terry. I was shocked to discover that I was telling the absolute truth.

26

THEN CAME ALMOST THREE WEEKS of Crash talking to me only through Betsy, who was talking to me only through Jeep. Actually, Betsy still talked to me, though just to the extent necessary to extricate me from my legal troubles. All other conversations were, according to my sister, "toxic," and she was very disciplined about avoiding them.

I consoled myself with the entirely bullshit rationalization that not talking was a form of love, too. I was pathetic. Then Jean found out about Betsy playing go-between for me and Crash, and that ended, too, so I became something worse than pathetic.

The police stopped calling me eventually. Once Laguna Beach PD had control over Colin's little empire, with a generous cut for the DEA, they stopped worrying quite so much about

Mutt's murder. Colin pleaded to manslaughter, adding more to his already extensive tally of guilty pleas. He did Emma a solid by pretending that the gun was his when she'd actually bought it from a meth dealer in Lake Forest. For that kindness alone, I would visit him regularly in jail. No one was charged for Simon's death by stupidity. The fact that I had saved the reality-television star from the clutches of the evil drug dealer must have taken the fun out of seizing any of my assets. They couldn't prove that the money I'd given Terry had been anything other than an expression of love, but when had that stopped them before?

The only question left to me was how the fuck did Terry get so far on the wrong side of things? No, it was bigger than that. The real question was how could he have let his mistakes, as horrible as they were, get in the way of his being there for that beautiful child? It didn't escape me that it was a good question to be asking myself, too. John Sewell's prediction that I would drive a permanent wedge between myself and my daughter had come true.

Meanwhile, Sewell seemed to have delivered on his promise to give Cathy her money. She moved to a nicer place in Irvine and was looking into starting an associate's program for nursing at Saddleback College. I went to see her and Paloma and Danny a few times, but I didn't ask many questions about Terry. It felt more important to simply be in the room with them. Particularly because I'd avoided diaper duty with Crash, I liked pitching in for Danny. Paloma had a lot of curiosity about my daughter, and I answered all her questions without letting on how much they pained me. Maybe that was more of my penance. While I spent time with the family Terry had left behind, John Sewell was off somewhere beginning the process of replacing me in my daughter's eyes.

Colin's downfall soon became just another cautionary tale about basement entrepreneurship in South Orange County. Life went on, and my own role—my failure to help my friend Terry and, maybe more important, a stranger, Mutt—was something I was learning to live with a day at a time. Sometimes I tried to imagine what that would have been like, helping Mutt. I had a track record with pseudo-tough guys; I would have been a good sponsor for him.

When I wasn't imagining myself sponsoring dead guys, I hid out at my shop. My A.A. family tried to turn me around. I was going to meetings again, and Wade and Troy and Emma used my house and my shop as though both belonged to them. Emma told me that MP—her new sponsor—had given her permission to consort with only two men in A.A.: me and Troy. This made me feel better about the possibility of getting back together with MP until I asked her if I should take it that way. At one point I had convinced her to stay at my house for a few minutes after she dropped Emma off. She drank a cup of herbal tea with me before she said, "Look at the safety you're giving Troy and Emma. Those two are flourishing. And they owe a lot of that to you."

I tried to care because MP wanted me to care. "Maybe they'd flourish even more if you lived here, too."

She finished her tea and said, "You're not the patient here today." Then she smiled and left me again. At least she smiled, right?

You'd think it would make me feel better, seeing the new

lives that Emma and Troy created in the wake of my disaster. Emma was working the steps with MP like her hair was on fire, and Troy had a plan for the next stage of his life that would have impressed the hell out of me if I hadn't been so malignantly self-centered: in a matter of weeks, he had become the computer fix-it guy of choice for Laguna Beach A.A., and he was getting himself together to apply for community college.

Troy's success meant that my house was filled with computers that he was working on. With his help, Emma had also turned one of my bedrooms into a small-scale video production facility from which she was posting to YouTube a meditation on every day of her sobriety. About half the time, the three of us would cook dinner together, and I had to admit, it was more entertaining than talking to myself. The two of them usually avoided doing the dishes by running off to a meeting.

The only thing that came close to comforting me was the hope chest I was designing for Paloma's quinceañera. In the Mexican culture, that's a combination fifteenth birthday party and debutante ball, and Paloma had been planning hers since before Terry died. Now that Cathy had been given Terry's insurance money, Paloma's quinceañera would be slightly less elaborate than her wedding—if she married the prince of Monaco. I was glad that Paloma could have her party, but I hated that the largesse had come by way of John Sewell.

The hope chest was based on an idea I'd had for Crash—and God knows I was planning on building one for her next. If you didn't look too closely, it was a regular old, distinctively American hope chest. Made with good wood and better fittings but pretty much the same design that had served young women for centuries. The kind of piece that should live at the bottom of a big comfortable bed.

That was only if you didn't look closely. When you did, you saw that the chest was bisected on the top and the sides by faint seams. When you tried to open it the old-fashioned way, it wouldn't: the hinges and the big brass lock were purely decorative. As you felt around, though, you realized that if you exerted a little pressure, those faint seams would separate and the chest would slide open sideways. The top rolled away at either side, like the ceiling of a football stadium, to reveal a warren of boxes. I'd made the boxes as complicated as possible, too. A few of them were large enough for sweaters and prom dresses, but it was the smaller ones that interested me. What would Paloma keep in them? Mementos of her mother? Love letters? Report cards?

If it's true, as an Art Center professor once told me, that "design is just a fancy word for problem solving," I'm not sure what problem I was trying to solve. How to show a fifteen-year-old girl that life was complicated but also beautiful? Maybe it was a lesson in how far a man who had lost what he loved most would go to occupy himself? Just figuring out how to rig the hinges took two full days. Good thing I had thrown away my life. I had the time.

One day, as I was finally getting satisfied with how the chest was opening and closing, Emma showed up at my shop. I pretended I wasn't happy to see her. Troy was away for a few days to visit his father in Seattle. While they were together, Troy planned to make the big amends. His absence meant that Emma had doubled up on the task of trying to distract me from myself. She was riding a moped with cool leather saddlebags.

"You notice anything amazing about me?" she said.

"There's nothing about you, dear, that doesn't amaze me. I'm amazed, among other things, that your head doesn't explode with all the crazy wonderful shit that's bouncing around in there."

She smiled. "That's actually a pretty good answer. *Bravissimo,* Randy."

After Emma figured out that she couldn't get me to focus on how she'd managed to snag such a mod ride, she took a laptop from the saddlebag and opened it on my worktable. I didn't have any reason to recognize the laptop that Cathy Acuña had given Troy the first time we met her, the one she said her boss had given her. By now, my house was awash in laptops just like it.

Emma said, "Troy would be really mad at me if he knew I was showing this to you."

I still wasn't that interested. I was using most of my brain to wonder whether brass hinges were better than platinum hinges, even though the platinum hinges were already a done deal. "Why would Troy be mad?"

"He's afraid you'll freak out and do something stupid."

Now I was interested. "Show me," I said.

"Promise you won't do something stupid?"

"Just show me."

It took forever for the fucking thing to boot up—God, I hate PCs—and once it did, the hard drive made enough noise to convince me it would die at any moment. Emma opened a video file, clicked on play, and immediately a woman who looked exactly like Claire Monaco was having sex with a well-beyond-middle-aged man. The video had those spooky drifting squarish gaps that corrupted video files sometimes get. It was a long video, and Emma gave me a quick tour through the rest of it: lots of positions and plenty of good shots of both their faces. I tried to imagine the circumstances of its filming. The camera was stationary, maybe on the other side of the room. Did these two even know they were being filmed?

"Where did Troy find this?" I asked.

"Right here on the computer," Emma said, "the one he got from your friend Cathy? Troy says that's why you should never put anything on your hard drive. We couldn't figure out why that chick Claire Monaco would be on Cathy's computer. God, that woman freaks me out every time I see her at the women's meeting—and I'm the one who freaks everyone else out. Troy remembered that this computer must have belonged to some guy you really hate? The one who's like stealing your daughter or something? Why don't you ever tell me anything? You don't think I want to hear about some guy who's stealing your daughter? Is this the guy?"

I'd tried hard to keep my Crash problems as far away from Emma and Troy as possible, but not hard enough. It wasn't John Sewell himself in the video. That wasn't how he rolled.

Emma kept going: "I was going to ask MP, but Troy said we'd better wait until he got back to town. I guess I thought this was something you'd want to see, that it could be important to you and your kid. I mean, it's probably some weird random video—I'm so fucking sick of porn—but I couldn't stand the idea of it sitting there and nobody dealing with it. You know what I mean? Randy?"

. . .

Claire Monaco had finished packing her bags and was almost on her way to St. Louis to start a new life with her son. She explained this to me when I reached her on her cell phone at Target, buying a few last-minute items for the long car trip.

I had taken the computer from Emma and told her I'd see her later at the house. I had started the call as I drove away in my truck. "You forgot to say goodbye, Claire."

"You think you can forgive me?" she said.

"For what?"

"For all that shit with Terry. For taking your money and doing nothing good with it."

"That was a long time ago," I said. "Are you having a good time with Alexander?"

She hesitated before she quietly said, "Yes."

"You're pre-forgiven, Claire. I don't have the strength left to judge you."

"You in legal trouble because of all this shit with Terry?"

"Not because of that," I said.

No one on earth was better equipped to understand. "Your wife is trying to take away your daughter."

"It's a little beyond trying. I never had custody to begin with, and now it's even worse."

"You sound like you're on the other side of it, though. I mean, in a good place."

"How do you figure?"

"You sound whipped." Claire laughed. "Terry used to say that was the best place to be."

"Terry said a lot of things."

I heard Claire's son, Alexander, ask her if he could have a cupcake. It sounded like they were near the checkout. I heard

her tell him, "Get some of those animal crackers. You like those."
I was oddly pleased to catch her in a moment of good mothering.

"Can I ask you some questions?" I said.

"About Terry? I don't know what else to say about him,
Randy."

"Actually, I want to know about you and John Sewell."

Claire sighed. She was about to enter her own purgatory, the
geographic cure. Around A.A., it was common wisdom that
moving somewhere else wasn't going to solve your problems.
Still, I kind of liked the idea that she was moving to St. Louis
rather than, say, Las Vegas.

"What did you find out?" she said.

"I've got some videos of you and Judge Fogarty. On a computer that used to belong to John Sewell."

"So," she said, "why are you calling me? You can't figure that
out?"

"I want to hear you say it. To a prosecutor."

"I have a bad history with prosecutors," she said. "No prosecutors."

"Because Sewell is funding this little trip out of town?"

"I'll tell you," she said. "But that's it. Fogarty didn't just retire. He was encouraged by a friend of ours to retire. I cooperated
with that process. There. That's my gift. Thanks for the money
when I really needed it. I gotta go, Randy. My son needs something unhealthy to eat."

She hung up. Viva St. Louis.

. . .

I called John Sewell and asked him to meet me that afternoon at
a certain condo in South Laguna that I happened to know was

up for sale. I told him I'd found something on a computer that once belonged to him.

It was Terry's old condo, the one where I worked most of the steps, the one where I paid Claire to leave Terry alone. It had gone on the market a week before, and the administrator of Terry's estate had called me. It was a simple thing to get a key from the Realtor. Meeting Sewell at Terry's old place was probably some kind of fucked-up nostalgia on my part. Also, privacy was important.

John Sewell was standing beside a carport underneath the condo, wearing a suit and a tie. After three weeks, his nose had healed, but it was leaning a little to one side. I opened the key box and let us into the apartment. The starkness of the place shocked me. There was nothing in it but some new wall-to-wall carpet that I didn't recognize: an imitation sisal that I couldn't imagine Terry ever liking. He was a plush kind of guy, took his shoes off the moment he walked in the door.

It had been a long time since I'd come over. How could I have forgotten there was a fireplace? A nice one, too: a big solid cinder-blocky thing, pushing its way out as if the room had been built for its pleasure. The broker must have started tarting the place up for a showing: there were framed pictures of couples and kids on that generous mantel. It looked like they'd been cobbled together from a few different families.

For lack of a better idea, Sewell stood beside the fireplace. There certainly wasn't anywhere to sit. He radiated impatience, which was how I realized that I'd been mooning over an empty room from my past. I walked over to him, admiring my remodel of his face. "Did you need surgery?"

"I will."

"What'd they give you for pain? Percocet?"

Sewell solemnly shook his head. "I keep busy."

"If I were you," I said, "I'd get the Percocet."

"You said you'd found something on a computer," Sewell said. "Can I see it?"

I held up the thumb drive that I'd brought in my pocket. "It's a sex tape of Judge Fogarty and Claire Monaco. You don't have to look at it, you just need to know I have the computer we found it on. I don't know much about computers, but it seems that erasing something doesn't actually erase it."

"If you were smart," Sewell said, "you'd put this all behind you."

"Have I done anything that makes you think I'm smart? If it helps me get the video into the right hands, I'll say I made it myself."

"You don't want to do this," Sewell said. "It's only going to cause you more trouble. You're Alison's father—she can't stay away from you forever. If I can get Jean to back down . . ."

"And Jean's going to share custody why, because you asked her to?"

Sewell looked at me with the seriousness of God on his face, like I was some poor fool about to be sentenced. "Jean will do what's best for her family."

I laughed. "You think you can control Jean, too? How about this? I'll destroy this video immediately and forget everything I know if you stay the fuck away from my daughter and her mother."

"Why does your life have to be so hard?" Sewell said. "That's what I don't understand. Why do you insist that everyone pay for their sins? The only person who's paying for his sins is you."

"Terry paid for his sins," I said. "So did Simon Busansky. And Mutt Kelly. So is Colin Alvarez. And now you're going to pay for yours."

"Look at yourself," Sewell said. "If you stay focused, in ten years you'll be worth as much as I am. But you ran around trying to get some kind of vengeance for your friend, and all you ended up doing was hurting more people. In five years, you'll be dead of a heart attack, and your daughter will be looking up to me. I'm trying to help you here."

"You want to know why my life has to be so hard?" I said. "Because I want it to be. I want to feel the bite of every goddamn stupid thing I've ever done. Some days that's all I have. The innovation is that now you're going to feel the bite of every stupid thing you've done, too." I figured that was a good time to walk out the door: dramatic, convincing. I even shook the memory stick at him for effect.

"You'll destroy that video right now," Sewell said, "if you want Cathy to get a single cent of insurance money."

A guy like Sewell never spoke carelessly. "You think you're going to take that money back?"

"I'm not taking it," Sewell said. "But with all you've brought to light about Terry's activities, his terribly guilty state of mind before he died, how hard will it be for the insurance company to claim suicide? He was ashamed that he'd become a criminal again, and he chose to kill himself. Am I wrong, or is that not basically the picture you helped draw for the police? That little boy can collect a million dollars when his father dies of a heroin overdose, but he can't collect anything if his father kills himself with a heroin overdose. That policy would have cost more."

"I thought she already got the money."

"I lent her some to tide her over," Sewell said. "The insurance check hasn't been issued yet."

"You motherfucker. You're going to blackmail me?"

"Blackmail? Please, Randy. There's a half-dozen attorneys looking for some way not to pay that million dollars. This was your mistake. But I can help you with the life insurance, too. I'm ready to put in a call for Cathy. I know some ways of doing business that you don't. Let's give it a good end. We both want Cathy to get the money. We both want Jean to calm down. Why can't we work together? You and I were bystanders to this mess, but if we resolve our conflict, there's no conflict left."

"It's not enough."

"I know you've had issues with addiction," Sewell continued, "but you're not like Alvarez or those others. You're not even like Terry. You have willpower; it's just misapplied. There's nothing wrong with wanting justice; you just can't insist on it. I'm a judge now, and even I can't insist on it. Wisdom is about knowing what you can ignore. It's time for you to leave some of these old ideas behind."

The thing about the devil, an old-timer named Billy once told me, is that he makes more sense than anyone else in the room. Whenever I thought Sewell was ordinary-smart, he proved himself to be smarter than anyone I knew. He was trying to divide me from the A.A. pack, and he was doing a pretty good job.

But that was something Sewell couldn't understand: there was no me outside of the me that A.A. had made.

"I need you out of my daughter's life for good," I said. "Or

I'm going to take this to the district attorney and let him figure out exactly how you got Fogarty off the bench. Make up your mind. You have until I can drive back down to Santa Ana."

I'd started to walk to the door when Sewell addressed me in a tone of voice I'd never heard. Maybe it was the voice he'd suppressed in order to perfect his will. It sounded so unlike him that I almost didn't recognize the symptoms of rage.

"Two things will happen before the end of the day," he said. "First, I will make a case to Alison for why she should never speak to you again. We've been taking walks a couple of times a week, just the two of us. I will explain to her the pattern of violence that she witnessed and how it stretches back to an incident when you were a police officer that I believe I'm right in saying she doesn't fully appreciate. Then I will make certain that no matter what happens, Cathy Acuña is unable to secure a cent of that insurance money. I will prepare a brief toward that purpose that even a first-year law student could follow. These are not threats, Randy. These are promises."

"Thanks for dropping the pretense," I said.

"Someone has to stop you."

Now that I'd reached Sewell on the deepest level, I had a fundamental insight. Was he a terrible criminal? No. Was he a bad man? Definitely.

He'd made a mistake, though, by getting angry. That was my neighborhood. I took out my old service weapon from the back of my jeans.

The gun had been stashed in a lock box at my shop—for years it had been stashed in a lock box at my shop—and taking it out today had been like reaching into another decade. I can't even say why I thought it was necessary. I didn't think about it again until I was pushing the barrel up under Sewell's chin. Which is what I did right after I pulled it out.

I quickly recognized that this was what I'd been moving toward for weeks. My whole life seemed to click into place. My heart got very, very calm.

Sewell looked scared, but not scared enough to stop talking. "Are you prepared to destroy your whole life?" Sewell said tightly.

"You tell me," I said, "how we would fucking know the difference."

I might have done it. I was that insane. I thought I'd found a way to make the world work. Maybe God didn't care about John Sewell's sins, but I did. John Sewell would die against the fireplace I couldn't remember in the condominium where I'd worked the steps. I was having a temper tantrum, for sure, but isn't that how most people get killed?

However, if insanity can be defined as doing the same thing and expecting different results, it was insane to imagine I could complete anything, even an execution-style killing, without Troy Padilla having a say in how I accomplished it.

"Randy?" Until he bounded through the front door, I thought I was hearing voices.

When he saw me, Troy crossed his arms, as though that gesture of disapproval were enough to prevent my faux pas.

"Aren't you supposed to be in Seattle?" I said. I barely glanced at Troy. I kept my focus on the matter at hand.

"Emma sent up the bat signal after you ran out of your shop. I told her not to show you that video until I got back."

"How the hell did you find me?"

"I called Yegua. He had heard you talking to the Realtor."

"Since when do you talk to Yegua?"

"Since we both agreed," Troy said, "that we should keep an eye on you."

"Awesome," I said. "Now go the fuck away."

"This is a permanent solution to a temporary problem," Troy said. "Give yourself a few more weeks. If you still want to kill him, I'll help you."

"What do you know about killing people?"

I did notice that Troy seemed remarkably comfortable with my holding a Glock about four feet from Sewell's chest. I shook my head. "Go," I said. "Now. You weren't even here."

"Listen, Randy—there's something I left out of my fifth step, and I should tell you before you end up in jail and can't be my sponsor anymore."

Both Sewell and I looked at him. This wasn't what either of us expected to hear.

"I told you that I lied about being from New Jersey, right? That wasn't the only lie. My dad actually is the head of a large criminal organization. I just felt like I should tell you this in order to finish my fifth step."

"Okay, Troy. You've told me."

"You still don't believe me."

"My God," Sewell said. "Is this a comedy routine?"

Troy walked up beside Sewell and inspected his broken nose. "Try to remember that I'm the only other person in this room who wants you to live." He turned back toward me. "Anyway, my mom's last name is Padilla. My father's Ukrainian. His last name is Isanov."

Sewell recognized the name, too. His back straightened decisively against the fireplace.

"Of Isanov Brothers Construction?" I said.

"My uncles and my dad."

In the Pacific Northwest, the Isanovs were as big as it got. Road construction, real estate, waste management, racetracks. The feds had wanted to take them apart for decades. I looked into Troy's eyes for the second time since he'd entered the room.

"So, listen," Troy continued. "I did what you said. I made amends to my dad, and he dropped everything to hang out with me. We took his plane down today after Emma called. He's here now."

"In Laguna?" I asked.

"In the carport."

. . .

Anthony Isanov was a well-dressed man in his fifties. He wore, believe it or not, the same blue Armani sport coat I owned myself. His soft blue shirt and stone-colored slacks were well tailored. Troy later told me he was a triathlete, and he had that sort of coiled strength. Also the most perfectly tended salt-and-pepper hair I'd ever seen, combed back over his head and seemingly trimmed ten minutes ago. He looked like one of those demographic-elevating, middle-aged J. Crew models.

Isanov pulled Troy close as he followed his son into the condo. "My God," he said. "This is him."

Like his son, Troy's father didn't seem particularly bothered by the gun idling in my right hand, but I stuffed it into my pants anyway. The Isanovs joined Sewell and me beside the fireplace.

"I won't say how grateful I am"—Isanov shook my hand fiercely—"because I'll lose it again."

Troy stood beside his father, and Sewell didn't move an inch.

"Mr. Isanov, this is John Sewell," I said.

Isanov turned to offer his hand. "Anthony Isanov. Happy to meet you, sir."

It wasn't possible for Sewell to be any stiffer, but Isanov's presence gave him at least another inch of broomstick up his ass.

"Whatever you need"—Isanov pointed at me—"I'll make it happen."

Such a gangster thing to say, but I believed him. He thought I'd returned his son to him, and maybe I had.

"I'd like to show Dad your houses later on," Troy said. "Randy builds beautiful houses."

"You told me that, buddy. I'm looking forward to it," Isanov said.

The pressure inside Troy must have been huge. His eyes bounced from his father to me. And then back to his father. And then back to me.

Isanov filled the awkward silence. "You used to dream about building houses when you were still, ah, on the police force?"

"No, sir. That was too big a dream to admit. I doubt it even crossed my mind."

"After you stopped drinking," Isanov said, "you started to dream?"

"I started to dream when I had no other choice."

Isanov laughed. "Sometimes the bastards have a boot on your neck and you can't do anything but enjoy the view."

Sewell looked like he had to pee. Badly.

"A friend of mine who recently passed told me that sometimes you have to take success and happiness like a punch in the face," I said. "You have to be a man about it."

Isanov laughed again. "Troy told me about him, too."

Troy beamed. If we'd been in my shop, I would have asked him to make coffee. Given him something to do.

Instead, I said, "Can I buy you a cup of coffee, Mr. Isanov? Has Troy told you about Jean Claude's? It's not Seattle, but it's an institution."

"That'd be great, Randy." He smiled his big smile. When it became clear that I wasn't moving on yet, Isanov said, "And then, maybe later, you'll let me buy you a meal. I'm staying at the Ritz-Carlton. We can eat there and then bring some cigars to the beach. Troy says you like cigars?"

Looking into his eyes, I said, "How about I catch up with you in a half hour?"

Maybe I imagined that the same pleasant denial which allowed the two of them to ignore the gun would extend to excusing me for a few minutes while I shot John Sewell. That I was completely insane at the moment was indisputable.

Isanov held my arm and gently drew me away from the fireplace, far enough so he wouldn't be heard, but I never took my eyes off Sewell.

"Can I be blunt with you, Randy?" he asked.

"Blunt is good," I said.

"Troy wants you to calm the fuck down," Isanov said, "and he brought me here to help you accomplish that."

"No disrespect, Mr. Isanov, but my being calm is none of your business."

"Bullshit, there's no disrespect. You use that gun, you disrespect everything you've achieved with my son."

Looking over at Troy, I had to give it to his father: this wasn't my finest day as a sponsor.

"You're a moron and my son is moron," Isanov continued. "But that's God's blessing on you. Maybe you're an artist, like Troy says. But don't make a mistake, Randy. The world is full of people like me, who live in the hell of *not* being morons. Please give me that gun."

I gave him the gun. The truth will set you free, but first it will really piss you off.

"Now," he said, "let's talk about this ugly business you're involved in. First let me tell you that if you get my son mixed up in something like this again, I'll kill you. Do you understand?"

"Whatever I do, Troy's going to make this life hard for you. It's his special skill. I know you think you're up for it, but trust me, you're not up for it."

"Do you understand?" Isanov repeated.

"Yes, I understand," I said. "Do you understand?"

"Better than you know," Isanov said. "Please take my son outside so I can fix this for you."

. . .

Troy and I walked around the side of the building, which was high above PCH. The ocean was blue like the blue on a map and oddly static—like if you threw yourself against it, you would bounce right off.

"What's he doing in there right now?" I asked.

"His thing. Which is good for you, because I don't think he's going to be doing his thing too much longer. We had a long talk today."

"Did I just put a judge in Anthony Isanov's back pocket?"

Troy laughed. "You really want me to answer that? All you need to know is that it's out of your hands now."

"I would be happily on my way to prison," I said, "if you hadn't forced me to do your goddamn fifth step."

"That's a beautiful thought. Me, I wouldn't have to make something out of my life."

Troy's father joined us on that pretty hill above PCH. "Judge Sewell won't bother you anymore."

"Thanks."

"Can you give Troy a ride to my hotel?" Isanov said. "I've got a few details to iron out before we have dinner."

I looked around the building to see if Sewell was still there, but his car was gone. Isanov got back into his rented Navigator, and he drove away, too.

27

AT SOME POINT NEAR THE END of my career as a Santa Ana police officer, I started to think that ironwork on doors and windows was beautiful, in the way that fire escapes in New York City are beautiful. The bars on Balthazar Bustamante's house were better than most: wild teardrops that looked like paisley. Sitting in my truck across the street, I wondered if I should have talked to Manny first so he could dissuade me. Maybe a quick café con leche at the *supermercado* to think it through. Now that I was there, though, my truck didn't seem to want to move, so I continued to admire the ironwork.

I had been on my way to Fullerton for Paloma's quinceañera after her Mass at St. Joseph's when my truck seemed to drive itself, like the arrow on some huge Ouija board, toward a small fortified home near Chapman Avenue.

The last known address for the guy who cost me my job and kicked my ass into A.A.

It had been four weeks since I took Troy's fifth step, two weeks since Troy's father had treated us to the best meal with cigars after that I'd ever experienced. And now I sat there watching a little old man I didn't recognize sitting in a lawn chair on the concrete porch. When I turned off my engine, he looked at me for a minute, then leisurely stepped inside. A minute later, a younger man came outside whom I did recognize. Eight years ago, Balthazar Bustamante had been a white-T-shirt-bandanna-under-the-baseball-cap scumbag. Today he was wearing a vintage polo shirt and green cargo shorts, and his hair was clippered at the shortest setting to camouflage his baldness. He rubbed the soul patch on his chin as he crossed the well-kept lawn. I couldn't remember Bustamante's street name. It was his full legal name that had been typed across my entire life.

"*¿Qué onda?*" I got out of my truck. "*¿Cómo estás?*"

"*Bien,*" Bustamante said. "Pretty fuckin' *bien.*"

Who knows what I expected, but this wasn't it. Bustamante smiled at me. "*Now* you speak Spanish?" he said.

"My new job requires it," I said. "Could have used it on my old job, too, I guess."

"I heard about your new job," Bustamante said. "You should give me a percentage. If it weren't for me, you'd still be a cop."

"This is true."

"Did you come here to apologize for almost killing me? For giving me headaches every day for two years? For costing my dad a shitload of money that he still doesn't have?"

"Not exactly an apology."

"Is this some kind of reality-TV show where the lowlife

cracker gringo asshole finds redemption and understanding by confronting his racist past?"

"No," I said. "Not that, either."

Bustamante laughed. "I'm taking a course at Cal State Fullerton: postmodern popular culture. I'm thinking there's a video camera in that van over there where some producer coached you to apologize but then get pissed off and start a fight because that's good television."

"You're in college?"

"Don't congratulate yourself," Bustamante said. "Maybe I'm trading crack for English papers and running volleyball players as whores."

"How much crack can you get for an essay these days?"

"You don't know shit about me." He pointed at my face. "You could live in my house and eat my food and suck my dick for ten years before you'd know less than shit."

He held my eyes for no longer than ten seconds, but it was the same bump in testosterone that almost killed us both eight years ago. This time I would have let him hit me. Eventually, Bustamante stared down at his feet. I followed his eyes, and maybe we were wondering the same thing: was he really wearing Birkenstocks?

"Why you here? You find fucking Jesus or something?" he asked.

"No," I said. "It's more like—"

"Because I did," Bustamante said. "My old man finally got me to go to church when I was still in the cast. The Holy Spirit hit me so goddamn hard, I thought I was having a stroke."

Laughing, I looked back toward his house, where his father

was standing in the doorway. "Nice shoes. Jesus tell you to become a beatnik?"

"With a name like Balthazar, you gotta feature yourself. The chicks at Fullerton dig it." Balthazar kicked at the grass. "Soon as my dad came in and said you were at the door, I thought, *Shit, that cracker motherfucker.* I kept thinking I was going to find you, explain what happened. I haven't sucked a pipe or had a drink since God whacked me over the head."

"Good for you, man. That's great. I'm sober, too."

Miracles, the old-timers say, are God's way of staying anonymous. It was hard not to be impressed. But I would never turn this into an inspiring A.A. story. We still hated each other. If anything, it had become a pleasant hatred.

"What do you guys call this thing you're doing so poorly?" Balthazar said.

"You guys?"

"You're in A.A., right? Just because I didn't drink the Kool-Aid doesn't mean I can't recognize cultlike behavior."

Manny would love this guy.

"We call it making amends," I said. I stood there for a minute.

"I'm listening," Balthazar said.

"Okay," I said. "I take responsibility for the whole deal. I was a homicidal cop, and you were an innocent victim of my rage. You can record that and take it to the grand jury."

"That's easy to say, Officer Chalmers, now that I've signed the settlement and I can no longer sue your ass."

"Would it have been easy for you to say?"

"Let's find out." Balthazar smiled. "I was a drug-addicted drug dealer bringing sickness and violence to my community.

And you can't record this because I won't hurt my father again."
That also had the ring of truth. I could see on Balthazar's face
that he thought so, too. My old enemy laughed and shook my
hand. "It's done. Take it to the bank. I forgive you."

"Just like that?"

"No," Balthazar said. I remembered his street name: De Niro.
Because of that scene in *The Untouchables* where the actor, playing Al Capone, kills a man with a bat, Bustamante's favorite
weapon. "I want you to do something for me."

"Tell me."

"Come to church with us sometime," De Niro Bustamante
said. "My dad will wet his pants with joy."

. . .

The restaurant Paloma had chosen for her quinceañera was
owned by an old character actor who'd had a long career as a
movie gangster. The hallway to the banquet room was thick
with pictures of the owner standing next to the guy who was
standing next to the guy who was standing next to Marlon
Brando. Or whoever. The restaurant itself was dizzying. The ceiling of the main dining room, which was twenty-five feet high,
was covered with toys and circus memorabilia. They had probably been assembled over the years—the dust said decades—with
no thought for any plan. It was an inexpensive place to eat Italian food, though, and the celebratory haphazardness of the
decor encouraged a good time. The waitpeople wore white tuxedo shirts and smiled in a way that didn't seem forced.

I turned from admiring the pictures on the wall to see my
own heart looking back at me. Crash was wearing a white blouse,
a brown skirt, and cowboy boots that her aunt had bought her.

The boots reminded me that I owed my sister my life, not only for getting law enforcement off my back but for encouraging Crash to speak with me again.

"I guess your mom didn't have time to say hello," I said.

Crash checked me out for a moment like she wasn't sure if she should stay. I took it like a man, mostly, and then I tried to meditate for the second time in my life, the way that MP had tried to teach me: I counted my breath, in and then out, in and then out. I got to a miraculous seven before Crash said, "I need to know something, Dad. Did you have anything to do with John going away?"

I took another deep breath. "More or less."

"What does that mean?" she said. "Did you do something? What did you do?"

"John made his own problems. Maybe I increased them. It's one thing I'm not going to apologize for. He would have hurt you and your mother eventually."

"More than you've already hurt us?" Crash said.

"I deserve that," I said. "And more. But I think you also know there's no force in the universe that could ever make me go away."

Crash smiled, so I put my arm around her and we entered the banquet room, which was festive with party dresses and paper flowers and a mirror ball hanging above it all. Paloma wore a tiara. Traditionally, the princess is escorted by several boys her own age—some of them relatives, some of them classmates— who wear faux military uniforms complete with epaulets and scabbards. The boys had begun dueling with their swords out-side the Mass at St. Joseph's and still hadn't stopped.

"Hey," I said. "After the party, you want to drive to Vegas, fill the back of the truck with fireworks, and blow up stuff in the desert?"

Crash narrowed her eyes. "I'm wearing a skirt, Dad."

"Is there some law that says you can't cause explosions wearing a skirt?"

She smiled, it seemed to me, with great compassion. As we made our way to the bar to get some Shirley Temples, I turned to face her. "Is it time to stop calling you Crash?"

"Alison is a nice name, too."

. . .

I danced three times with Cathy, twice with my daughter, but only once with Paloma—the kids with the swords had kept her busy. I'd just finished some kind of Mexican hokeypokey, and Alison and I were watching little Danny practice his smiles, a skill she assured me he'd mastered only in the last hour.

Paloma had joined us, and she argued that Danny had been smiling before Alison started making faces at him, a point that Alison conceded by putting her arm over Paloma's shoulder. I was wondering what would result from bringing my daughter to a party where she could become friends with the secret daughter of her almost stepfather when I looked over to see Troy and Emma dancing. That made me wonder how soon before they would be sleeping together. When Troy held out a chair for her after getting her a soft drink and a plate of cookies, I thought, *Good for you, buddy. Good for you.*

It wasn't a bad night for me, either. I think that was Emma's doing, but I didn't ask. When I found a legitimate break in the action, I asked MP to dance. It was a slow dance, uncharacteristic for this party. I didn't say anything for a while. Then I said,

"Can it be time for you to go on a date with me?" She pulled herself closer and said, "It can be that time not next Saturday but the Saturday after that."

Even Wade found his way to the party via cell phone. As part of his coursework for his masters in social work—why should Troy be the only one going back to school?—he'd arranged a ride-along with Manny, and he wanted to let me know that he was in the patrol car right now. I invited both of them over for a piece of cake later on.

With all my life clustered around me, I shouldn't have been surprised when the bartender tapped me on the shoulder and told me that I had another friend who wanted to talk. I found Sean sitting on a bench outside the front door of the restaurant. We'd been going to meetings together almost every night for a couple of weeks. A few nights ago, he'd told me that his boss wanted him to do a couple of late shifts, that he'd start catching a few more meetings during the day. That wasn't the entire truth. There was a thickness around him like shame. And like being drunk.

"I'm assuming you did something really stupid," I said.

"Pissing inside my supervisor's locker?"

"Did anyone see you?"

"Dude, that's half the fun."

As we talked, my daughter came through the doorway with Danny in her arms. She helped him wave to me, and both Sean and I waved back.

"Is that Terry's kid?" Sean asked.

"You can't tell?"

Alison turned, still waving Danny's hand as the heavy wooden door closed behind her. For the first time in forever, that squeaking Styrofoam ice chest in my head was quiet. The world was only the world: the coolness of the night, the slatted wooden bench under my ass, the traffic noise from Orangethorpe.

Once I was sure that my new sponsee was on the right side of things, I brought him into the restaurant. As the decor dazzled him, I asked the bartender to make us both cappuccinos.

Who knew if Sean would ever get sober, but I loved him. The way I loved Terry and Wade and Troy and every other loser I'd known in A.A. Or, as an old-timer named Joey Buttons once told me: Jesus didn't hang out with the thieves and whores because he wanted to save their souls. He hung out with them because they were *more fun.*

As Sean devoted himself to a plate of lasagna with a side of tamales, I watched Alison and Paloma charge around the room as though they'd been friends all their lives, navigating the happiness of the party with an intensity that was half modern dance and half street hockey.

When Cathy sat down beside us, she gave Danny to me without so much as a nod. I can't understand why anyone ever trusts me, but I'm always moved when they do. Danny slept in my arms.

I started talking to Cathy about Terry. I'd never spoken to her this way. Sean looked up from his plate of food but then must have realized that it was just an A.A. story, one that he'd either heard before or would hear again, so he went back to eating. It was, in fact, the Italian food that had reminded me.

. . .

When I finished my certificate program at Art Center, it just happened to be the same week as my second A.A. anniversary. Terry and Wade were so proud of me that they decided to throw a party. They got it catered by this Italian restaurant in Newport Beach, and they decorated the courtyard of Terry's condo with streamers and balloons and signs. They told me that all I had to do was invite anyone I wanted. They repeated that instruction many times: anyone you want. They were preparing "a big shindig"—that's what Terry called it—and there would be plenty of food to go around.

When the evening came, they were in for a shock. Although I'd met and was friendly with hundreds of people in Laguna Beach A.A., I'd invited only five. The Italian sausages alone would have fed sixty. Wade had printed out from his computer a huge banner that said CONGRATULATIONS RANDY! The few of us milling around underneath it looked pathetic.

Terry must have been pissed. He made sure everyone had enough to eat before he retreated to his living room, where he smoked a cigar and left me to guess how much the whole deal had cost.

Afterward, when I was hiding in his backyard on a chaise longue, he came out to sit next to me. I was still addicted to cigarettes, and I'd made it about halfway through a pack of Camels. Terry chewed on the dead plug of his cigar. Neither of us spoke for a while.

It felt like graduation, and I had to wonder what came next. Especially if I had alienated my friends.

"I know what happened," Terry said. "And I'm not mad at you."

"What happened?" I didn't know myself.

"It was my fault," Terry said. "You didn't feel like you deserved the party. I should have thought of that before I told you to invite people. You had a bad case of low self-esteem."

Terry leaned back in the other chaise and threw his cigar butt over the fence. Any other day, he would have choked on an expression like "low self-esteem." I offered him a Camel. I dug out my lighter and gave him that, too.

"Here's the thing." Terry stopped to pick a bit of tobacco from his teeth. "You *don't* deserve it. There's nothing you've done in your whole life that means you deserve this party. Not this party or anything else that's happened. Not this deal at Art Center—none of it. You don't deserve the love of your daughter, either. You really don't deserve that."

He had my attention. He was going to tell me the absolute truth about something. I couldn't imagine what.

"Because it's a gift," Terry said. "It's not about deserving or earning or being a good guy. God loves you because that's just what God does. Wade and I throw parties for your sorry ass because that's what we do. It's not about you, Randy. Which is mighty good news, because if it were about you, our lives would be a fucking nightmare."

. . .

Cathy threw back her head and laughed—it was a version of Danny's father that she recognized. But then she stopped laughing. We looked at each other.

"You know," I said. "I never even asked how you met him, how you two came together."

"He came over to the building a few times with John," she said, "and then he showed up once by himself. At first he pretended he was trying to find John. And then he just started coming by. He understood Paloma better than anyone, the way she could be angry and then happy sometimes in the same minute.

When she was upset, he never took it seriously. He taught me how to take it less seriously."

"He would have been a great father," I said. "Hell, he *was* a great father."

"I didn't want to do it again after John," Cathy said. "Another lawyer. But he was inside my heart before I knew what was happening."

At just that moment, little Danny burped, though he didn't wake up. I looked at him and then at his mother. "Cathy, I'm going to ask this once. And it's only because I'd like to know, not because I'm going to blame you for anything. Do you really not know who was with Terry that night?"

As she gently touched Danny's foot, Cathy sighed. "I knew Thomas for a couple of years. He worked for John, used to fix the building, come by for coffee sometimes. Terry liked talking with him when he came by, said he could find him some work. Thomas was good with Paloma, too, but different. Not so much like a father, more like a brother. I knew he had problems. He called me because he didn't know what to do. He was telling me that my man was dead, but it was because he himself was lost, not because he cared about me. I kept his secret anyway. Maybe I shouldn't have. It wasn't his fault how Terry died. Thomas was like a child. Terry could have been a kind of father to him—like I think he was to you—but I guess Terry was lost by then, too."

. . .

When Terry was first having trouble getting off heroin—long before I knew him—a group of well-meaning recovering alcoholics accosted DUI Dave, his sponsor, in the parking lot of the Coastal Club. They told Dave—for his own good, mind you—

that if he continued to work with Terry, the most unpromising newcomer anyone had ever seen, both of them would end up drunk. And those sweet, concerned guys didn't want that to happen.

Dave—who is long dead now, of asbestosis and mesothelioma—told those fellows his exact thoughts on the subject: they could go fuck themselves if they thought they had any fucking say in how he did his fucking twelfth-step work. Terry was sleeping on Dave's couch at the time, and Dave would bring Terry along to construction jobs in Riverside, where Terry would detox by walking around and napping in Dave's truck.

Those guys in the parking lot of the Coastal Club were actually right. Terry wasn't, in fact, a good bet, and maybe Dave could have spent his remaining years more productively. Alcoholics like to see a good return on their investment with newcomers, and the best return is when someone dies sober.

. . .

I knew exactly what had happened to Terry. It's one of the oldest stories in A.A., but also the story that hardly anyone ever talks about. How could we? It's too terrible and too absurd. I should have known, though. I, of all people, should have known.

Because as much as I had learned, there was always the one thing that I couldn't wrap my mind around: why did he shoot drugs two days after his son was born?

In spite of his many fuckups—and they were legion: Busansky, pot dealing, and a hole in the integrity of his A.A. program the size of a moon rocket—in spite of all that, Terry realized that he was going to get everything he wanted. Cathy was going to have his baby, and he would be a beautiful smart boy. The rest of it could be handled—he knew lawyers who had come back from worse. Terry would marry Cathy if she would have him, but even if she wouldn't, well, there was the baby.

It was what he'd wanted since forever.

Then he looked down deep within himself and realized that it didn't make a goddamn bit of difference. Didn't even put a dent in the thing. Not a fucking dent.

And then there was the thought about that body under the house, which just seemed like more of the blackness that was already pouring out of his heart. It wasn't just that he'd fucked up. It was worse than that: the fuckup was older than the world, inescapable and total.

Terry must have spent a day pretending that he wasn't heartbroken. Most addicts have at least one big idea hidden in their heart: *I will be okay when.* Even with all the step work and therapy and success, people still imagine they will be okay when they are rich. Or married. Or have a baby. Life for an alcoholic is often a process of discovering all the things that don't make any difference.

Not that, either?

It was during that day and a half when he ran with Troy and sought comfort with Claire and shot drugs with Mutt Kelly. According to Cathy, he never saw his son. The *not even this?* must have been too horrible to face.

He found his way to Mutt Kelly because Mutt was an addict who was still in the game. Terry could have even convinced himself that he was going on a twelfth-step call—that he was going to help Mutt with his drug problem, with the Busansky mess, with whatever. Maybe that was even true as he was driving over to Mutt's house. But he was also looking for drugs, something that Mutt would know about and Terry, after a fifteen-year vacation, would not. The transition must have been seamless: one minute he was a guy looking to help another struggling addict, the next minute he was a guy looking to cop. Maybe it felt like he had never stopped being a guy looking to cop.

Here's the really ugly part: the Terry Elias who saved my life didn't die right away. I'm betting he persisted through most of the afternoon and evening. I can't help but imagine that Terry was talking about sobriety all the way to Santa Ana and even once he had those little plastic bags in his pocket.

He was probably talking about it even while he was high. What else would he talk about?

Maybe it pissed off Mutt, but I'm guessing it didn't. I'm guessing that Mutt was inside the same kind of warm, fuzzy insanity. Maybe they had talked themselves into believing that it was the last time for both of them. That's in The Big Book, right? The part about finding out for yourself that you can't control your addiction, that you have to surrender.

I bet my name came up. And Wade's. Terry might have even told a dusty story about DUI Dave. Maybe he was struggling even after they copped the dope, telling himself it could still become a story about the day he almost lost everything. But there was also this great aching—the thought of that baby coming home to him—and the aching, which had become acute in the hospital, might have seemed like a wave that he needed to ride to shore.

In the last moments of Terry's life, Mutt was the coward who didn't call 911, even if he called Cathy two days later. I don't blame him: cowardice is part of an addict's job description, and considering how I myself dropped the ball with Mutt, how can I blame Mutt for anything? But maybe Mutt was a little braver than that as Terry fell. Maybe he held him. And maybe, when my friend's heart stopped and everything let loose inside him, that stupid biker said a prayer.

I don't think so. I think Mutt was gone before any of that happened.

Maybe I'm wrong. Maybe Terry was happy at the end. Sometimes when people binge after a long time clean and sober, they don't regret it. They think: *What fucking idiots they all are to deny themselves this pleasure. This pleasure is worth everything.*

I don't wish that for Terry, not even right before he died. I want to believe there was a moment when he stumbled against the bed, or knocked over a lamp into a bottle of vodka, a moment when the great happiness of the drug was pierced and he saw himself as a fool who had squandered a great gift. I want him miserable, fighting himself, and ashamed of his failure. I hope he felt like he let every one of us down. And it's not for my sake that I want this. Not for Wade, not even for little Danny. Self-hatred can be a kind of grace, and that's what I want for Terry, the best friend God ever gave me: a grace of the severest and most durable kind.

Sweet and powerful enough to carry him home.